THE MUDDY GOOSE

Guide

TO THE

WEIRD
NORTHWEST

A PLAYABLE ADVENTURE

Edited by **ERIK GROVE** • *Series from* **FRANCES LU-PAI IPPOLITO**

DEM▲GOGUE PRESS
MAKER OF GAMES AND BOOKS

Edited by Erik Grove
Series from Frances Lu-Pai Ippolito
Interior design by Brian W. Parker and Believe In Wonder Publishing
First Edition
Paperback Edition:

The book is published by Demagogue Press LLC
www.demagoguepress.com

ISBN: 4 979-8-9887299-2-1

This Book Belongs to:

____

Dream bold,
Wander far,
Tell good stories

—the Muddy Goose Adventure Society Credo

The Rules

1. Leave no trash behind; make the world better (if you can) than you found it.
2. When someone has a story to tell, listen politely. (You'll get your turn.)
3. Always say hello to friendly dogs.
4. If you've got enough, share.
5. Wipe your feet.

Contents

How To Play This Book

The northwestern corner of the United States is a lot more than coffee shops and Sasquatches.

Oregon and Washington are a patchwork of contradictory places and cultures. Thriving big cities hug the interstate from the Canadian border to California while the Pacific Ocean crashes against chilly rocky shorelines to the east and mountains loom in the cloudy horizon. The northwest is small towns and hiking trails, big tech playgrounds, and pop culture punchlines. It's mushroom hunting and micro brewing, backyard gardens, rushing rivers, flannel clad rock 'n' roll legends, high deserts, and old growth forests you can lose yourself in. But most of all, the northwest is stories. Funny, brutal, contemplative, or bizarre—when the rain comes down or the sky turns a perfect July blue, the words come out onto keyboards or paper, in front of bookstore crowds, or over a game table at home with your friends.

That's what we wanted to share with you in *The Muddy Goose Guide to the Weird Northwest*. This is how we tell stories here. With a little magic, a lot of heart, and a hint of the sinister, we imagine stories in unexpected places too big to be simply contained with text on paper and we want you to join in. This is a Playable Adventure after all.

So how do you play?

This book offers you three ways to "play" each adventure. You can read the stories at your own pace, in order or by whatever title catches your fancy. We're proud of the variety and distinctiveness you'll find between these covers. We've got fantasists and poets, novelists and new voices, masters of the macabre and fairy tale dreamers. The stories are very different but complementary, an eclectic cross section of the thriving northwest creative community.

The second way you can play these adventures is using the cover itself as a board. You'll find game rules and cut-out playing pieces in the back. Inspired by the Royal Game of the Goose, one of the very first board games dating back over 500 years, each one of our stories is represented with a numbered square on the board. Careful though—some spaces hide nasty surprises.

The final way you can play is by stuffing this book in a bag or your back pocket and venturing out to any of the 25 real world locations featured within. We invite you to go beyond the pages, to transform these stories into experiences we never could have imagined. We've included places within this book to record your experiences and track your progress. Think of it like a video game where you want to get all the achievements and find all the Easter eggs but with hiking boots instead of pixels. For locals, you'll see familiar spots and hidden gems. For visitors to the northwest, you'll find a map that takes you from the obvious to the mysterious and offers a journey that will introduce you to our weird, wonderful home.

Who knows? Maybe you'll stay for another game.

—Erik and Frances

The Rituals of the Fremont Troll
by Patrick Hurley

In Seattle, a troll lives under the Aurora Bridge. The local council of Seattle's Fremont neighborhood, which also lies beneath the bridge, will claim they came together in the 90's to construct the troll, and this is true in a literal sense, but in other ways, the troll was already there, had been there since the Aurora Bridge was first built almost 60 years earlier. The sculptors, artisans, and volunteers just laid concrete, steel rebar, and wire around the troll, giving him form, allowing him to rest easy, protected from the elements by a sturdy coating of gray silicate.

The Fremont Troll sleeps with one eye open. His great hand covers a rusted, sealed Volkswagen Beetle. During the day, tourists and locals visit him, taking pictures standing atop his enormous head or gathered around his dusty Beetle. Several feet away, along the troll's sidewalk, sits a plaque with a little metal box for donations, and during the day, pilgrims leave coins and bills as tribute.

At night, things are different. At night, there are many games, rituals, and wardings that may be enacted with the Fremont Troll, beneath the Aurora Bridge. Some pedestrians utter little prayers as they pass by the troll on a summer's evening for good luck. A few walk by and affectionately pat his hand or head. Others shuffle past him fearfully, certain if they don't keep one eye on the looming creature at all times, the troll's great hands will unclench and snatch them up. Of all the little rituals these passersby partake, there are three that have emerged as the most likely to elicit a response from the Fremont Troll.

A Night Offering, Under the Three-Quarters Moon

A second, smaller donation box, made of whorled gray driftwood, lies atop the troll's great head. It's invisible during the day and can only be seen when the moon is three-quarters full. Those who feel lovelorn or guilty may place a love note or written confession within the driftwood box, though it's a dangerous game. If the note contains true sentiments of particular emotional resonance, and the troll deems it appropriate, it nods its great head but once, causing a small tremor in the ground and a great jolt in the bridge above. Have care, for with this nod, you may have your wildest love returned or your darkest sins shriven.

However, if the offering is particularly callow, poorly written, if the sin is too grievous, or even if the troll is feeling particularly peckish that evening and the three-quarters moon is harvest red, another even rarer event occurs.

The Fremont Troll opens its other eye. While the troll's perpetually open eye is regularly painted different colors to match the changing holidays and seasons, none know the color of the troll's hidden eye. Some say it's the color of time, reversing in on itself. Others claim it's the color of the nothingness that existed before the Big Bang. They say to look into the troll's closed eye is to witness the deepest truths of the universe and the worst parts of oneself.

Not all have the constitution for such reflection.

Those who emerge from beneath the Aurora Bridge after looking into the troll's closed eye are said to have changed. They are wiser, more somber. Some can hear a music on the wind when all anyone else hears is silence. Others, their sense of safety in the universe devoured, are driven to despair and will do anything they can to forget what they saw in the troll's secret eye. They live eventful lives, often achieving legendary feats or wreaking terrible horrors upon the world, yet their great secret is that it was all in an effort to escape that lurking eternal wisdom.

The troll seems well fed and content after such encounters, and the flowers and weeds around his lair blossom crimson, as the winds blow through Seattle, beneath the Aurora Bridge, under the three-quarters harvest moon. His open eye gleams with reflected streetlight, keeping his secrets.

The Finger Trinkets of the Troll

Should you not wish to test your soul against the shoals of eternity, there are other games you may play, other tests to be taken.

One is a test of agility and song. The Troll's other hand, the one not grasping the car, is dug deep into the earth, his great fingers punching into the dark loam beneath the layered cement. Foot to foot, you must leap between the gaps of his fingers, touching only ground, going west, then east, then west again. As you leap between his fingers, hum a tune. "4 and 20 Blackbirds" works quite well, but "All 'Round the Mulberry Bush" can be dangerous. Foot to foot, never two feet within the same gap. Each misstep takes away one year of life, and you mustn't ever stumble, lest your bones be added to the troll's hill. Should you hit all the gaps equally, the troll asks you, borrowing a voice of creaking iron and steel from the Aurora Bridge's aging joints, to choose which finger you would like him to lift.

There are no wrong choices, but it's not clear if there are any right ones. What lies beneath each troll's finger is different for everyone who's passed the test. Trinkets from lost loved ones. Old family photos, long forgotten. Ripped pages from a diary containing passages about you, written by someone you never suspected thought of you at all. Their words may be damning with faint praise or the truest things about yourself you've ever read. Whatever you find, you will never forget what lay beneath the troll's finger. Some try to take their prize with them, but always it vanishes after a day, becoming dust and dead leaves, just like fairy gold.

The Blessing of the Troll

Still others, hoping to escape the confines of our mundane world with its rigid physics and static history, make pilgrimage to the Fremont Troll, seeking its blessing. If you would seek the troll's blessing, be sure, be oh so sure. The blessing of the Fremont Troll isn't idly given, and those he judges as unworthy have cause to regret their temerity. The troll is always hungry.

First, know that the blessing of the Fremont Troll can only be sought during periods of great change. What a stone troll judges to be interesting times is very different than humans who dwell in the land of the quick, so have care not to visit on an auspicious day by mortal standards.

The most reliable periods are solstices and equinoxes. There, as light gives way to dark, (or vice versa), and warmth and cold exchanges places, as the world begins its period of dying or renewal, supplicants may ask for the troll's blessing. This, too, must be earned.

The Fremont Troll will ask you one of his many riddles. Not with his mouth. Were the Fremont Troll to ever open his mouth, the earth would scream, the Aurora Bridge crumble, and Seattle would be covered in a poisonous cloud of dust.

Instead, the Fremont Troll will pose one of his riddles by borrowing the voice of the wind, blowing off the Fremont Cut, emboldened by the icy waves from nearby Lake Union. The would-be blessee must answer quickly, whispering into the troll's hidden, hair-covered ear before the wind dies. If you guess wrongly, the wind will tell you so, and you will never sleep fitfully while in its presence again, no matter how gentle the breeze. Yet if your answer is correct, then you stand ready for the Troll's blessing.

With a groan and a sob, the Fremont Troll unclasps his car-clutching hand. It pains him to do so, so only those who've passed the test are allowed this rare honor. The sealant around Volkswagen Beetle vanishes, and the locks behind its rusty doors click open. The supplicant must enter the Beetle and lie on its floor as the door closes. Then comes the waiting.

Some emerge quickly.

Others open the door and stumble out after many minutes, which for them might have been days. There's a smell as they open the door to the Beetle, a scent of fresh pine and damp earth. As if, during the few minutes they lay on the musty floor, the supplicants were transported somewhere else, another world in which our seconds lasted for hours and our minutes took days.

For this is the troll's blessing: a gateway and passport to his plane of origin.

The land of the trolls is not a place visited lightly, but there is treasure to be found there, and wisdom as well. There, the aesir sip golden mead from the blood of a dead philosopher while old blind crones measure out the lives of kings and queens on purple threads, cutting them with silver shears. There, dragons hoard treasure, the cursed gold twisting through their veins and into their nightmares, until, they hope, some would-be entrepreneur with dreams of a start-up comes to plunder their venture capital. This has happened several times before.

There, gnomish peasants roam the wilderlands, tending yaks and unicorn with hides of rough leather and fur of bristly iron. There in the land of the trolls, goblins and elves wander freely under sunlight, meeting with trolls and dwarves for dances and trades and weddings.

There are many pockets from our world to theirs, many thin places, many quests and riddles to be solved. Not all supplicants come back. Not all want to.

Yet those who return from their sojourn in the sealed-off Beetle of the Fremont Troll do not speak of what they saw on their journey, though they're almost always changed in some way. Wiser perhaps, a little more forgiving. Impatient with cruelty. Less willing to give up on family and friends. Those who've partaken of the dragon's hoard come back with a burning gleam in their eye, yet there is something sad and empty about them, something lost in their fake smile.

Still others never return from the Beetle at all. When this happens, the troll's open eye closes, the Beetle reseals itself, and he clasps it tight once more. No one knows what happens to those vanished few. Perhaps they changed too much to return to our mundane sphere of reality. Or perhaps they couldn't change at all.

In Seattle, a troll lives under the Aurora Bridge. Some will say it's just a clever art installation. Others will say it's a symbol for a bohemian neighborhood's creative spirit. Still others will claim it's a wellspring of our collective unconsciousness, filled with mythic resonance. How else to explain a city where so many make their living from imagination and music? How else to explain a place where wizards gather on the coast to weave magic and design dungeons, where adventurers find paths and so many brilliant programmers build games of the mind?

But those who know the truth, the true-truth, beneath the literal and symbolic history of Fremont Troll, discerning what *should* be, know different. They know that the Fremont Troll is no symbol or totem but a creature unto himself. He is a guardian, a gift-giver, a bestower of blessings and devourer of lies. Perhaps one day, he'll grow weary of us and our little games. Or the day might come when he can no longer stand his staid and unchanging concrete form (for trolls are capable of changing shape at whim in their own world). Perhaps he will retreat back to his land through the Beetle portal we've given him, leaving nothing behind but a hollow statue. Perhaps he already has. But if so, the world is a poorer place for it, and there will be one less passage through the thin places between worlds, to the land of the trolls.

Green Lake: The Game
by Camden Rose

An immersive board game based on the real-life Green Lake in Seattle, WA, USA

66 fans on BoardGameRatings.com

"This game helped me fight for my inner peace." - Anonymous

"Truly, a game like no other. Once you start playing, you can't play anything else." - Jane from JaneWantsKids.com

GAME COMPONENTS

1 flashlight

1 water bottle

1 pair of walking shoes

1 coffee from a local shop (optional)

1 empty womb

GAME OVERVIEW

Green Lake is a 2.8-mile loop formed from the Vashon Glacial Ice Sheet. Its dredgings have produced volcanic ash, goose poop, and questionable muck. When the Olmsted Brothers updated the lake, they diked and filled until it shrunk by almost 100 acres.

Today, hundreds of people enjoy its scenic offerings. Small children, bikers, families, and dogs all loop around the lake, almost if they are searching for something, as if they've forgotten something and know that if they keep going around the lake, maybe, just maybe, they'll find the end and what they need.

What do *you* want though? Why are you here? Well, that's up to you to decide. For now, let's go with the simple: You're here to find courage.

Ready to start your quest? Once you have your game components, proceed to GAME SETUP and let's begin.

GAME SETUP

Go to Green Lake right before sunset. Tell yourself you'll finish before the sun goes down. Park in the lot everyone knows about. Walk past the fields of empty soccer nets. Walk down the gravel road, past the smaller parking lot near the stadium. Wonder how a stadium can look like it's floating on water. Wonder why you didn't park in the closer parking lot.

Hope that you can FIND COURAGE on this walk.

Keep walking. Find the beginning—or your beginning—of the trail. Green Lake is a circle. It has no start and has no end. It starts only when you want and ends only when you want. Relish in the choice. Try not to think about how it doesn't actually end or start, only continue forever. Try not to think about how it is as endless as your worries.

Try not to think about the *thing* that has been following you since you started this journey, waiting for you to LOOK BACK. Your therapist recommended a walk in nature, and so you must walk.

When you have made it to the start or the end or the endless beginning, proceed to PLAYING THE GAME.

PLAYING THE GAME

TAKING A TURN

To take your turn, move one step in front of the other. As you proceed around the lake, keep your voice off. Keep your steps silent. Let nature take over but try not to let it take over too much.

No matter what you do, don't LOOK BACK. Don't LOOK BACK. If you LOOK BACK, proceed to GAME END.

As you travel throughout Green Lake, you reach common and uncommon destinations. Read about them below.

COMMON DESTINATIONS

The common destinations are THE LONG STRETCH, BATHROOMS, and ENTRANCES/EXITS.

COMMON DESTINATION: THE LONG STRETCH

Green Lake has many of these long stretches. When you reach one, you have no option but to use your turn to walk and walk and walk. Don't RUN through these stretches. Don't use your flashlight, as much as you want to. You aren't allowed to see around the corners just yet.

Sometimes you can see expensive pastel-colored houses to the right. Sometimes you can see a glimpse of the small island near the center of the lake. Sometimes all you see is grass and trees and the path, endless. Sometimes you feel like THE LONG STRETCH is a metaphor for waiting.

You can look at whatever you want to look at as you walk, but don't LOOK BACK. If you LOOK BACK process to GAME END. If you RUN, proceed to GAME END.

COMMON DESTINATION: BATHROOMS

Depending on which bathroom you enter, your experience will be different. Only go if you need to. Try not to listen to the noises in the stall next to you. Try not to think about how you left your flashlight, water bottle, and (optional) coffee from a local shop outside of the stall.

Preen your focus. Focus on the stained toilet, the missing toilet paper, the broken lock. Don't focus on the red drops on your pad. Don't focus on the clinking in the stall over. Don't focus on the *thing* outside of your body, waiting for you.

When you have finished, leave the stall. Make sure to turn right out of the bathrooms, or you will enter THE LOOP. If you enter THE LOOP, proceed to GAME END.

COMMON DESTINATION: ENTRANCES/EXITS

Know that once you leave through an exit, whether it be concrete or gravel, when you return—for you must return—your return will become your beginning, and you'll begin walking around the endless circle again.

If you stop, you must start again. If you leave, you must return. You must accept that you don't have control. It is all up to your body and your partner's body to do what they need to do to give you what you want, and you are just going through the motions, taking your turn, and hoping that this time it'll be different. This time it'll work, and you'll get what you want.

If you leave through an exit before you are meant to leave, proceed to GAME SETUP. The game must start again.

UNCOMMON DESTINATIONS

Uncommon destinations are THE SEATTLE PUBLIC THEATER, GREEN LAKE COMMUNITY CENTER AND EVANS POOL, and STADIUM. If you see any one of these destinations more than once, proceed to GAME END. You are experiencing THE LOOP.

UNCOMMON DESTINATION: THE SEATTLE PUBLIC THEATER

If there is a performance at the theater and you have tickets, enjoy the show. Maybe there is a showing of a parody of Christmas Carol, or maybe a political satire about women's healthcare. Whatever it is, know this: Nothing can hurt you at the theater. The theater is a magical place where you can forget about the *thing*, your desire to have kids, and your relationship with your partner.

When you finish the show, use your excitement to power you through the rest of the trail. You are so close to finding courage. You might not be pregnant yet, but you can FIND COURAGE. If you do FIND COURAGE at the show that is strong enough to propel you through the rest of the walk, proceed to GAME END.

If you do not have tickets or there is not a performance, keep your eyes on the theater for as long as you can. It will keep you sane. Don't look at the ENTRANCES/EXITS to the other side. If you do, proceed to that game destination.

UNCOMMON DESTINATION: GREEN LAKE COMMUNITY CENTER AND EVANS POOL

Move between the docks and the BATHROOMS. If you end up at the BATHROOMS, proceed to that game destination. When you get to the community center, keep your eyes on the road. When the road splits, take the path to the right, the one closest to the center.

If you take the path to the left, you are taking a different loop than you are meant to take. You will never leave the lake. You have entered THE LOOP. If you enter THE LOOP, proceed to GAME END.

If you take the path to the right, stay to the side, near the closed ice cream store. You can look in the windows if you'd like, but it won't get you ice cream.

Ice cream reminds you of the kids you can't have. Ice cream reminds you of the money you've spent on fruitless pregnancy and ovulation tests. Ice cream reminds you of the ways your body has failed. Ice cream reminds you of your partner's insistence that you try, and try, and try again. He seems to have courage to keep going, while you're still looking.

The night is cold and brisk, and the clouds are blocking the stars and moon.

It couldn't be darker.

UNCOMMON DESTINATION: STADIUM

If you have reached the stadium, your cycle is complete. Ignore your beating heart and FIND COURAGE. Go to the exit. Walk along the gravel. Feel your body physically relax as you get further away from the lake and closer to the parking lot. Take out your flashlight and use it to guide your path. You might have been scared to use it before, but now you're safe. If you have made it here, you FIND COURAGE. Proceed to GAME END.

GAME END

There are many ways to end your game of the Green Lake walk. You can end the game with THE LOOP, RUN, LOOK BACK, or FIND COURAGE. Proceed to the option that is for you.

THE LOOP

It seems to continue forever, like a marble going around a circle ramp. Around and around and around until finally it falls through the hole.

You keep circling. With each loop, you're unsure what you've seen before and what you haven't. You're unsure if you've ever seen an exit or entrance, if you've ever started this game or if you've always been playing it.

You will keep circling Green Lake, wondering if it really is different this time or not. Because it's different this time, yes? Just like how every bout of conception is different.

Except it's not. It's a holding pattern. You are a plane, circling, waiting to land. You are in a bed, underneath your partner, yearning for someone to love. You are a woman, walking around a lake, hoping that maybe you'll enjoy it this time and the journey will be as exciting as the reward.

It's all the same. Every time is the same. There's desire, there's hope, and there's sorrow.

As you walk more, you become more convinced that you've always been walking this lake, playing this game. You're as old as the Vashon Glacier. You're as old as the volcano. You're immortal. You can't have kids because you can't die, no matter what your body has gone through.

You lose. Even though your bones ache, you won't stop walking. You'll never stop walking, even if your heart isn't in it anymore.

RUN

Your feet are loud against the concrete as you run as fast as you can. You look for an exit, an entrance, anything that you can save you. But it's too late. The lake is everywhere. The trees are everywhere. The *thing* that has been following you is everywhere. Running is pointless, you know, but you keep going and going. More steps join your own until it sounds like there's a whole army behind you. A whole army of all the kids you could have had.

You decide to end things with your partner. You know he wants kids, too, but you can't handle the way his face looks every time he tries, every time he hopes. If you leave him, if you run away, you won't face more failure. Before you can take another step, the shadows deepen. You can't see anything.

You lose. There's nowhere to run when there is no path.

LOOK BACK

Your eyes, seemingly on their own, find the shadows lurking just beyond, right behind you. You've been followed by the very thing you've been trying to avoid. It comes toward you and, just like all the times before, find that you can't move, can't make your body move.

You feel your brain and heart, your tired brain and heart, seemingly float above your body, as though they are separate. Because they must be separate, right? If you had control of your body like you do of your brain and heart, then maybe you'd be able to have kids. Maybe the joining of you and your partner would work just this one time. Or maybe you could force yourself to move on, to not mourn every possible loss.

But if this cycle, this walk, these cycles of conception, have taught you anything, it's that you never were in control. You never had a choice. You can do whatever you can to run away from the fact that your body is a failure which means you're a failure, but the fact of the matter remains.

No matter how much you want kids, the *thing* inside of you—your womb—refuses.

Except it's not inside of you anymore. It's been outside of you for years now, bleeding and broken but hungry. You didn't feed it for too long, and it left. It gave up.

You watch the *thing* slide to you like a snake, fallopian tubes wrinkled and shriveled like a prune. It turns its vagina—your vagina—toward you. It wraps you in a tight, motherly hug.

It consumes.

You lose. At least your death is quick.

FIND COURAGE

You turn to face the *thing* with determination. You throw your flashlight, water bottle, and (optional) coffee from a local shop to the side and hold out your hands. It wriggles toward you, but you're ready this time. You grab the *thing* by the tubes and pull down your pants. Then, with the same movement you'd use to put in a tampon, you force your womb up into you.

It settles nicely and almost seems to sigh in relief.

Congratulations! You have completed your quest for courage. You're ready to try conceiving again.

You win. The *thing* has decided to stay inside you for now.

Bridge Walk
by Gigi Little

The Burnside Bridge just would not stay put.

Even though staying put is what bridges are good at. Late-late at night when no cars were driving around on him, when no one was walking or biking on him, the bridge would leave his post on the Willamette River and go trekking around the city.

He didn't stay out long. After all, there are always people wanting to cross bridges. He just took one short hour each night—which was one hour too many according to the other bridges in town. It gave him a reputation for being kind of a flake, but he didn't mind. No one but the bridges knew about his nightly jaunts. He visited the Portland Rose Garden and smelled the roses. He visited Mount Tabor, which is a volcano in the city, and he was so excited that when he returned to his post, he stationed himself backwards by mistake. Luckily, the Burnside Bridge is pretty symmetrical, so no one noticed. He visited Powell's City of Books, but he was way too big to fit through the door, and the place was closed at that time of night anyway, so instead he read the billboards on the street. They weren't as interesting.

On Monday night, or rather Tuesday morning, at two o'clock, the start of his favorite hour, the Burnside Bridge was waiting for a lone car to clear his deck, when a small voice came to him.

"So, where are you going tonight?"

Startled—because usually he was so good about making sure he was alone before heading off on a walk—the bridge looked around. A tiny figure, a girl, stood on top of him at the railing, in the dim gold streetlamp glow.

"I know you roam around at night," she said. "I know everything about all the bridges in town."

She had a red coat over what looked like striped pajamas, and her hair was smushed under a blue knit beanie like she'd been in bed and had suddenly decided to leave the house in the night.

Was she eleven? Twelve?

It's hard for bridges to tell people's ages.

She leaned back against the railing, casual, like talking to a bridge at two in the morning was nothing out of the ordinary.

"How did you know I roam?" he asked. "It's not like I tell people."

She pointed her chin to a house just off the bridge by a block or two. "I live over there. I can see you from my bedroom window. Lots of times, this late, I look out, and you're gone."

Behind her, moonlight glittered on the water, and the lights of the city studded the dark.

"This is late for a kid to be up looking out a window," the bridge said. "Or standing alone on a bridge, for that matter."

"I always wake up in the middle of the night," she said.

"Do you really know everything about all the bridges in town?"

The girl pointed at the next bridge in the line of bridges that crossed the wide river. Its structure didn't contain any fancy arches or suspender cables, but the concrete of its piers, the two thickest columns that extended down into the water, were decorated with colored light. Tonight those lights were a deep pink. "That's the Morrison Bridge. It was built in 1958. At thirty-six feet tall, it's the largest mechanical device in the whole state."

"That's right!" called the Morrison Bridge, listening in.

"The bridge after that," the girl said, "is the Hawthorne Bridge. Built in 1910, it's the oldest vertical-lift bridge still in operation in America."

"Amazing!" called the Morrison Bridge.

"And you," the girl said to the Burnside Bridge, "were built in 1926. You're a Strauss-type double-leaf bascule bridge two thousand two hundred and forty-one feet long."

"I'll take your word for it," he said.

"You have two Italian Renaissance-style towers."

"Those come in handy," he said, "for storing the orange traffic cones I like to put out at the water's edge to keep cars from, you know, falling in the river whenever I take a walk."

"Hey, kid," the Morrison Bridge raised her voice out over the water to them again, "maybe you can talk some sense into this guy, stop him from gallivanting around every night."

"I just want to have fun," the Burnside Bridge pouted. "I just want to see my city."

"That's not true, Bernie," the Morrison Bridge called. "You're really looking for that other bridge."

The Burnside Bridge was quiet a moment. Then, "Okay, fine, whatever, I'm also looking for that other bridge."

"What bridge?" the girl asked.

The bulbs in his tall streetlamps glowed brighter. "Prettiest bridge I've ever seen. Seriously, you wouldn't believe how pretty. I've seen them around and I think they're just… I'm not sure of their pronouns, so I use they/them."

"The bridge's pronouns?" the girl asked.

The Morrison Bridge sang out. "He thinks he's in love."

The Burnside Bridge made an exaggerated shrug of his handrails. "Alright, what's wrong with that?"

"Bernie," the Morrison Bridge said, "you haven't even met them. You've just seen them from afar."

"Well, that's what I'm trying to do," he said, "Meet them, get to know them."

"I'll help you find them," the girl said.

The Burnside Bridge blinked his streetlamps at her. "You will?"

"I know everything about all the bridges in Portland," she said. "In fact, I bet I know which one you're talking about. It's the prettiest Portland bridge in my opinion. I'll take you there."

"Oh great," the Morrison Bridge rolled her eyes, or would have if she had eyes.

"Wow, thank you," the Burnside Bridge said. "Gosh, I haven't even asked your name."

The girl put her hand out as if to shake but then just patted the surface of the bridge's railing. "I'm Edy."

Edy helped the bridge set out his orange traffic cones, plus a couple signs reading "Bridge Closed," at each side of the water's edge. Then he disconnected himself from the roadway and they were off with Edy pointing the way. They headed north and a little west, following the river.

A bridge walking around at night isn't a simple thing since bridges really don't have any sort of feet. But if they raise themselves into an arch shape, their ends, left and right, can be used pretty well as legs. In order to keep from making like Godzilla and creating a path of wanton destruction in his wake, the Burnside Bridge tiptoed gingerly between buildings and houses. Still, he had a long leg span—or I guess you'd call it a bridge span—and moved fast through the streets. Edy held tight to the rungs of the railing and watched the dark city slip by.

"I don't get how you can do this every night and no one sees you," she said.

"Oh, I just turn on my forcefield," he said. "Keeps folks from seeing me."

And yes: now that he said that, Edy thought she could see this forcefield, a pearlescent haze hugging the space around the bridge. She wondered if she was invisible, too, inside its magic.

A warm buzz of thrill sat at the top of her stomach.

She said, "If all bridges can project these magic forcefields and move around invisible, why aren't your friends all roaming the streets at night, too?"

The bridge shrugged, nearly bouncing Edy off her feet. "I guess none of them have wanderlust like me. The only other one I know who does is—well, guess."

"The pretty bridge?"

"I've caught glimpses of them in all sorts of different places," he said.

"Then why haven't you been able to meet them?"

"Well, I haven't seen them at night," he said. "Only during the day, when there's too much traffic to leave my post."

Edy pulled off her beanie and let the chill two o'clock air stream through her hair.

"But yeah," the Burnside Bridge said. "They have wanderlust just like me. That's why I think we'd make a good pair."

When Edy and Bernie pulled up alongside the St. Johns Bridge—its beautiful, minty green gothic towers (four-hundred feet tall, Edy would tell you) rising into the black sky—Edy could already see that the Burnside Bridge was disappointed.

"I'm sorry," he said. "This isn't the bridge I've been looking for. I know the St. Johns Bridge. He's super handsome, yeah, but the one I'm looking for is colorful."

"Come on, this one's colorful," Edy said. "Look at that cool green."

"Oh, yeah," he said, "very cool, but the bridge I'm looking for has more colors."

"Hey," said the St. Johns Bridge, "I don't know who you're talking about, but my opinion is, you don't need loads of colors when the color you have is awesome."

The Burnside Bridge introduced Edy to the St. Johns Bridge, and even though they hadn't discovered the bridge they were looking for, the three of them hung out and had a nice time, including some cake the St. Johns Bridge had baked that morning. The Burnside Bridge told the St. Johns Bridge how Edy knew everything about all the bridges in Portland.

"Edy, tell John what you know about him," the Burnside Bridge said.

"Well," she said, "you're a steel suspension bridge and the tallest bridge in Portland. You have a one thousand two hundred and seven-foot center span and a total length of two thousand sixty-seven feet."

"Hey!" said the St. Johns Bridge. "You're good!"

"I'm sorry we didn't find your bridge tonight," Edy told the Burnside Bridge.

His parapets, the safety barriers running along his length and holding up his handrails, looked droopy and disappointed.

"I realize," she said, "I haven't been thinking about this right. Of course it's not the St. Johns Bridge. I don't think it's any of the twelve regular Portland bridges. Otherwise, why would you see it roaming around in the daytime? If any of the regular Portland bridges that are stationed on the Willamette River were to go wandering around in the daytime, people would notice them missing. I think this is a rogue bridge. If we're going to find it, we need to look somewhere other than the river."

On Tuesday night, or rather Wednesday morning, Edy and the Burnside Bridge visited Sauvie Island. They enjoyed the beach and picked some strawberries but didn't find any pretty, colorful bridges. On Wednesday night, or rather Thursday morning, Edy and the Burnside Bridge checked out Forest Park. There's a walking bridge there. Fiberglass pultruded decking with a cedar handrail, Edy would tell you. They asked him if he knew of any pretty, colorful bridges. He said he didn't but he'd keep an eye out.

On Thursday night, or rather Friday morning, they visited the Portland Japanese Garden, which was super neat, but the only bridge they found there was a tiny footbridge over a little pond. Redwood structure with copper finials shaped like lotus buds, Edy would tell you. They asked the footbridge if she'd seen any pretty, colorful bridges hanging around, and she had lots to say, but they didn't understand Japanese.

Later, when Edy and the Burnside Bridge had returned to his post at the Willamette River, his parapets were drooping again. "Argh, I'm never going to find my mystery bridge!"

Edy, tired and a little discouraged herself, sat on his deck with her back up against his railing. "We'll keep looking. Tell me again what they look like. They're pretty…."

"So pretty," the Burnside Bridge said.

"And colorful."

"*So* colorful!"

The Morrison Bridge, eavesdropping again, piped up, "You want colorful? What do I look like, a freeway onramp?" And she flashed the LED lights, purple tonight, that decorated her concrete piers.

"Your lights are nice, Morri," the Burnside Bridge said, "but not as colorful as the pretty bridge. No offense."

"None taken."

"So," Edy said, "how many colors are we talking? Like three?"

"More," the Burnside Bridge said. "There's red, and orange, and yellow—"

"Sounds kind of gaudy to me," the Morrison Bridge put in. "No offense."

"None taken." The Burnside Bridge thought some more. "Let's see, there's also green, and blue...."

"And purple?" Edy asked.

The Burnside Bridge blinked his streetlamps. "True! How did you know?"

"And the colors sort of sit on top of each other in bands?" Edy asked.

"True!"

"And all together it's shaped like one smooth arc of colors?" Edy asked.

"True! True!"

"And you say you only ever see this bridge during the day? Is it only when it's raining?"

"Well, usually when it's sort of rainy and sunny at the same time," the Burnside Bridge said.

Edy stood quick, put her hands on her hips and tipped her head back, proud of herself for solving the mystery. "What you've been seeing is a rainbow."

Bernie's gold streetlamps blazed bright. "What? Are you kidding me? You figured it out? Who is this Rainbridge?"

"Rainbow," Edy corrected. "And it's not a who, it's a what."

"It's a what?"

"It's light," she said.

"Most bridges are pretty heavy," he said.

"It's made out of light," she said. "It's not a bridge at all. It's a scientific phenomenon caused by the refraction and reflection of the sun's rays in drops of rain."

"It's...." The Burnside Bridge was quiet. Then: "Not a bridge at all?"

Instantly, the pride drained out of Edy. She was left with a dull weight in her stomach.

He said it again, but not a question this time: "Not a bridge at all."

True, she almost said, but didn't.

Across the water, the LED lights decorating the Morrison Bridge's concrete piers turned a dim blue.

For a moment, though, the Burnside Bridge's voice sounded light and eager again. "Well, how do we meet this Rainbridge?"

"Rainbow," Edy corrected.

"Rainbow."

"Unfortunately, we can't. A rainbow isn't something you can meet. It's not a bridge you can talk to or drive on or walk on or touch. You can never reach it. You can only see it."

"You can never reach it?"

Edy put her hands in her pockets and looked down at her feet on the bridge's deck. "Never."

The bulbs in the Burnside Bridge's streetlamps faded into dark. "That doesn't seem fair," he said. "Why should there be something beautiful that you can never reach?"

On Friday night, or rather Saturday morning, Edy was back again.

"You came," the Burnside Bridge said as he felt her footsteps tap across his back.

His voice sounded both sad and pleasantly surprised, like he hadn't expected her to return since they didn't have any mystery bridge to go seeking anymore.

"Sure!" Edy said. "I wanted to see you."

That made the span of the bridge's parapets rise in a smile. But then he sighed. "I'm not feeling much like going out tonight."

"I'm sorry we couldn't find your bridge," Edy said.

"I feel like such a dope," he said, "for looking for them for so long and then finding out it was nothing but a rainbridge."

"Rainbow."

"Rainbow," the Burnside Bridge said. "I feel like maybe I'll never go roaming again."

The Morrison Bridge, eavesdropping as usual, called out, "That's the smartest thing you've said in a long time."

"If it makes you feel any better," Edy said, "I think we had a really good time looking."

The Burnside Bridge thought about that and then said, "True."

"Hey, kid," the Morrison Bridge called over. "Why do you keep coming out in the middle of the night, anyway? I'm sure you have a nice, warm bed, and a family who'd be horrified to learn you were sneaking out."

"Yeah, I shouldn't be doing that," Edy crossed her arms on the bridge railing and looked out over the water to the glitter of city lights. "Remember when you said you just wanted to see your city?" she asked the Burnside Bridge.

"Sure," he said.

"Well, me too," she said. "I want to… it's just…" and then she spat it out fast like if she didn't, she'd never be able to say it out loud. "We're moving."

An early morning car shushed across the bridge, its headlights spraying silver on the roadway.

"I don't want to go." Edy's voice wasn't the usual lively chirp she used when she was reciting bridge statistics. She sounded small and unsure.

The Burnside Bridge's streetlamps dimmed.

Then they brightened.

"Hey!" he said, "I'm going to take you on a tour of the city. Just for you."

Edy turned, eyes sunny, "Really?"

"Oh, great," the Morrison Bridge mumbled, "here we go again."

"Let's get the cones up," Bernie said, cheery. "And then hold on tight. This city is full of magic. I'm going to show it all to you."

He really did mean magic. They visited the troll who lives under the Hawthorne Bridge and the gargoyles who guard the old cement building on Madison Street. They had a quick chat with the shapeshifting griffon who lingers in the shadows of Old Town. Some of the magic they visited wasn't magic-magic, but regular magic—the type of magic you miss when you forget that there's true magic in regular things. Like the murals of roses painted all over the city. And the statue of Joan of Arc gleaming gold in the moonlight. They looked at art in gallery windows and found poetry tacked to telephone poles. They visited Mill Ends Park, the smallest park in the whole world, just two feet wide and containing a handful of flowers and one tiny tree. Sweeping along on the Burnside Bridge, seeing so much of her city, Edy felt sadder to have to leave—and then she felt happier for having seen it all.

"I'm going to miss this place," she said when they got back to Bernie's post on the Willamette River, "and I'm going to miss you."

"It'll be sad for sure," he told her, "but the best friend in your life might be waiting to be found in your new home."

"There aren't even bridges where I'm moving," she stood at his railing, staring off across the water to the shadowy shape of her Portland house.

"No bridges? None at all?"

"Well, no big river ones, not like you."

"That's tough," he said.

A man on a bicycle, dim in the early morning darkness, rode by behind Edy and off across the bridge.

"Does it rain where you're moving?" the Burnside Bridge asked.

"Sure," she said.

"Good," he said.

"Why?"

"You'll be able to see the Rainbridge."

Out of habit, Edy opened her mouth to correct him, but then she smiled at him instead. "True." She patted his handrail. "Rainbridge."

Go, Goose, Go
by Erik Grove

No one knows for sure why they call him Goose

 An old story maybe

folklore we've lost to the whisper of leaves

or is it the way he laughs?

   loud and too honest

       head back to the gray and blue

He's always sunburnt in wet shoes

 trail stubble on ruddy cheeks, night club stamped and a paperback in his back pocket

drinking coffee and leaping puddles

library carded in cable knit

   erudite in the names of moss and sidewalk preachers and birds that fly away

 the places Elliott sang and Kurt said goodbye

 indie movie stores and vinyl record players

    craft cocktails

    hops and smoke

    a kiss that tastes like rivers and Sounds and the 7th deepest lake in the world

if you open your windows on certain half deserted nights and call his name

 Goose, Goose, Goose!

 (and honk —don't forget to the honk)

he will take you while the evening spreads out against the sky

    (or the morning or the time you have left)

    on an adventure

    (or an afternoon)

        to the trails and avenues, the concrete evergreen contradictions

the mistakes we've made and amends we've yet to give in cherry blossoms and middle school lunch trays

the promises we mean to make and the hopes we hesitate to say out loud in the storm-strained light

but let's go, he says

  to the high desert and dunes

    to the rainforest and neon towers

    to the best phō place in Fremont and the city of books

    to the stumps and tea houses

    to the sideshows and coliseums roaring

        across bridges

        so many bridges

        and more bridges

        and more

    to the food carts and micro brews

    to the mill towns we forget and the trails that never end

        mushroom covered, derelict, and wild

        our muddy backyard

          waiting

no one knows for sure why they call him Goose

    long gone our thinned-out flannel friend

        but we can laugh still

        like him

and we can roam still

like him

and we can

    and we will

        go

Beached
by Luciano Marano

Tanner smelled the corpse before he saw it.

Stench rolled off the whale's body like the waves through which it once swam, overpowering the otherwise typical seaside stink of drying seaweed and iodine. An immense mound of splotchy blue-gray blubber and muscle spread across the rocky shore of Manitou Beach, the macabre spectacle of it was revealed gradually as Tanner walked along the curve, staying just beyond reach of the whispering surf.

Dawn lit the sky, banishing the night's chill. Wisps of fog danced up from the warming ground and quickly vanished. On the distant ridge, a row of pointed silhouettes stood out starkly against the rising sun, making each house seem larger and trendier than the last. Certain residents of the exclusive neighborhood were supposedly petitioning yet again to limit public access to the beach except on weekends.

Tanner tried not to take their efforts personally, but it was hard. All his life he'd felt left out and picked last. Even at work, when his supervisor insisted everybody else in the Seattle office return in-person at least parttime, but never once broached the subject with Tanner. Just the idea of a confrontation, either with his boss or some nearby homeowner, made Tanner's stomach hurt. At this hour, though, and being more than two weeks after Labor Day, he had the beach to himself—for better or worse.

The tide was drawn back to its lowest point, laying bare the land it recently covered so completely, and glorious treasures were revealed for a brief precious time. Gorgeous shells and sea-polished rocks. Driftwood, smooth and white as clean bone. Bottles, watches, and other miscellaneous fragments of civilization. To say nothing of the tiny wriggling, scuttling wonders trapped in the pools left behind by the water's retreat.

And today there was also the whale.

Soon, Tanner knew, the water would begin its inexorable rise and this portion of Bainbridge Island would become unreachable again. Shoes crunching over the pebbly ground, the day's first find, a flat pink shell, all but forgotten in his hand, Tanner moved closer. In the years he'd been walking this stretch of beach—a kind of emotional bracing before the scope of his world became a computer monitor and spreadsheets for the day—and despite the many prizes he'd brought home, Tanner had come across nothing like the whale. Not even close.

His eyes roamed over its constellations of scars. He always thought of whales as gentle and graceful creatures, but life in the ocean was clearly more savage. The smell was nearly palpable, thick and weighted, and he imagined the stink permeating his clothes, like campfire smoke or cooking grease. It seemed insufficient, so ethereal a souvenir being his only keepsake from this strange encounter. He went slowly forward to touch the body and saw himself partially reflected in the whale's enormous cloudy eyeball, threatening and unfamiliar. Just another scavenger.

Back the way he'd come, out of sight beyond the bend of the shoreline, Tanner heard a dog's excited barking. Probably Big Mac and French Fry, he thought, picturing the stocky bearded man tossing a frisbee to his shaggy mutt. Only a few regulars frequented the beach this early in the off-season, so Tanner generally knew everybody he was likely to encounter. Big Mac worked nights as some kind of security guard in the city, and bringing French Fry to the beach was the first thing he did after finishing his shift—that is, the first thing he did after enjoying a hefty belt or three of Jameson, to judge by the smell of him.

Big Mac was nice enough in small doses. The dog, however, was friendly to a fault. Notorious for leaping upon anyone and everyone who came along, French Fry had supposedly earned a specific mention in local residents' latest petition—and not without reason. More than once, Tanner himself was badly scratched by French Fry's eager nails and soaked in his slobber. The overly enthusiastic dog chased birds, crabs, waves, frisbees, and beachgoers with equal obsessive determination. Tanner expected Big Mac would have a difficult time keeping him away from the whale.

The barking grew louder as Tanner circled the body, still taken aback by the sheer size of the whale. It almost didn't look real. Being so close made him feel very small. The day was heating up quickly and sweat trickled down Tanner's neck as he came around the tail of the beast, giving its largest fin a wide berth.

Inside the arc made by the curve of the whale's body squatted a young woman. She wore tight neon pink shorts and matching sports bra, the long braid of her hair pulled through the back of a baseball cap. A white fanny pack was fastened snugly around her narrow hips, out of which she'd taken her phone and was busily snapping pictures.

Sprinter—that was the name Tanner had given the woman, having seen her running hard along the beach many times but never exchanging more than a nod—turned to regard Tanner as he came around the tail. Her face wore a thin sheen of sweat and the expression of grave concentration. Beneath her battered Nike running shoes, the ground was stained with dark fluid.

"Have you ever seen anything like this before?" she asked.

"On TV, mostly," Tanner said. "And from the ferry once. It was swimming pretty far off, though. Couldn't see much."

"No." Sprinter stood and pointed at the whale's side. "I mean anything like *this*."

A savage gash, maybe four feet long and several inches wide, had been cut into the whale. The skin and blubber to either side was peeled back revealing layers of flesh of different color and texture. The blackness at the wound's center was absolute and Tanner wondered how deep it really was. How far away was the heart of this magnificent creature? What could possibly do *that* to something so large? His mind reeled.

"That isn't a normal cut," Sprinter said. "It almost looks like something came out of it, right? I mean something inside the whale."

Tanner was more than a little disturbed by the wound, though he could not say exactly why, and both excited and unnerved by the interaction. That morning began with his usual everyday routine: a short drive from his apartment in Winslow, stopping for coffee on the way, then walking along the shore, picking up whatever treasures and trinkets caught his eye. Now, all of that seemed pathetic. What exactly was he searching for? Anything interesting, yet nothing in particular. Nothing that really mattered.

Perhaps, Tanner realized, he merely hoped to find distractions among the rocks and sand. A new bauble to offset the drab, loneliness of his apartment. A new friend, maybe. Somebody who would smile and wave when they saw him coming.

French Fry's barking was closer and he heard Big Mac shouting. The waves continued lapping the beach in their usual steady rhythm. Such normal sounds happening around something so fantastic and unexpected as the whale only added to the uncanniness of the moment. Pain shot through his hand as Tanner found he'd been squeezing the pink shell tightly enough to cut himself, and quickly dropped it.

"I'm not a marine biologist." Sprinter turned back to the whale, raising her phone for more photos. "But I am a doctor. A dermatologist, actually. And I can tell you that's a weird laceration. More like a rupture of some kind."

French Fry came around the body in a noisy blur. Skidding to a stop in the rocks and sand, he turned to face the whale, barking frantically and growling, hair on his neck sharply raised. There was nothing friendly about the noises or posture, no trace of the unruly but loveable creature Tanner knew. The dog glared beyond Sprinter, staring fixedly at the whale's gaping wound, teeth bared and glistening.

"This happens all the time," Sprinter spoke louder, to be heard over French Fry, while

Tanner took a step back, away from the madly barking dog and increasingly pungent reek of the whale. The woman's eyes blazed intently as she took more pictures. It had grown noticeably hotter, and Tanner's clothes stuck to him uncomfortably.

"More and more whales are beaching themselves every year and nobody really understands why. I just watched a documentary all about it. They said it may be a sickness. Or it might be the effects of sonar or climate change. Underwater earthquakes. It could be something else, too. Something we don't even know about yet."

Big Mac hurried around the whale, breathing hard, gut straining against his Oregon Ducks sweatshirt, which was faded, sleeveless, and dotted with stains of different colors. His thick arms were pale beneath smudged tattoos.

"Jesus Goddamn Christ," the big man gasped, hands on his hips. "You just about gave me a heart attack. Come here right now. Get away from that nasty thing." He took hold of French Fry's collar and tried, unsuccessfully, to pull him away from the corpse. "Come on, buddy, knock it off already. The damn thing's dead, it ain't going nowhere."

Finally, Big Mac managed to drag French Fry back a few feet, though the dog continued to bark ferociously at the whale and struggle against him.

Sprinter whirled around, holding up her phone. "You've been warned before, Macklin. That dog needs to be on a leash. There's a sign!"

"You need to be on a leash, honey. And there's only one ball-busting harpy allowed to call me *Macklin*, okay? She's got the divorce papers to prove it."

"Just so you know, I'm recording this right now."

"Well, make sure and get my good side, princess." With his free hand, Big Mac reached into the left pocket of his cargo shorts and pulled out a U of O flask, unscrewed the cap using just one hand, then took a large swallow. "You want some?"

Tanner could only grin and shake his head dumbly in reply. How they could possibly care about such petty concerns in the presence of something so incredible mystified him. Couldn't they see that none of it really meant anything? Were *these* the sort of people he'd hoped to befriend by coming to the beach?

"Nice." Sprinter sneered from behind her phone. "Do you even know what time it is? And there's no alcohol allowed on the beach. There's a sign!"

"For your information, this is kombucha." Big Mac winked at Tanner and drank again while the dog growled and pawed the rocks at his feet.

Sprinter turned her attention and camera back onto the whale once more. "I don't have time now, hillbilly. I'll deal with you later. There's a procedure for this, I think. Somebody specific you're supposed to call when a whale is beached. The Coast Guard, maybe? I don't remember and reception sucks out here. I can't look up who to report this to."

"Why don't you call the police?" Big Mac said. "Go ahead and report the whale for trespassing. You know you want to. Maybe we could write up a petition about it?"

Sprinter shouted something at him, then she and Big Mac were both yelling. Like he was struggling to be heard over their fight, the dog began barking again—desperately, it seemed. But Tanner heard it all faintly, as if from far away, while gazing into the inky center of the whale's enormous wound. There was something in the blackness, he thought. Crazy at it sounded, unreal as it seemed, *movement* had caught his eye, something glistening in the dark.

For a moment Tanner imagined he could see straight to the middle of the whale. Something was there, he was certain. A new and wondrous treasure to be found if he only looked closely enough. Something more than he'd ever dared hope to find.

Something he could keep.

The blackness suddenly gave way to white, which shifted and squirmed as if turning over down in the dark wet depths of the carcass. A pulsing band of ivory moved up through the slowly decomposing meat quickly—almost eagerly, Tanner thought—toward the light, growing larger and forcing the sides of the wound to stretch as it emerged. Starkly white against the mottled flesh and congealing gore through which it slithered, but like a pearl, faint shades of pink and blue shimmered across the creature's skin.

French Fry leapt from Big Mac's grasp and tore off down the beach, back the way they'd come. His feet tossed up a cloud of sand and rocks as he ran, a strange new sound trailing in his wake. A wailing cry of fear, perhaps, or longing.

"What the hell?" Big Mac ran a hand through his beard as he watched the dog flee. "He must be going after something."

Tanner's mouth struggled weakly around half-formed words that might describe the strange creature emerging from the whale, the incredible birth happening in front of them. Part of him wanted nothing more than to share the moment with somebody—anybody!—who might recognize its importance. But, try as he might, he could not make himself speak.

In the distance, French Fry struggled with what looked like a big piece of driftwood, head thrashing back and forth as he worked to tear his prize free of the sand. Releasing his quarry from the vice of his teeth just long enough to manage a brief terrible yowl of agony when it reared up and wrapped around his neck.

"What is that?"

The gravity in Big Mac's voice silenced even Sprinter, who stepped away from the whale, without seeing the creature emerging there, and turned to scan the beach, face blanching when she found the dog. Instinctively, she raised her phone and began a new recording, eyes wide and unblinking. Together, she and Big Mac watched, frozen in disbelief, as some kind of ivory serpent twisted around the dog in slowly pulsing coils.

But Tanner could not drag his eyes from the creature's twin, weaving its way through the balmy air of morning, pulling more of itself from the whale, snaking tentatively forward to explore this strange new world of air and light.

For what, exactly, did it search? Tanner suspected he knew, but found it hard to form any kind of coherent thought as he watched the worm apparently "see" him as well, though it had no visible eyes, and turn its rounded head swiftly in his direction. Countless tiny legs lined the underside of the worm. Fluttering wildly, seeking fresh purchase, they almost seemed to be waving at him.

Sprinter finally saw it and began screaming. Backing away, she tripped and collapsed onto her butt in the sand, phone gripped tightly in both hands and held out before her like a protective talisman.

Big Mac paid them all no mind, humans and worm alike, watching in horror as one end of the first monster—the head, presumably, though it appeared identical to the tail—began to slowly push itself into his dog's mouth, which was stretched wide as it struggled to breathe.

Forced from the safety of its quickly cooling home inside the dead whale, and the temporary shelter of the sand, the worms evidently had no sense of scale, did not realize their own girth. And in its obvious hurry to escape the cold and bright world in which it found itself, the one penetrating French Fry did not care. It was much too large for its new intended host, though, and the sound of the dog's struggle, his jaw bones slowly breaking, were shockingly loud against the soft sound of the waves and Sprinter's sickened moan.

"Fuck that shit!" From inside the right pocket of his shorts, Big Mac pulled a black pistol. Tossing down his flask, he noisily raked the slide.

Dazedly, as if she might faint, Sprinter looked up at him from the ground and said quietly, "No guns allowed on the beach. There's a sign."

As he raised the weapon and charged toward French Fry, with the nightmarish worm seemingly determined to force its way into the whatever warm darkness there was inside the dog, Big Mac shouted, "There's also a goddamn constitution!"

Lost in contemplation of the swirling shimmering hues as they danced across the advancing worm's smooth flesh, Tanner barely registered the single gunshot which punctuated the morning, echoing down the long empty beach. The short piercing scream that followed, so quickly cut off as to leave one questioning whether it really happened, he tuned out completely.

French Fry's weak and wounded barking grew faint as, for the first time in his life, the dog ran *away* from something. He might survive, but he'd be alone. Tanner knew all about being alone. He never once thought of running.

Sprinter was pleading, her voice high and frantic, as the sand around her began to writhe. Lured out of hiding by the heat of human bodies, perhaps, or maybe the day's temperature as it climbed along with the sun, the wriggling mass of creatures surfaced and swarmed the screaming woman, seeking entrance. Access. *Sanctuary.*

Flesh is a boundary as transient and nebulous as the tide. And when it's shifted, Tanner thought, when it's peeled away and new vistas are bared, who knew what wonders might be revealed? His jaw began to ache and Tanner found that his mouth was open.

To scream?

To speak?

A greeting, maybe?

A warning?

He could not decide.

As the head of the worm drew nearer his face, Tanner's eyes filled with tears. He could not see, but that didn't matter, not anymore. He squeezed them shut and waited in darkness to be transformed. Suddenly, he felt huge. Tanner was certain he could be a giant—big as a whale, even. He could contain multitudes. He could be somebody's home, their entire world.

Here, finally, was what he'd searched for so long hoping to find. A treasure worth carrying away. A true connection. Something wondrous enough to put everything—his empty apartment, his terrible job, the petty disappointments of his life—into proper perspective and ensure he'd never feel lonely again.

Something to touch his heart.

White Stag
by Joe Streckert

"Amanda, this is crazy."

Their apartment building was still standing. It had bent and twisted in the great quake, but the old supports held. The rest of their downtown Portland block wasn't so lucky. Brick structures had cracked and snapped, and old metal had broken like twigs in a child's hand. Concrete turned to dust during ninety long seconds of shaking.

"He needs us," said Amanda. That wasn't strictly true. Simon was in good hands in the NICU. It was the best possible place for him to be. But phones and electricity were out. Amanda and Becca needed to know if their tiny son was still alive.

He'd been born at thirty weeks. Fortunately, Amanda and Becca lived a mere two miles away from the best NICU in the region. Until about twenty minutes ago it had been an inconsequential commute. Now, the Willamette River and a collapsed highway stood in their way.

"I can't convince you to wait until morning?" asked Becca. "There might be falling debris. Or aftershocks."

"You don't want to wait," said Amanda, meeting her wife's gaze.

She was right. Becca needed to see their son, too.

Their doctor had prepared them for a long stay in the NICU. It would be two months or more until Simon could come home. In the meantime, they'd visited him every day. Long workdays, meetings, and even inconveniently scheduled pickleball hadn't been able to stop their daily visits. Neither would the quake, apparently.

Their street was dark. Nothing electronic was alive. Here and there candles and flashlights flickered in windows and doorways. It was a clear night, and a half full moon hovered in the black sky. They each carried flashlights and made their way to the river.

"Do you think any of the bridges are still up?" asked Becca.

"At least one of them has to be," said Amanda. "The newer ones were designed with earthquakes in mind. Or we hire some guy with a boat."

"What do you mean 'Some guy with a boat?'"

"You know," said Amanda, "a boat guy."

"It's 1 in the morning," said Becca. "I think the guys who live on boats are still sleeping off last night's booze."

"Nah," said Amanda, "if the quake didn't wake them up, they were still smoking weed and looking at the stars. We'll find some ancient Deadhead who will be more than happy to give a pair of nice ladies a ride."

"Sure," said Becca skeptically.

"How hard can it be to hire a nautical hobo?" said Amanda. "I've got cash. We'll be fine."

"How about you don't say stuff like 'I've got cash' out loud while we're walking through a literal hellscape?"

"Hey," said Amanda, "Downtown has its problems, but I think 'hellscape' is a bit much."

The blocks between their apartment and the Willamette were an inky passage of shadows and echoes. Most of the buildings were empty commercial spaces filled with shattered office glass. A few bars buzzed with activity, lit with candles and the light of unconnected phones. "I don't have any bars either," said more than one voice.

"Maybe we should ask for help," said Amanda. "Go into that dive bar. See if anyone knows a boat guy."

"Let's just get to the river," said Becca.

It took them little time. During daylight hours the Willamette was a short walk from their home. In the dark they got there in perhaps twenty minutes as they navigated debris and damage. When they got to the waterfront an immense shape loomed against stars.

"What the fuck is that?" Asked Becca. Her flashlight played on the behemoth object, half-submerged in the Willamette.

"Oh. Oh no." As Amanda replied as they each figured out what it was. The Morrison Bridge, a drab but functional expanse of concrete, had collapsed in the quake. The main extent of the structure was twisted and bent at a sharp angle. It jutted up from the river like a stick in the bottom of a marsh.

"I hope no one was on that thing when it collapsed," said Becca.

"It was 1 am," said Amanda.

"People still drive at 1 am."

"Hello!" Shouted Amanda. "Is anyone there? Do you need help?"

No answer came from the fallen bridge.

"Just as well," said Becca, turning northward. "We don't want to be delayed. We have… What the hell?"

"Light!"

Some distance north an electronic glimmer shone in the darkness. A neon sign was still lit atop a cracked building.

"How on earth?" said Becca. "Is that the White Stag sign?" Becca was old enough that she called it "the White Stag sign."

"It is!" Said Amanda, her voice rising with excitement. "And the Burnside Bridge is still standing. Becca, let's go!" Amanda started off northward, toward the light and the still-standing bridge. The sign, a symbol of the city, was somehow still powered. The leaping neon stag still glowed, and the sign still spelled out "PORTLAND, OREGON," in incandescent lettering.

"Amanda," said Becca, "there's no way we're taking the Burnside. If the Morrison collapsed, then the Burnside is probably just about to fall. They're both old concrete."

"It'll be fine," said Amanda. "It's not going to give way under our weight. If it survived a quake and can survive two people walking on it."

"What happened to finding a boat guy?"

"Bridges are quicker than boat guys," said Amanda. "Our boy needs us. Would you rather swim?"

Becca followed her wife.

The neon stag bathed the bridgehead in a brightness not quite like day. "How is that still on?" asked Becca.

"No idea," said Amanda. "But if the sign works that's a good sign for the hospital. Their electricity is probably better protected than some old lights."

"Okay," said Becca, "that's a good point, actually."

"Let's go," said Amanda.

The concrete span was spiderwebbed with cracks and fissures. The White Stag's light was just enough that Becca and Amanda could see almost halfway across the bridge.

"You're fucking crazy for crossing that thing!" Behind them a ragged homeless-looking woman yelled in their direction. "But good luck. Don't die!"

"Yup," said Amanda, waving at the woman.

"Let's do this fast," said Becca. "This thing looks like it's ready to join the Morrison for a swim." Amanda nodded. Neither of them spoke as they set out across the drawbridge. Broken pavement crunched beneath their feet, and one of the small, sentinel-like towers on the side of the Burnside had tumbled into the Willamette. Amanda kept her eyes forward, lighting the way with her flashlight.

"Holy shit," Becca stopped abruptly toward the midpoint of the bridge.

The Burnside was two drawbridges that met in the middle. The span they were on was more or less level, as flat as it had been before the quake. The other was askew. The right side tilted downward toward the river. The left slanted up into the air.

"Okay," said Becca. "That's not good."

"It's only angled a little," said Amanda. "It'll be like walking on the side of a hill."

"Yeah," said Becca, "but let's try to hold onto something."

"Left or right?" Asked Amanda, indicating the sidewalks and handrails on either side of the structure.

"Left," said Becca, nodding toward the side that tilted upward. "If the damn thing is going to collapse it'll probably fall down, towards the right. Best to not be there."

"Good thinking," said Amanda. They stepped across the gap where the two halves of the drawbridge met, onto the crooked side of the bridge. Becca half-expected it to creak or groan when her foot hit the angled concrete. The Burnside did not respond.

"Okay," said Amanda. "We're doing this. Okay."

They crept toward the sidewalk on the left side of the bridge. It wasn't entirely unlike hiking on a sloping trail. Each clung to the handrail on the side of the structure, Amanda first and then Becca, taking care with their steps, as if they could shatter the whole thing with a wrong step.

"We're almost there," said Amanda after a long silence.

The structure creaked beneath them. Becca froze.

"No," said Amanda, looking over her shoulder. "Wrong reaction. Keep going."

"Yeah," said Becca. "You're right. Yeah."

Something large splashed and sunk into the river beneath them.

"What was that?" It was Amanda who spoke.

"Probably a big chunk of concrete," said Becca. "C'mon. You just told me to keep going."

"We should run," said Amanda. Her hands held tight on the handrail.

Becca said nothing but exhaled in a way that Amanda knew all too well. They both began to sprint.

Seconds into their run the scream of breaking metal filled the air. Sounds adjacent to gunshots cracked through the night. For a moment it looked to Becca like the entire world was rising up and taking off into the sky.

In a fraction of a second, she realized why: The bridge was falling and taking her with it.

Becca didn't know what else to do. She held on as the drawbridge span hit water. The river met her with a sharp impact and a screaming splash that eclipsed other sound.

She was underwater. She'd let go of the handrail in the fall. Becca opened her eyes and saw nothing but she felt cold river water hit her eyes, which somehow made the blackness deeper. She didn't know which way was up. The fall had scrambled her sense of direction.

She didn't know where Amanda was. There was no light to guide her. Maybe she could find the handrail again. Where was Amanda? She wanted to scream but didn't dare open her mouth. As she held it shut, the waters of the Willamette rammed against her lips, like some tiny but determined siege engine. If she waited too long the river would invade her mouth, her nose, her lungs.

She remembered that she was wearing boots, jeans, and a jacket. She knew how to swim, but not when encumbered by so much clothing.

Becca tried to remember her old scout training. She'd learned what to do when drowning. Was it keep your mouth closed? Or open it? One of them was the right answer. She couldn't remember. She was supposed to take off her shoes. How on earth was she going to unlace her boots in the dark? She'd learned swimming and survival but in the moment none of it floated to the top of her memory. She flailed around in the watery dark. Amanda. Where was Amanda?

There was pressure in her lungs. She recalled something about carbon dioxide and holding your breath. Becca desperately wanted to open her mouth. She couldn't just flail like this. She looked toward what she thought was upward. She'd go there. That was up. She knew that was up. She'd swim that way, break the surface, and finally open her mouth.

Becca turned her head around just to be sure.

Light.

She'd been wrong. Had she followed her instincts she'd have swam toward the depths. She turned around, pointed herself at what still intuitively felt like the wrong direction, and swam toward the light.

"Becca!"

Amanda's voice rang in her ears as she surfaced. She breathed out and in, letting the night air fill her lungs. Amanda swam toward her, treading water in white light. "C'mon," she said, "we've got to climb before this thing collapses. I swear, I thought you were about to swim to the bottom."

"My direction got fucked up," said Becca. "I saw the light. I guess it was the moon? I dunno. Let's climb."

The handrail was still attached to the side of the bridge. The span of the Burnside that had once rose into the air to let boats pass was now hanging off the structure like a bit of skin dangling from a cut. They could climb it, get back to street level, continue their journey.

"We can do this," said Amanda. "Aren't you glad I got you into rock climbing? Let's go."

"Let's go," echoed Becca. "I just hope this thing doesn't…" She didn't finish her sentence. Becca realized that she hadn't seen the moon at all.

Something was on the bridge above them. It glowed with white light and neither Becca nor Amanda could make out its exact shape.

"What's that?" asked Becca, slowly ascending via the handrail. The bridge wailed beneath its collapsing weight. Small bits of concrete fell off into the Willamette like stone rain. The glowing thing above them seemed to move from side to side like an attentive yet lightly distracted wild beast.

"Antlers," said Amanda. "It's… glowing antlers."

As they climbed the thing came into focus: An illuminated white stag with blazing neon tubes forming a tree-like rack of antlers. The creature's fur glowed with inner light, and Becca somehow knew that if she were to see its coat up close each strand of hair would be a tiny neon tube, abuzz with brightness.

The stag looked down at them, twitching an ear with idle curiosity.

"Is… is it going to attack us?" Becca was unsure if stags were territorial or not. She knew enough about wildlife to know that "herbivore" did not necessarily mean "friendly."

"I don't think so," said Amanda. "I think it's lighting our way."

"What happens when we get to it?" asked Becca.

"It's not like we have any choice," said Amanda. "Keep climbing."

The metal of the handrail was cold and wet in Becca's hands. Old paint fell off under her grip, and much of the structure had rusted away. Becca was indeed grateful that her wife had gotten her into rock climbing. Amanda had insisted that it would be a good way to meet people, especially other queer women. And it had been. But Becca had struggled with the actual climbing. She'd always been athletic, but she was the bulky and muscular sort. Had she been a man, fathers and coaches would have encouraged her to play football. She enjoyed power lifting and college rugby, not hoisting up her own considerable mass. But now the only pathway was up.

Amanda, who was lithe, agile, and would have been dead meat on the rugby field, was already near the top.

Becca's hands were covered in blood and rust. The handrail was not designed to be used as a climbing aide. The ornate, filigreed metal dug into her fingers and palms. It wasn't at all like the carefully sculpted handholds of her climbing gym, or the comfortable knurling of a powerlifting bar.

She had to remember to breathe. At least there was light. Climbing would have been much more difficult without the strange light of the stag.

Her clothing was soaked with river water. Becca wondered how much mass that added to her climb. How many pounds of Willamette was soaked into her denim? It was enough to make a difference. She went slowly, hand over hand, one step upward at a time, resting one limb while the others strained with effort.

She started to get tunnel vision. Black bars at the edges of her visual fields closed in on the bright light.

"Becca, focus!"

Amanda was already at the top. She was kneeling down, extending her hand.

"You can do this!"

The immense neon stag loomed behind Becca's wife.

Becca knew she had to climb. She would reach the top of the dangling span, or she would die.

Her arms felt like they belonged to some other being. The pain-filled things that were hands seemed to exist outside her experience. They did not immediately obey her mind's commands.

"Becca, take my hand!"

Amanda reached for her, but Becca couldn't move.

Simon, she thought.

Her son was waiting for her. Simon might be dead already. He might be screaming in the darkness of an unpowered NICU. She imagined him in his bed, hooked up to a powerless CPAP, crying for nurses who had been killed by falling debris.

She saw her wet, tired hands in the neon light.

She would see her son.

Becca dragged herself through the pain and lifted her body upward. Amanda was just a few feet away, surrounded by a neon aura. The handrail was cold, wet, and slippery beneath her palms and fingers. At one point a flake of old paint lodged in the side of her hand like a shard of glass. Becca couldn't help but wonder if there was lead in the paint, or if the cut would become infected.

She had no way of knowing that now. Her pain and injuries did not matter in the moment.

Amanda's extended arm was just within reach. Becca's fingers brushed against hers.

"Take my hand!"

Her boots slid on wet metal and concrete. Blood was running down her arm. Becca's body was so full of pain she didn't feel it anymore. Amanda was right there.

She grasped upward. Amanda's hand was in hers. Becca's wife was not a large woman, but her strength was enough to matter. Amanda pulled Becca up, enough that she could scramble to relative safety.

At the top Becca stood up on the Burnside's cracked concrete and immediately collapsed.

Her world went dark. A moment later she came to, upright in Amanda's arms. They were soaked with river water and blood.

"You did it," said Amanda. "I… I thought I'd lost you."

"That was a bit harder than anything at the climbing gym," said Becca.

 "I caught you as you passed out," said Amanda. "Glad you didn't make the climb just to hit your head on the concrete."

A creak of iron and shattering of cement broke through the night air. The dangling remnant of the drawbridge fell into the Willamette, kicking up river water and debris.

"We need to move," said Amanda.

"Agreed," said Becca. "And… what's with that?"

The stag regarded them from the center of the roadway. The buildings and streetlights behind it were entirely dark. Its neon antlers and glowing fur were the only electric light amidst the quake's devastation.

"It's a glowing deer?" said Amanda.

"Okay," said Becca. "A glowing deer. Sure."

"Let's go," said Amanda. "Before the rest of this falls. Move." They started walking at a fast clip. The cold night air stung on Becca's wet skin. She realized that neither of them had a flashlight anymore.

"We don't have light," said Becca. "How do we…"

"The deer?" said Amanda. "We follow the glowing deer."

"I don't think the deer is going to the hospital," said Becca. "I mean… why would it?"

"Uh… I don't know," said Amanda. "In stories white stags are good omens. I think. It means you're going the right way. Besides, it's the light we have."

"Don't the Narnia kids follow a white stag?"

"Yeah, it brings them home."

"They go from being kings and queens to kids in World War II," said Becca, "is that a good thing?"

"You almost died," said Amanda, "and you're thinking about Narnia."

Becca heard a wet, falling sound. Pieces of the Burnside Bridge were collapsing into the river below.

"Hospital's that way, right?" Said Becca, indicating north.

"It is," said Amanda. "And… well, looks like the stag is going toward it."

The neon animal strode through the dark, pouring white light into the world. The area around the beast was clear and visible, almost but not quite like daylight. Becca wondered if she heard the low hum of a neon sign coming from the creature, or if it was just some trick of her exhausted mind. Becca and Amanda followed as the stag poured its light into the cracks of broken buildings and shattered streets.

"It's going in the right direction," said Amanda. "We might as well take advantage of the light."

In the stag's vicinity they saw downed power lines and teetering utility poles. They gave damaged brick walls that swayed in the night a wide berth and avoided hazards like streets with cracked-open sewers. At one point they saw something run away from them and stop in the distance. It was a coyote. No, it was several coyotes: They were bloody, battered, and desperate to feel something besides pain. They did not go near the stag or its neon halo. The great beast was not prey to them.

"It can't be going to the NICU," said Becca. "Wherever an electric deer is going, it's not our way."

"Becca, we're following a giant, glowing post-apocalyptic stag," said Amanda. "Obviously it's going to lead us in the right direction."

Becca was silent for a moment. "This isn't post-apocalyptic," she said.

"Sweetie, take a look at that," said Amanda, pointing to a hulking ruin on the horizon.

"Okay," said Becca, "the stadium caved in. That does not an apocalypse make."

"An earthquake is a local apocalypse," said Amanda. "Still counts."

The stag walked onward, leading them toward a place where they could cross a highway in relative safety, avoiding a fallen overpass and a pile of crashed cars that smoldered in the distance.

"Do you think anyone's still alive over there?" asked Becca, nodding toward the cars.

"It's been a while," said Amanda. "Everyone involved in that pile-up is either escaped or dead. Besides, we have an infant who needs us." Becca was surprised that Amanda wanted to proceed past the smoking vehicles. But she was right: Simon was their priority.

"Apocalypse means 'revelation,'" said Amanda.

"What?" Becca replied. The white deer led them through ruins that had only been functional buildings under an hour ago.

"It doesn't mean the world ends. I mean, it could. An apocalypse is all about a wiping away of the old order and the creation of something new. That's the important part."

"I think the loss of life is the actual important part, darling," said Becca.

"Yes," said Amanda. "But…"

"Are you seriously going to 'yes, but' the human costs of a fucking earthquake?"

"Okay," said Amanda. "You have a point. I know how that sounds."

"Yeah," said Becca. "Thousands of people are probably dead. Our son might be one of them."

"He's not dead, Becca." A flame of anger rose in Amanda's voice. Becca decided she didn't want to have the fight.

"Okay," said Becca. "He's waiting for us. And we're coming to him."

"The stag wouldn't be leading us toward a dead kid," said Amanda. "That's not how these things work."

Life, Becca thought, didn't adhere to rules of narrative or myths or stories. Sometimes people just died.

But also: they were following a colossal glowing ungulate, like something out of a knightly romance. Alive or dead, they were heading toward their son.

"Amanda, do you know where we are?" Becca was realizing how dependent she was on her phone to get around.

"Yes," she said. "We're heading north. We just crossed the highway. The hospital is very slightly northwest of us."

"You're not just saying that because of the glow stag?"

"We're going in the right direction, Becca."

The stag crested a hill. Its antlers dipped out of vision as it crossed to the other side, but the white neon glow remained.

"C'mon," said Amanda. "We should be close. It's just over…"

When they got to the top of the hill the stag was gone. The white glow they saw was not from their guide, but the hospital itself. They'd been closer than they thought.

"How…?"

"They probably have their own generators," said Becca. "It makes sense that they would." They ran for the entrance.

A man was sitting at the administrative desk with gauze on his head. Becca and Amanda recognized him. He was one of the workers they saw on their daily visits to the NICU.

"Hi," said Becca, "we're here to see…"

"I know," said the man, "I remember you. You're going to have to take the stairs. The elevator's out."

"Thank you," said Amanda. "Did you hit your head?"

"A stapler hit me," said the man. "Flew off the desk and got me good. Bled a bunch but I'm not concussed. Go see your kid."

"Thank you," said Amanda. "Uh. Feel better!"

They ran up the stairwell, their footsteps echoing on the blank walls. Several stairs had deep cracks, but none was broken or untreadable. When they got to their floor, they knocked on the locked door to the NICU. At some point in their ascent Amanda had started to cry. She threw her arms around Becca with heaving sobs.

"He's alive," said Becca, returning her embrace. "You said so. You know he's alive. You know."

Amanda's tears flowed onto Becca's shirt.

"Why won't they open the door?" she sobbed.

"It's been thirty seconds," said Becca. "They'll be here."

"I just… I don't know what I'll do if he's gone."

Becca held her wife. "He's not gone."

A nurse in bloody scrubs answered the door. "You're Simon's parents, yes?"

"We are," said Amanda. She stared at the nurse's scrubs. "How is he? Is he hurt?"

"He's hurt," said the nurse. "He's…"

Amanda bolted down the hallway. Becca ran after her, into their son's room.

Simon was in his crib, asleep, as usual. His CPAP mask was on his face, and his heart rate and O2 monitor clicked away. He had a bandage on the side of his head.

Amanda screamed.

"Oh god," she said. "Oh no. Oh god. Oh god."

"Amanda," said Becca, "he's alive. Look! His heart monitor's on. He's breathing. It's okay. It's okay."

"Becca, what if…"

"He took a bad hit," said the nurse, coming up behind them. "The quake knocked him around and he hit his head. The doctor wants to keep an eye on things. Right now, everything looks as good it could, though."

"But if his brain is bleeding…"

"Amanda, his brain isn't bleeding," said Becca.

"We don't think it is," said the nurse, "but it's good that you're here. The doctor does want to do some imaging later, just to make sure."

"I want to hold him," said Amanda.

"Of course," said the nurse.

Amanda held their tiny son against her chest. He woke up as soon as they lifted him out of his crib. "He opened his eyes," said Amanda, her tears flowing freely. "That's good, right? That's good."

"That's good, yes," said the nurse.

Amanda held Simon against her chest for well over an hour. Becca rested on a hospital cot and they both looked out the window. The pale pink light of dawn crawled through the sky.

"My god," said Becca. "The city is…"

"Still here," said Amanda.

Becca was going to say "devastated," but Amanda was right. Downtown Portland was a collection of shattered glass and cracked walls, but most of the buildings were still upright.

"Look," said Becca, "the stag sign."

"It's lit up," said Amanda. "Somehow. Doesn't that thing turn off during the day?"

Becca put her hand on her wife's shoulder. Simon rested peacefully in Amanda's arms.

"Most of the time," said Becca as the neon stag glowed in the distance. "But I don't think the light is going out anytime soon."

Scabs on the Earth
By Karen Aria Lin

As I pulled into a parking spot for the Downtown Bellevue Park, my brindle rescue dog unfurled from the backseat and scrabbled onto the center console with alert ears and tail. My chest tightened as I ran my trembling hand over Yao-Yao's protruding ribs. I'd avoided finding her shadows to eat for weeks.

On my phone, I double-checked the internet forum posts that had drawn me to the park tonight:

My dog keeps digging and whining at this one spot in the grass

Mine too! Is it gophers? Buried bodies? LOL weird!

My heart had jumped when I first found these posts (search keywords: dog, digging, weird). I was sure the mystery spot was a scab on the earth where buried shadows of the past yearned to break free. Normal dogs could dig all they wanted, but only shadow feeders like Yao-Yao could release them.

This late at night, the park's expansive grass field and playground were deserted, except for a couple making out on a bench. I was relieved for an excuse to delay our confrontation with the shadows, which couldn't happen until we were alone in the park. I needed time to collect myself. My hands had been shaking all day, during my long hospital shift and the drive over from Seattle.

Would today's mission be like our trip to Oregon, where Yao-Yao had summoned a gold rush town with smoky saloons and grungy hotels? Or like Tacoma, where she'd released an indigenous village with peacefully chatting basket weavers?

In San Francisco, Yao-Yao had even landed us in the middle of a skirmish between prehistoric humans. We escaped fast enough for Yao-Yao to find and feast on some shadow acorns. But when we returned to the hole she'd dug, a warrior had leapt out from the bushes and driven his spear into Yao-Yao's leg. Her scream of pain has haunted me ever since.

That was when I learned that the shadows, despite being imprints of the past, could inflict violence upon us.

And then—my hands tightened on the steering wheel and my breath went shallow—there was the time Yao-Yao had summoned a logging mill in Everett. She'd been gorging on shadow apples near a tree, when a man had tried to capture her with a rope. When I threw him judo-style to the ground, I'd only meant to buy time for Yao-Yao and me to escape. I wasn't prepared for the sickening crunch of his skull against rock, the way his whole body went limp in my arms, the tangy smell of blood—

"Mizuki, these are just nightmares," my therapist liked to tell me. She couldn't understand how solid and real the shadows felt in my mind and body. I had to quit teaching judo because every time I sparred with a student, I imagined their skulls cracking open on the mat.

I startled when Yao-Yao whined in my ear. The necking couple had finally driven away, leaving us alone in the park. Yao-Yao, sensing what was to come, skittered to the rear door.

When I stepped out of the car into the cold night, my legs shook. I was in a bad state to face the shadows, but it didn't matter. Yao-Yao was hungry.

She bolted from the car on her leash, nearly yanking my arm out of its socket. She pulled me past a row of thin trees and the dirt jogging path, over a bridge previously occupied by scattering geese, and onto the circular grass field. Tail up and nose to the grass, she sniffed vigorously for the spot where shadows pressed against the earth's surface.

Near one of the trees at the field's center, she finally dug her paws into the grass and swiped frantically. I stood off to the side to avoid flying clods of dirt. My body wouldn't stop shaking. Deeper and deeper she went, expanding the hole.

When the hole was a foot deep, wisps of shadows began to coil up. I shivered when chilly shadows brushed against me on their way out of the ground.

My grip on Yao-Yao's leash was so tight, my fingers ached. I couldn't let her run amok until I knew what piece of history was emerging from the hole. Shadows poured out faster and thicker, coalescing around us and blotting out the modern world. Bellevue Park's grass field faded into the backdrop, replaced by a scene growing clearer under the moonlight.

Rows and rows of crops formed around us, low leaves curling over my feet. The smell of soil filled my nose. I inspected the plants, but nothing was growing. I was light-headed with adrenaline. Somehow, the vast farmland seemed even more menacing than town streets. Nowhere to hide.

Please, no humans. Please, let this be abandoned farmland.

"Kisama nanimono da?" A deep voice shouted behind me.

I turned—

—and found a man looming over me, his glinting metal shovel brandished upright, his shadowy face contorted with anger.

Dimly, I was aware of Yao-Yao yelping as I yanked on her leash.

And then, I was running. Yao-Yao sprinted at my side between the row of crops. I wasn't running *to* anything, just *away*. My heart thundered in my ears. My feet pounded against dirt. When more farmers materialized in my row, I trampled sideways through the crops. A wooden cabin popped into view, and I turned sharply to avoid it.

"Stop!" someone shouted. I kept running. Images stabbed my mind. *The man rushing Yao-Yao. My body slamming against his. His skull cracking open against the rock. Life rushing out of his body.*

Shrieks and shouts filled my brain. From me or the shadow people? Didn't matter. None of it was real. None of it—

I collided into something hard. A shadow man. Yao-Yao and I tumbled to the dirt.

When I got up again, a fist coiled around my forearm. Without thinking, I flung out my other arm. My fist smashed into the man's face, cracking against a cheekbone. He released me with a cry and stumbled back. Other farmers circled me like a pack closing in on prey.

"Get back!" I shouted. I crouched in the dirt and pulled Yao-Yao to my chest.

The man clutched his face where I'd hit him. He gazed at me from a few feet away and held up his other hand.

"We won't hurt you," he said calmly. "You're safe."

Safe?

My body froze in its tight, coiled position. My mind was spinning to dark places, assessing weak points in the farmers' throats and kneecaps and groins. The man was middle-aged and unarmed. I should go home, make a run for the hole Yao-Yao had dug up. I should use the man's overall straps to pull him in for a hip throw.

The man stepped closer, and I stepped back. I glanced around for the farmer who'd threatened me with the shovel.

"He didn't mean to scare you," the man I'd hit said. "You startled us with your sudden appearance, that's all."

"I'm dangerous," I said, forcing the words out through a lump in my throat. "I don't want to hurt you, but I might."

"Dangerous?" he said gently. "You just look like a scared young woman. And her scared dog."

I looked down at Yao-Yao. She was wriggling desperately out of my grip. I hadn't realized how tightly I was squeezing. I released her. But when I moved to touch her, she shied away with her tail between her legs.

My breath hitched at the fear in her wide eyes. Was she sensing more danger in me than the shadows? Did this mean that the farmers really weren't going to hurt us? They weren't advancing on us, after all. Just watching with concerned looks on their faces.

I am safe, I told myself, and to my surprise, I believed it. I let go of my fear, and my body collapsed inward, my head to my knees. Tears prickled my eyes. I felt the farmers' gazes on me. I wished they would look away while I tried to contain the emotions pouring from me. I took deep breaths like my therapist taught me. The farmers weren't attacking me. *I was safe. We were safe.*

After a while, the man said softly, "Where did you come from?"

I chanced a look at him. It was hard to see the contours of his shadowy face through my watery eyes, but he looked Asian. The shovel-wielding man had shouted "Kisama nanimono da?" *Who are you?* All these farmers must be Japanese immigrants.

I tried to summon the Japanese I spoke with my parents.

"Watashi no—" I started weakly, but the man cut me off.

"You can speak English," he said. "I was born in America." He peered at me. "So, it seems, were you."

I said, "Yes. I was born in Seattle." I couldn't quite meet his eyes, so I gazed at his chin.

He smiled. "I'm sorry I grabbed you. I couldn't have you trampling all over our crops. The strawberries need to be carefully cultivated to survive winter."

My cheeks flushed with embarrassment. I cleared my throat and said, "I—I'm sorry I hit you. Are you alright?"

He touched his cheekbone and winced, but then said, "Yes, I'll be fine."

"I'm sorry to intrude on your fields," I said. My voice sounded unnaturally loud. "My dog was hungry."

I reached out to Yao-Yao again. To my relief, she let me touch her head.

The man rubbed his chin. "Why don't you help us tend the plants? Then I'll find something for your dog to eat."

I hesitated. I'd never done a speck of farming in my life. I couldn't imagine performing manual labor right now, when exhaustion from my panic and my workday was hitting me all at once. More importantly, could I work with the man after hitting him? After I broke down in front of him and all the farmers?

"Dad!"

We startled and turned at the sound of footsteps. A 14-year-old girl ran toward us from the wooden cabin. The distress on her shadowy face seemed too heavy for a teenager.

"Dad," she cried again, stopping in front of him. She paid me no attention. "There's a war started. The Japanese have bombed Pearl Harbor."

The farmers around me broke out into uneasy mutters. My stomach twisted. I knew exactly where we were in history now. I knew what would come next—the executive orders to board trains bound for crowded, inhumane internment camps. These strawberry farms would be wrested from the farmers' grasp and turned into restaurants, concrete-metal office high-rises, and the Bellevue Park.

The man said nothing, just looked at his daughter. His spine had gone stiff. Now that he was the scared and vulnerable one, I had the urge to comfort him. I stood up slowly with Yao-Yao's leash in hand.

"Sir," I said tentatively. "Sir, I'll help you tend your plants."

The man said to his daughter, "Go back to the house, Rae." She took off at a run back to the cabin. Then he picked up a rake lying nearby and pruned the plants silently. Had he heard what I said? His expression was dazed. He knew the Japanese bombing Pearl Harbor wasn't good news for him and the other farmers.

Then he said, "Don't call me sir. I'm Tom. Tom Matsuoka."

"I'm Mizuki," I said.

He handed me his rake.

I led Yao-Yao to the end of the crop row and tied the leash around a stake. She didn't protest. She seemed to sense that I had a purpose to serve first.

I followed Tom around with my rake and copied the way he covered the strawberry plants with straw mulch. I had a thousand questions for him. My parents had immigrated to Seattle in the 1980s, but I'd always wondered, *what if the war had been part of my story?*

I asked Tom, "Why strawberries?"

He laughed, a delicately troubled sound. "We grow all sorts of crops. But strawberries are most important because we contribute to the Strawberry Festival every year in the spring."

You won't be around next spring, I thought. But I kept quiet. He deserved as much peace as possible, even if he would cease to exist in this form once I kicked the soil back in Yao-Yao's hole.

Tom passed me to some older farmers, some more fluent in English than others. The physical exertion of breaking apart straw bales, pushing wheelbarrows, and pruning weeds calmed my body. Working with the older Japanese famers felt like regrowing something in me that had been destroyed, like a reminder I was still good inside. My therapist had told me to find community, to stay mindful of the present. How funny that my present moment meant connecting with the past.

I'd almost forgotten about Tom, until he returned from the cabin with a bucket. Inside was a rainbow of crops—strawberries, cabbages, beans, and even meat scraps.

"Here," he said. "For your dog."

My "thank you" felt inadequate. I brought the bucket to Yao-Yao. She gobbled up her decadent meal, then licked the empty bucket. I scratched her behind the ears.

With Yao-Yao fed, there wasn't much reason to stay any longer. I almost hated to leave the peaceful farm, but it was quite late. I drank in one last look at Tom and the others as I led Yao-Yao back to the hole she'd dug. They watched me curiously.

"Goodbye," I said.

I kicked soil back into the hole. Tom, the crops, the farmers, the cabin, and the darkened sky dissolved into smoke-like wisps. They brushed past on me on the way back into the hole, warming me this time. The garden lamps, benches, and trees of Bellevue Park returned to focus.

I found I wasn't ready to go home yet. Standing in the middle of the park, I looked up Tom Matsuoka on my phone. Soon after Pearl Harbor, his family was forcibly relocated to California. Without the Japanese farmers, the Strawberry Festival was cancelled in 1942. The farmland they cleared across Wilburton, Clyde Hill, and other Bellevue areas became shopping malls, high rises, and multi-million-dollar homes. Tom's brother returned to Bellevue after the war, but Tom didn't.

As sadness and remembrance sank into my bones, I wandered through a curious stone archway near the grass field. There, Yao-Yao and I found a sheltered walking garden lined with bare cherry trees. I stopped to read a stone plaque near my feet: "To Honor the Bellevue Citizens of Japanese Ancestry Who Have So Enriched Our Community. May 20, 1993."

I said another silent thank you to Tom. I crouched down to hug Yao-Yao, who felt less bony already. She kissed me on the face.

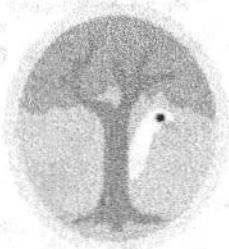

How Do You Like Them
by Curtis C. Chen

"Wow. That is without a doubt the fugliest apple tree I have ever seen."

"Jeez, say it louder, why don't you? Aren't we supposed to be keeping a low profile here?"

"Oh, don't worry, we're completely inconspicuous. Just two normal contemporary tourists strolling around lovely Fort Vancouver, seeing the historical sights, checking out the Old Apple Tree, what have you. See? Nobody's paying any attention to us as we approach the target in broad daylight."

"Maybe don't say words like 'target' right now. You remember the plan?"

"Sure. I'm on lookout duty while you hop the fence, and—whoa. Hold up. You see that sign over there?"

"What sign—hey! Come back! Low profile, what the fuck!"

"Never mind all that! Look here. Look at the date on this signage."

"You're joking. We landed in the wrong year *again*? I told you, we need to get a cutting from this tree no more than six days before it dies in June of 2020—"

"Yeah, yeah, I'm aware. But now we know which side of the target we're on! And there's one more charge left in the gauntlet."

"Um, don't we need that to get home? And don't we need to know *how far* we are off target in order to actually get this right?"

"Oh, that's easy. I'm running isotope dating on this sign now. That'll tell us how long it's been here, and then I'll use that time-delta to recalibrate the gauntlet for our next leap."

"Can you please stop calling them 'leaps'? It makes it sound like we're jumping off a cliff or something."

"Or into a river? I don't understand why you don't like the water metaphor."

"I am not having a philosophical discussion about temporal mechanics while we are trapped in the past."

"You could have just said 'I am not having a philosophical discussion about temporal mechanics,' dude."

"So you don't deny that we are trapped in the past."

"Only temporarily! Look, I've got the isotope dating, now I just need to do the math for this next leap."

"Really committing to that, huh."

"I will absolutely die on that hill. Okay, check my numbers here?"

"You still haven't explained how we're supposed to get home if we're using the last charge in the gauntlet to get to the target."

"Yeah, don't worry about that, okay? We'll be fine."

"Don't worry——? I'm sorry, I am *very much* going to worry about being stuck in the ass-backwards twenty-first century for the rest of my life! What aren't you telling me?"

"I'm sensing a real lack of trust in this relationship right now."

"We don't know each other at all! I don't even know your first name!"

"It's Whiteclaw."

"I will have questions about that later!"

"What's your first name, by the way?"

"*Later!* Please tell me how we are supposed to 'leap' back to our home era if there's no more power left in the gauntlet!"

"Okay! I wasn't supposed to tell you this, because we have a very clear division of labor on this assignment—I handle the time travel, you handle the biological sampling—but if it will make you feel better, I'll tell you. But you can't tell anyone that I told you, like in the debriefing or anything. I could get into a lot of trouble."

"Fine. I won't tell anyone that you violated this crucial piece of mission protocol by sharing with your partner what the travel plan was."

"Wow. And you say *I'm* sarcastic."

"Please just tell me what's supposed to happen."

"Once again, this is outside the scope of your responsibilities on this assignment, so you really don't have to worry about this. But once we get to the target and you've collected all the samples you need, I will be able to recharge the gauntlet for our leap home. It'll just take an hour or so, probably, during which time you can chill out and get some lunch?"

"Sorry. You really weren't going to tell me until *after* I got the sample that we were going to dawdle in this era before going home?"

"I thought you wanted to try some ancient foods. They still have chicken here! Haven't you always wondered where that phrase comes from, 'everything tastes like chicken'?"

"Don't change the subject. How are you going to recharge the gauntlet?"

"You don't really need to know that, do you?"

"Dear gods. Are you going to murder someone? Hold on, are you going to kill another time traveler and steal their shit? Is the plan to commit cross-time homicide?"

"No! Of course not! That's completely and totally illegal, not to mention it violates a ton of durable mission protocols."

"Just tell me what you're going to do for an hour that will recharge the gauntlet."

"*About* an hour."

"ANSWER THE QUESTION."

"Okay, but first, how much do you know about how the gauntlet works?"

"I know that it's powered by some kind of exotic matter that scientists captured from a dying star or a black hole or something like—"

"You can't capture anything from a black hole. Nothing can escape the event horizon."

"Whatever! Why is this part important anyway?"

"I just want you to be clear on the details, since you want to know about my part of the mission responsibilities. So yes, we need that exotic matter—it's called *solarium*, by the way—"

"Wait, isn't that... a room? Like a sunporch in a house?"

"It's an overloaded term. Chemistry and architecture are two disciplines that don't usually overlap, so I guess nobody minded very much when they picked the name. Anyway, solarium is pretty hard to come by even in our era, but fortunately for us, a small amount was discovered here in the past, encased inside a meteorite that's currently on display in a local museum."

"So the plan is to steal something out of a museum? How is that better than murder?"

"Wow. I don't even know how to respond to that."

"And how do you know that this special meteorite will still be there? What if some other time traveler already nicked it? Did somebody check before sending us back here?"

"Oh, no, that's the genius part of it, see? We've known about this special solarium resource for years, since pretty much the beginning of the gauntlet program. So every time someone needs to use the meteorite to recharge their gauntlet, they just log it in when they get back to our era, and we fabricate a new meteorite and someone else takes it back into the past to replace the one we took."

"So you're telling me that the rock we're going to steal... probably isn't even the actual original solarium-bearing meteorite?"

"Oh, it's definitely not. And it's not 'we,' it's just me. I'm going to go run this errand while you enjoy a chicken popsicle, remember?"

"Do you even know what chicken is?"

"I'm not the biologist. Anyway, like I said, it'll just take an hour or so—"

"Oh hell no. You are not leaving me alone here, and I am not leaving you alone. Shouldn't that be one of your 'durable mission protocols'? Never abandon your partner?"

"It's not a big deal. You'll know exactly where I am."

"And where will that be, exactly? Just in case something goes wrong, she said, rolling her eyes histrionically?"

"Not far. Just the other side of this metro area. I think the region is called—Beaver-town?"

"Wait a minute. Do you mean *Beaverton*? Beaverton, *Oregon*?"

"Yeah, that's right! How do you know so much about ancient geography?"

"Because I read the mission briefing! And, two things: one, it's going to take you at least half an hour just to get there, according to the map I saw; and two, you can't get there from here on public transit. We're on the other side of the Colombian River right now, in fact we're in a whole other province, *Washington*, so how the hell is this 'errand' supposed to take you only an hour? I'm coming with you."

"There's really no need for that."

"Are you going to steal a private vehicle?"

"I believe they're called 'cars' in this era."

"Are you going to steal a fucking car?"

"...Maybe."

"And this is something you've done before? In this historical era?"

"I've had plenty of simulator training—"

"Oh for fuck's sake. We're going together. Forget the whole stealing-a-car thing, you are not pulling a museum heist by yourself. It's just not happening."

"Well, I won't refuse the help. And I'm touched that you care so much."

"I just don't want to get stuck here! Ten million things could still go wrong with this so-called plan, and you're the only one wearing a time machine, so I am not letting you out of my sight, Whiteclaw!"

"Well, this is highly irregular, but I'm flexible. I do appreciate your concern, by the way."

"I'm concerned for myself!"

"Since we're talking about the plan. And *this* apple tree is still here, albeit not in a usable form—do you want to make sure your sampling equipment will work correctly? Before you do it for real?"

"I'm just taking a cutting from the tree. As I understand, these people do it all the time. I'll hop the fence, snip a branch, seal it into a sample container, shove that into my vest pocket, and then we go home."

"We'll also have to conceal ourselves when we leap."

"There's that tunnel right there."

"Right next to the road? In front of the freaking restaurant? Not very secluded."

"Okay, how about up on that, uh, land bridge then?"

"Hmm. Let me check the overhead map... Yeah, that would work. We'd be higher up, farther away from any other paths. We'd just have to wait until nobody else was nearby."

"Actually, no. I forgot we need to go grab that rock. We are not going to stay here after I get my sample. You're going to have our getaway vehicle ready, I'll run back to you, and then we drive out west to do our museum heist."

"What? No. Are you saying we leap out from the museum? No, no, that's totally against protocol."

"Why? We wouldn't have to come all the way back here again. It would save us at least half an hour. More, if there's traffic."

"Because the vehicle we appropriated would be out of place! Haven't you ever heard of the butterfly effect?"

"Is this some stupid time travel thing?"

"It is a foundational principle of temporal mechanics!"

"Like you said, I'm not the expert. Why do I care about this right now?"

"It's also basic chaos theory! Don't you study nature and shit?"

"Oh, wait, maybe I do know this. Is this the thing where a butterfly flaps its wings, and a thousand miles away, there's a thunderstorm or something?"

"Exactly! The smallest action will ripple outward and produce consequences that are difficult or impossible to predict, and the bigger the action, the more likely that those ripples will have larger effects down the timestream."

"Okay, you're right. The water metaphor does help."

"My point here is, we need to return the vehicle we're going to borrow back to where we found it, so it doesn't have an appreciable impact on its owner."

"But we're going to have it for an hour or more. Doesn't that mean we'd also need to know the owner wouldn't miss it for that length of time?"

"This is why I didn't want to get into the weeds with you on this. Yes, and I have that information available to me through the gauntlet. Are you willing to trust me to do my frickin' job at this point, please?"

"Okay! Fine! I do trust you. Honestly, I wouldn't have traveled back in time several centuries with someone I didn't trust. This assignment's too important."

"Right. And normally I don't ask too many questions, but since you brought it up—why *is* this old apple tree so important, anyway? We've got plenty of apples in our home era, so it can't be a preservation thing."

"Actually, it kind of is. Turns out that this particular apple tree is genetically unique in the world, and it doesn't exist in this form in the future. We don't have access to its full genome, and we need it for—well—I can't really tell you that."

"Seriously? After I told you literally everything about my part of this mission? Come on, dude."

"You can call me Sam."

"Nice to meet you, Sam. Want to share some more info? Like about *your* mission?"

"Look, I would tell you if I knew. I actually don't know. I was handed this assignment by my boss, most of my file's blacked out, all I know is that having the full genome of this old apple tree is crucial to some highly classified secret program back home."

"And you don't have any concerns about that?"

"What do you mean?"

"In my experience, highly classified secret programs don't usually have a track record of doing *good* things for the world."

"Isn't this whole time travel thing also a highly classified secret program?"

"Touché. But there are some clear and obvious reasons for restricting who has access to a time machine. You're just talking about a fruit tree."

"How dare you. Do you have any idea—of course you don't, I'll give you the short version, different apple cultivars are produced by—"

"Sorry to interrupt, but did you say 'carnivores'?"

"Cultivars. Meaning 'cultivated variety,' referring to a cultivated plant that humans have selected for certain desired traits, and whose traits are retained when propagated. You've probably seen different names for apple varieties at the hypermart? Like 'pink lady,' 'cosmic crisp,'or 'anhedonic ambrosia'?"

"Yeah, sure. So this old apple tree is genetically unique, you said, special in some way? Are its apples unusually delicious or something?"

"No, they're actually pretty awful tasting, from what I understand. I suspect that my bosses want the full genome so they can try to connect the dots, so to speak, between this cultivar and some other, ultra-specialized cultivars that have emerged in our home era."

"Why is that important?"

"Because the ultra-specialized cultivars of concern in our era are poisonous."

"Oh. Wait, what?"

"Yeah, I know, it's a cliché, but poison apples are a thing. And they're especially hard to detect if they're grown to be poisonous from the ground up. No obvious tampering of any kind, just all-natural neurotoxins deadly to humans baked into their plant genetics."

"Bio-scanners won't pick it up?"

"Funny story, these particular chemicals aren't toxic until they interact with human saliva. So yes, you can cut open an apple and then spit on it to see if it starts foaming and smelling like burnt almonds, but that's not really something that's done at polite dinner parties."

"Now I know why we always cut our apples."

"Fun, right? Anyway, whoever bred these poison apples obviously didn't share their records with the rest of the scientific community, so we've had to reconstruct the family tree, so to speak, that led to them. Mapping the genetics has been one of the best ways to pinpoint divergence, and from there we can extrapolate who might have been working on it and where."

"So your eventual goal is to track down whoever made these poison apples and... apprehend them?"

"Come on, Whiteclaw. You work for a secret time travel program. Do the math."

"Oh! So you're going to stop them before they actually make the poison apples."

"Ideally, we'll leap in and catch them red-handed."

"Hey! Sam! You said 'leap'!"

"Fuck."

"Well, that is a noble goal and a great plan. I hope it works out for everyone. And hey! Maybe we'll get to work together again! Wouldn't that be great?"

"Ask me again after we do this stupid museum heist road trip."

5 *Uncommon Ways to Get to Pike Place Market*

(an excerpt from Muddy Goose Quarterly issue 54, Fall 1991)

1. While carrying exactly 9 quarters, 2 dimes, and 11 pennies minted before 1982 in your left pocket, enter "PPM" for the 4th highest score in Space Zombies 3D in Tilt Arcade, Springfield, Oregon; step through the resulting space time portal.

2. Give a strawberry ice cream sandwich to the Grays Harbor hippogriff and say, "I'm feeling feisty!"; hold on tight.

3. Dial-up EmeraldNET BBS and post "Pick me up, please" on the Pike Place Rides Bulletin Board; wait for Leo to drive over in his Volkswagen.

4. Stroll down Pine Street following the slow slick rain as it rolls drop by drop toward Elliott Bay; consider how perfect this moment is, a late May Sunday morning wearing your headphones with your favorite song playing, thinking of a good friend you'll see soon and the questions you'll ask, the memories you'll share and what you'll get for lunch; know that you are alive and it is hard sometimes, hard for everyone, but it will be okay and it will be lovely also, as lovely as your favorite song and an easy walk, and you are simply enough and always will be and you will remember this, remember when you were content and you felt new, and Pike Place Market is across the street now and the pain au chocolat at your favorite French bakery is always worth the line; don't forget to say hello to dogs.

5. Whale catapult.

Desolation Jack
by E. Michael Lewis

Desolation Peak, Mount Baker National Forest, Washington State

August 1956

Jack Kerouac sat on the latrine, pants around his ankles, when the poet Hanshan leapt from behind the fire lookout. The old Chinese poet was dressed in brown rags and a cap. Bent and stooped, he twirled a rattan stick like a baton. Dancing madly past the fire lookout, he whirled and laughed with a wide-mouthed smile and sickly brown teeth. Jack opened his own mouth to shout "Hello" or "Watch your step" or "I admire your work" but the noise strangled tight in his throat. The ancient Haiku master waggled his finger at him, as if to say, "Pull your pants up and get to work." Then he danced away, a mad march of kicks and high steps that carried him behind the lookout and out of sight. Jack stood and started to run but fell, his feet trapped by his pants. He struggled up and followed the man behind the lookout. No one was there.

Jack bent down and looked closely at tracks in the dust, odd tracks, like the ones from wooden sandals he'd seen for sale in Frisco's Chinatown. He admired them in their perfection, the dry dust stomped flat by parallel bars like mathematical equations, a crazy dance of equal signs across the rugged face of Desolation.

Jack smiled a little and straightened. A rock caught his eye, half buried in the soil. He pulled it free and looked underneath. There was no poem written on it.

Of course not, he thought. This is not Cold Mountain, this is Desolation.

Jack pitched the rock over the cliff.

At 4,400 feet, Desolation Peak was devoid of trees but not of life. The ground around the lookout had been scoured clean of everything except grass. It grew thick between patches of light brown soil and bare rock, with species of wildflowers Jack could not name buzzing with bees.

The sides fell steeply away into undisturbed forest, sloping east into a wide valley and west down to Ross Lake. Fifty feet away from the lookout was the doorless outhouse, a peaked-roof single-holer covering a waste pit. A half-used bag of quicklime and a shovel sat next to it. One hundred feet on the opposite side of the lookout, next to the trail that led down off the mountain, was the garbage heap, well away from the lookout as a precaution against wild animals. Rusted cans, spent food wrappings, even old clothes mixed with unidentified bits of rubbish and melted into the hillside with many passing summers and winters.

Surmounted by a scorched lightning rod, the fire lookout itself was a small, square, dingy-white cottage with wide, single pane windows on all sides and shutters that could be braced open or fastened shut. There was a woodstove for cooking and heat, and cabinets for his food. Inside the cabinet was a six-inch knife with the Boy Scouts of America insignia on its handle, its pitted bladed spotted with rust. There was a bookshelf with four books. He eventually read them all when his own Buddhist text, his Diamond Sutra, failed him. The two-way radio was his only link to the outside world. The wood framed bed had a mattress that used coils of rope rather than metal springs, in case of lightning strikes.

In the center of the cabin was the Osbourne Fire Finder. The wide flat circle, emblazed with a map, rotated on a mount that extended down into the stone of Desolation Peak. By sighting the smoke and using a set of simple calculations, he could pinpoint a forest fire with a high degree of accuracy. Jack looked on it as his instrument of divination. Whatever land I gaze upon through its sight, he thought, will one day burn.

Or be logged, he hastily added. Cut, split, pulped, chipped, and shipped, until all the tall, majestic trees wound up in America's bathroom stalls, unrolling slowly into the ass cracks of a million lazy Americans.

Better it burn, he decided.

Looking north toward Canada, Mount Hozomeen pierced the sky with its twin peaks still covered in snow. Silent, looming and slate dark with ragged basalt cliffs, it reminded Jack of a discarded blade planted handle first in the ground, waiting to stab the foot of some wandering giant.

They paid Jack to come to Desolation Peak to look for forest fires, but he came to write, to experience, to meditate, to find The Void. He knew from the moment he was first alone here: Hozomeen was The Void. It was the center of all things for him, an insensible and uncaring pile of sharpened earth, alone with itself as only a mountain can be, not caring about the sky, or the rain, or forest fires or poet Jack. To the south was Jack Mountain. Though it carried his name and spiraled taller and truer into the Western Washington sky, it did not fill him with the awe, with the terror of The Void. Hozomeen looked out at the world without seeing him. It taunted him, forming that nothingness which all good Buddhists sought, the one Jack struggled to internalize, even when faced with a tremendous example.

Without a doubt, it was the most beautiful mountain he'd ever seen.

Now that he was by himself, rolling his own cigarettes, free of booze and Benzedrine and women, he found himself terrible company. He wrote in journals. Part of a novel. A long continuous letter to his mother. Uneasy, broken haikus. He turned off the radio to do it, which irritated the boys at Fire Command. Far from providing him with the freedom of distraction that he hoped would produce memorable work, he found himself lonely, bored, and yearning to return to the civilized world.

It occurred to Jack, while he stood on his head on the little patch of grass next to the fire lookout, gazing up to the twin spires of Mount Hozomeen, that the whole world is really upside down. Every person, great and small, is held to the Earth by the invisible hand of gravity—the closest thing to divine will that science allowed. Gooseflesh he couldn't blame on the chilly wind rose on his arms. Tasting bile, he moved his eyes from the mountain to his feet, which swayed gently above him, keeping his balance. Beyond them, the sky yearned to swallow him in an ocean of endless, open space, an abyss of blue that taxed his mind and added weight to his thoughts, until he fell, bent and graceless in the dirt.

The darkness unsettled him. He had been in the wilderness before, atop mountains even, but even so, the darkness on Desolation Peak crowded Jack into the lookout, forcing his shoulders to hunch as he scribbled his journal by kerosene light. The windows acted as mirrors to the dark, and every time he looked up, he saw himself in the act of looking up, his pencil hanging just above the page. The darkness sealed him in, forced him to look at himself. At thirty-four, he already felt past his prime. Yet in the half-light of Desolation, he could still look charming, even handsome.

The wilderness was also quiet, but that was fine. He had lived and slept both in noisy cities and quiet towns, but it was never truly silent on a mountaintop. There is the wind for one, moving in one ceaseless exhalation across the face of Hozomeen. There were also the noises of the mountain's citizens, as numerous as the inhabitants of Times Square. The drone of the errant mosquito, or the angry, stupid buzz of a bee, or the scritch-scritch-scritch of mice that crawled and crept just out of his field of vision, always daring him to look. These noises were magnified by the darkness. Any sound from outside, from the rat he caught sitting like a king atop the trash heap, to the skittish fawn that loped past him that first night, sounding like an elevated train.

Sometimes, after starting at a noise, he would stop to listen and hear nothing. Sometimes he would open the door and just stand there, breathing in the musky scent of the alpine flowers and waiting. He had been warned about the creatures he might see atop Desolation, the ones who might come around at night, the ones that roamed the forest and the mountains unopposed. Even knowing this, he sometimes left the door standing opened and cast himself into the night, looking at the stars and the ancient dull orb of the moon play around Hozomeen. Sometimes he would take the kerosene lamp with him to the latrine, hurrying and yet feeling childish for doing so, like a child on Halloween, waiting to be scared—knowing it was coming, knowing it deep in his stomach for a solid irrefutable fact. The darkness that held sway on Desolation Peak nattered at Jack Kerouac. It pushed inside his skull, hid there, hunkered down. It was the only thing bigger than Hozomeen.

Until he heard the thunder.

The poet Hanshan had written that many people who climbed Cold Mountain grew afraid. One night, Ned, the lookout on Sourdough Peak, called Jack and asked if he was getting lightning. Jack told him that the sky was clear with a bright moon—the truth. But then the north wind turned, and the clouds came in, and sudden, shocking golden patches appeared at intervals in the clouds. Jack signed off the radio so that he could dim the kerosene lamp and go outside. He paced about the lookout, thinking of his poet friends Gary Snyder and Allen Ginsburg and how they'd view this sight, Desolation Jack with a few days' growth, talking to himself in a lightning storm. With the first clap of thunder, he went inside, turned up the lantern, and lay down, face to the wall, blankets pulled tightly over him.

In the dream, Mary Carney came to him, loved him, offered him the promise of love and happiness and luxurious freedom. She flew into the lookout like an angel and pulled him into the sky, and they soared together like Wendy and Peter Pan, hand in hand. They winged low over the valley, brushing their fingers against the wispy treetops, moving from landmark to landmark as if the Osbourne Fire Finder had become the world. Mount Terror. Mount Fury. Mount Despair. Mount Baker, huge in the distance. Three Fools Creek. Lightning Creek. Freezeout Creek. They looked in on the other sleeping fire lookouts, like Jesuit Pat on Crater Peak and Ned on Sourdough, whose fire it would be. Mary laughed at them. She had a laugh that Jack liked. It reminded him of champagne. They flew over Jack Mountain, so low and so close that the snow clung to his hair and eyebrows, which he brushed away laughing.

Jack tried to steer her toward Hozomeen. "It's the prettiest. Like you."

Mary smiled and held him back. In her familiar brogue, she said, "Hozomeen is The Void."

"I know."

They had stopped now, suddenly back inside the fire lookout, falling horizontally into his sleeping bag. "Don't you want to see it?" Jack asked her.

"I've already seen it, silly." Her back arched and her skin changed to the color of dark granite. Her brogue was gone now as she said, "I am The Void."

Some mornings, fog enveloped Desolation. It huddled at his doorstep like a frightened child, bringing dampness into his bed. His world shrank to the confines of the lookout. When he talked aloud to himself, the fog made it sound as if a pillow had been placed over his head. In one of the books left by past lookouts, the author described the fog as female—if so, this girl-child was a cold, damp little skank, motherless and indigent. But the author was a hack, the story dull and predictable. Still, Jack liked the book, a pulp western with a lawman and his six-shooter on the cover, the thrilling title in bold letters, high desert scrub and dark sand in the background.

When he emerged from the lookout to use the latrine, he imagined himself lost in the wilderness, emerging from the forest and finding a trail, following it as it led up a rise, stopping and seeing the lookout looming there in the mist. It could almost be mistaken for a pagoda.

Mice infested the lookout. He could hear them moving around at night, unquiet scratches on the wooden beams, windows sills and cold floor. Isolation had emboldened them, as Jack learned when a mouse, brown with smart, twitching whiskers, nearly jumped from the Osborne Fire Finder into his stew as he cooked it on his little stove. And later, despite the fact that the cabinets were fastened tight, Jack found that the mice could somehow get inside, make off with even the tiniest of crumbs, and leave their little turds behind. Some nights it was hard to sleep, and more than once he felt the light pressure of sharp feet on his chest and awakened in the predawn to see the lengthening shadow of a tiny furry hump.

Once he opened the cabinet and found a mouse in the open. It had white fur and a long brackish tail. Neither of them moved. The little creature reminded him of his football days, of the cold look of an opponent. He slapped his hand down on the shelf—bang—but the mouse remained still. Only when he had lunged for the tiny beast had it moved, fleeing before Jack so quickly it could have dematerialized. After that, Jack used a rucksack and rope to bundle up his most precious food and hang it from a beam that ran the length of the lookout.

When he awoke in the next morning, it was light enough to see the sack of food swinging ever so slightly. He sprung out of his sleeping bag and punched the bag like a prizefighter. When it came loose and landed on the floor, a mouse tumbled out of its folds. Before he could stop himself, he threw a can of food at it, then his notebook, then the rusty knife. That speared it. The mouse skittered in place, then lay still. Now awake and in full joy of a lucky kill, he whooped and swore and shook his fist that the other invisible mice, who he felt staring at him from nooks and crannies when his back was turned. Jack the mighty hunter.

He picked up the skewered mouse and examined his handiwork. There was hardly any blood. He walked outside with it, intent on flinging it into the latrine, when he heard footsteps. A small shape held the corner of his eye, and he turned his head, expecting it to become more indistinct. Instead, it became crystal clear.

It was a small boy, no more than eleven. Gerard.

"Ti Jean," his dead brother called him in Québécois. And Jack remembered the mouse.

Gerard had cried over the death of his little mouse, so upset and angry with this awful world for inventing death and thrusting it upon those around us who didn't want it, didn't understand it and didn't care for it. Jack remembered how his big brother had fought his parents to keep it, to care for it, how he told his younger brother to value life, to cherish it, at all costs.

He looked again at what had been his clever destructive feat just a moment ago. He felt the weight of the knife increase in his palm, like it was becoming real. It reminded him of the knife he'd helped Lucien Carr get rid of over a decade ago. His stomach turned. He looked back to Gerard, who looked to him pale yet happy. Also, shorter. Jack realized that he saw Gerard for the boy that he was, not the big brother he had been.

"I'll take care of it," Jack said.

He went back inside and took a spent tin can, removed the label, rinsed it and shook it dry. Carefully, he scraped the mouse from the blade and deposited it inside. Outside, he filled it with wildflowers and walked to the garbage pit with his shovel. He removed a single scoop of earth, dropped the casket into the hole and filled it up again. Then he threw the knife into the latrine. Gerard had gone long before Jack had finished.

Jack's boots were in sad shape when he'd arrived at Desolation on horseback, so he had stopped wearing them. He hadn't used his salary advance to buy new ones—after all, there was nowhere to walk. The ground outside the lookout was not uniformly level, but the rocks were not all sharp. The warm grass felt good between his toes while he performed his daily exercises.

He was afraid to do push-ups, however, lest he bow his head to Hozomeen and raise it to find the mountain gone. Hozomeen turned a blind eye to Jack, busy being a mountain.

He was cooking split pea soup from powder. The smell delighted him. The mix was very precious and he was glad not to have lost it to the mice. As he moved to secure it in the cupboard, the light caught two beady eyes, fixed, it seemed, on him. He moved and his shadow exposed the mouse, not moving, brown with a daub of white on its forehead.

Instinctively, Jack's hand rose to swat it, to smash it before it could eat his food, his food that cost him fifty dollars in credit at the store in Concrete. But he didn't move. Neither did the mouse. They stayed in stalemate until it came time to stir the soup. He took his eyes away for a moment, and the mouse was gone.

The next morning, his took a pinch of the soup mix and scattered it over the other mouse's grave. From then on, he heard the mice but never saw them.

It was a black bear, most likely, whose scat he examined along the trail to Starvation Ridge, near the rubbish heap. Jack found the garbage pile disturbed and teeth marks on a tin can he'd used earlier in the month. He searched for tracks and found none but kept finding his shoulders hunched in apprehension. He now knew the primordial fear keener than that of dying, but of being eaten alive, of winding up not as a corpse in the ground for the worms to eat, but as a pile of shit along some forgotten animal trail deep in the forest of the Pacific Northwest, serving as little more than a warning for his prey. He wondered, how long will it be before they come to look for me, if I failed to make a radio check? What if I were injured, instead of killed outright? Would the bear pull my body into the forest, away from the prying eyes of Hozomeen, and finish me off? Would he leave me to bleed to death on the threshold of the lookout, arm outstretched to the radio?

The fog came again and huddled at his doorstep. Jack waited.

Coming down the mountain. When he got the call from old Blackie Burns, joy filled him and he hastily packed up everything, going down the checklist. It took the better part of the day, but the rain had returned, and the fire season was over, and with August complete, it was time to go.

The trail was a long series of switchbacks that led forty-four hundred feet down to Ross Lake. There was no escaping the need for footwear. Jack used his favorite pencil to trace the outline of his foot onto part of a cardboard box, then carved it out and whittled it down to fit inside his boots. Before he started out, he put on two pairs of socks. He took a moment, as he surveyed the lookout one final time, to take a knee and offer something like a prayer. Then he turned, hefted the seventy-pound pack on his back and started down. He was careful not to look at Hozomeen.

After three minutes of hiking, his boots were already letting in small rocks, and he wondered how he would make it down to the lake and keep his feet intact. His thighs burned and as he reached nearby Starvation Ridge (the name secretly thrilled him—who had starved here, he wondered), Jack stopped to smoke. He wrote a little. He could no longer see Hozomeen, but Old

Jack loomed above him, coldly indifferent. Below, the waters of Ross Lake were almost indigo. The day was clear, the temperature just edging on hot, with the wind hushed, as though weary. He looked at the forest ahead of him, but instead of thinking of Thoreau and his writings about Walden, it was Hawthorne's story Young Goodman Brown that came to mind. His loneliness overpowered him for a moment, then switched into a sharp fear that he could meet something in the woods, like the bear, or worse—an intruder. Someone who should not be here. Someone who could kill him—or bargain for his soul. The sweat on his forehead grew cold as he wondered which was worse.

He had to get off this mountain.

At the bottom, Fred would be waiting with a boat. If Jack got there late, Fred Berry would be gone. Jack didn't carry a tent or any real outdoor survival gear, and the radio was locked up tight on Desolation. No way would his shoes last a trip back to the top. He did not want to stay another night in this God-forsaken, God-filled wilderness. He thought of his life, living forever alone in Desolation. His eyes traced the trail into the shadow-shrouded canopy of trees. Then he pictured himself on the little blue tugboat, on his way to Seattle, then San Francisco, then Mexico City.

Yes, by God, it was time to go.

Jack entered the forest. The trail consisted of packed dirt strewn with stones at random intervals. The trees that surrounded him huddled together, smelling of damp earth and sweet sap. The branches created a ceiling irregularly pierced by thin beams of sunshine, giving the light an inconsequential quality. Douglas fir and Western Red Cedar grew side by side, some with trunks as wide as dining room tables. Between them, younger lodgepole pines flourished. At their feet lay decaying trunks of fallen trees, some charred, some rotten, each covered with ferns and moss. Jack felt like the youngest being in the forest. After a while, he found himself turning and looking back in the direction of Desolation as he walked. He had to tread more carefully because of his boots, and because of the uneven ground, and sometimes he had to duck under a branch or push one out of his way. Still, he looked back. He realized for the first time that the fear he felt had at long last built up inside him, a fear that something would happen and that he'd have to return to that inconsequential shack on the inconsequential peak in the middle of nowhere, a stone's throw from Canada. A fear that it could follow him, this Desolation, into the world—the one waiting at the end of his boat ride. A fear that Hozomeen's terrible indifference would stay on him like a stink, like a stench he could never wash away. Jack was afraid that the mountain was following him.

He ran.

After a moment it was more of a hobble as his pack swayed dangerously on his back, threatening to upset his balance. Slivers of pain stabbed his feet as his soles split open and admitted sharp, course gravel. Of the two pairs of socks he wore, the outer one was threadbare, so he imagined that as he hastened, he could hear the socks ripping. Still, he moved, until he came to a stop with a gasp, leaning on a tree, letting it shoulder the weight of the pack as he panted.

Until now, the forest had been hushed but not silent. Now there was a dreadful stillness filled only by the sound of his struggling breath.

Then a crack, like a rifle report, filled his ears and he threw himself to the ground by instinct. From above him, movement in the canopy—then a tree limb as long as two men fell on him and covered him in a skeleton of dead branches. He shoved it away, snapping it in two in the process. Its bark was gray as driftwood. Jack looked up and saw that the tree he had leaned against was dead. While it looked healthy for the first ten feet, the bark peeled away and exposed the point where, some decades ago, it had been struck by lightning. This was a dangerous tree, a 'widow maker', a tree that stood despite being long dead. In a forest fire, a widow maker could erupt like a roman candle or explode like a bomb.

Jack tried to stand, but his pack held him down. He slipped free and, after tossing the branch that had struck him, pulled his pack down the trail and propped it against one of the widow maker's living relatives. He smoked with trembling fingers and ground out the butt with the heel of his broken boot.

No sound but me, he thought. No sound but me. He struggled back into his pack and started walking.

The pain in his feet worsened. He tried to tread gingerly over the rocks, but they worked to defeat his efforts by pitching him askew. The tiny round pebbles, meant to give pack horses more purchase on the dry earth, sought and found their way into his shoes and lodged there. Jack stopped several times to shake them out.

One time, as he examined the cardboard inserts that were fairly well ruined, he turned his head sharply to listen. From above him, on the hillside, he heard something. A crash, and a trickle of stones and soil, dislodged as if under the pressure of a footfall.

Another branch, he thought. Just another branch. No one else is out here. Nobody.

Jack's mouth went dry as he heard the sound again, nearer now, defiantly coming from the trail above him, something moving fast. He squinted and thought he saw something—a shape among the shadows. He hurriedly stuffed the disintegrating inserts into his boots and put them on without tying them. Panic gripped him and set him in motion down the hill.

Fast. He swung his arms wide, not only to add speed, but to keep balance. As he ran, he tried desperately not to think, about what may be behind him, about what was behind him, what was coming down the mountain, following him, coming after him. But he did think. He began to mutter to himself, a mantra to get him down the hill—"the boat, the boat"—his thighs stung, and he could feel bruises forming on his feet, their blue-blackness spreading out from his arches, the skin under his toenails maroon, the nails themselves misshapen. Still, he ran.

He came to a fallen snag that, on his journey up, had required the party to dismount and lead their horses under. Now it was fully on the ground. Jack scrambled to get a leg up but found that it wouldn't swing that high. He tried to push himself, but it was too awkward with the pack. As the noise behind him sounded again, he pulled himself up and belly-crawled just enough to get a foothold, and in an awkward moment, found himself on the ground beyond the tree. As formidable a barrier it seemed, he somehow knew that it wouldn't stop what chased him.

He continued on, now cursing, saying every vile word he knew against God and the Devil and Buddha and Jesus and the rocks and himself and Hozomeen and Desolation. The trail grew dusty in places and running stirred it up, so that it passed through the sunbeams in paisley patterns, and Jack thought, that might be the last beautiful thing I ever see. Clouds of mosquitoes also hung in those patches of sunlight. As he crashed through them, they entered his nose and mouth, and he swatted them away cursing and spitting. In those moments, Jack wanted every insect in the world to die.

Through the trees ahead, he thought that patches of blue were beginning to form. The lake, he thought, I must reach the lake. His torrent of curses slowed and was replaced by whimpers. He could not go on. Despite coming all this way, he would never get off the mountain. He would die here, far from his mother in Lowell, far from Mexico City or New York or San Francisco. He would die and when the rangers came to look for him, they'd find his pack torn open, and his bones gnawed and mashed and poking out of a pile of shit. The rain will have come and made everything wet, and his precious notebooks would be sopping and torn and rendered meaningless.

"The boat," he cried. "The boat!"

Then, a yell came from below, from the lake. He responded by putting his fingers in his mouth and whistling. He heard water splashing on its hull and disrupting the rhythmic lapping on the shore, a sound which he had until just then equated with his own pulse. He stifled his whimpers and slowed, still cursing quietly, and walked down. The noise from behind him had ceased.

From the boat, Fred asked a question. Jack Kerouac couldn't hear him over the frenzy of his panic, over the delight of his relief, over the screaming of his suffering feet. He called back, "Huh?"

A Letter Found Among Records Recovered from a Historical Mystery Capsule, Opened on the Hundredth Anniversary of its Burial in Astoria, Oregon*
by Mark Teppo

July 19th 1924

Mr. Houdini,

Guided by the remit of your outstanding arrangement with my employer, the Pinkerton Detective Agency, I am writing to inform you of the matter regarding a mysterious cargo carried by the British ship, the *Peter Iredale*, which ran aground on the Oregon coast on the night of October 25th, in the year 1906.

The *Peter Iredale* was a 285-foot, four-masted, steel-hulled barque, and it belonged to a fleet managed by the ship's namesake, out of Liverpool, England. On its last journey, which began on September 26th, 1906, in Salina Cruz, Mexico, the *Peter Iredale* was listed as carrying 1,000 tons of ballast, slightly less than half of its available tonnage, and twenty-seven crew.

On the aforementioned night, shortly after sighting the Tillamook Rock Lighthouse, the ship altered course to enter the mouth of the Columbia River, where, afouled by mist and tide, it was pushed shoreward by heavy winds. Captain H. Lawrence responded in a manner befitting his commission, a manner vetted by the British Vice-Consulate during an inquiry in November of that year, but his efforts to jibe away from shore were confounded by a sudden squall. The ship grounded on a nearby beach, formed by sedimentary deposits from the Columbia River. The crew were rescued by the use of a breeches buoy, along with two stowaways.

As the crew of the *Peter Iredale* and the members of the inquiry board were all British nationals, I had little hope any of them would still be in the Pacific Northwest. To my surprise, however, I managed to track down three of the crew—one, in Seattle, Washington, and the other two, in Portland, Oregon. I spoke to each man separately, and each displayed a reticence to recall the events of that night in 1906, a reticence that I could not fully attribute to an impassioned devotion to their former captain. These interviews provided details that ran counter to the official record, and which I wanted to investigate more fully before presenting them in a report.

Following these interviews, I visited the wreck of the *Peter Iredale*. It is located on Clatsop Sands, a stretch of land not far from the township of Astoria, Oregon. The shallowness of the water along this stretch of beach makes salvage from the ocean overly complicated. Realizing the allure of actually visiting a wrecked ship, and the attendant increase in tourist revenue in regards to this activity, local authorities have made little effort to remove the ship.

As it has been nearly twenty years since the ship grounded, much of the wooden structure of the *Peter Iredale* has been compromised by the unforgiving weather of the Oregon coast. Though I did attempt to board the wreck, going so far as to hire a local fisherman to facilitate and guide my efforts, I was unable to spend any measurable time aboard the ship, which frustrated my efforts to verify and illuminate the contradictory details gleaned through my interviews with the crew of the *Peter Iredale*.

At this time, I was presented with a bit of providence. My guide was a local named George P—, a third-generation fisherman, whose father was present during the attempts to recover the *Peter Iredale*. As the hull was made of steel, damage to it was minimal, and it was altogether likely that the ship could be towed back out to sea. However, the weather at that time of year was both harsh and unpredictable, and before an attempt could be undertaken, the *Peter Iredale* began to take on water. As it listed to port, it became more deeply mired in the sand. George's father went aboard the ship several times, and, according to his son, was witness to an inordinately large crate, partially filled with rank-smelling straw, that was stored in a forward compartment of the ship. On the interior of this crate were a number of deep scratches that appeared not unlike those markings made by bears, who mark trees in their natural environment in an effort to denote their territory.

Having exhausted my leads locally, I directed my inquires to the origin of this mysterious box as well as the possible identity of the two stowaways, individuals who I believe were known to the crew of the *Peter Iredale*, and who were merely marked on the official record as 'stowaways,' a not uncommon occurrence aboard ships and freighters that plied the Pacific, in an effort to disguise their identities. As my request for funds to facilitate international travel have been rejected by my superiors, my inquiries have been limited to those persons who I have been able to reach by telephone and who have responded to my efforts at correspondence. Please consider the following details to be highly speculative and uncorroborated, though I hope the possible conclusion presented thereafter is of interest enough that you might provide assurances to my superiors for the necessary funds to facilitate a more in-depth investigation into these items of conjecture.

In 1902, and again in 1905, the Swiss physician, photographer, and mountaineer, Jules Jacot-Guillarmod attempted to scale K2, one of the mountains in the Himalayas. He was accompanied on both of these expeditions by a British mountaineer named Aleister Crowley, who later became more widely known as a ceremonial magician and occultist. I, of course, trust you need no further background on this man, as I am sure his claims of "magic" are very much within the scope of your ongoing efforts to combat fraudulence and chicanery in matters spiritual and esoteric.

Both of these expeditions were failures. The first was beset with mishaps and medical conditions exacerbated by environmental conditions. The second was unsuccessful due to extensive conflicts between Jacot-Guillarmod and Crowley as to the pace, purpose, and direction of the expeditions. Jacot-Guillarmod, it would appear, was invested in scaling this mountain. Crowley, on the other hand, whether due to some lingering effect of the illnesses and snow blindness suffered on the previous expedition, seems to have been searching for something. The 1905 expedition met with tragedy when several members of the company were killed in an unexpected avalanche, after which Crowley unexpectedly left the expedition.

Previously, in 1904, Crowley, along with his new bride, Rose Edith Kelly, spent some time in Cairo, Egypt, where he claims to have been visited by an incorporeal entity named "Aiwass," who spoke to him over the course of three days. This visitation became *Liber AL vet Legis*, also known as the *Book of the Law*, which became the basis for Thelema, Crowley's esoteric religious movement.

I am not an exceptionally educated man, Mr. Houdini, though the Pinkerton Detective Agency prides itself on hiring men of reasonable intelligence and learning, and while I have scoured Crowley's text multiple times, I have been unable to find a concrete reference therein that would facilitate and properly illuminate my forthcoming conclusion. That said, I do believe there is a connection between something that Crowley saw, or thought he saw while in the grips of malaria-influenced delirium on the slopes of K2 in 1902, and what he received from Aiwass in 1904, that propelled him to undertake the second expedition in 1905, as well as his decision to unceremoniously abandon the expedition.

Following his departure from the mountain, Crowley made his way across India. First through British-ruled United Provinces, where he purported engaged in some sport hunting, which may or may not have been related to what he found on the mountain, then to Calcutta, where some manner of altercation occurred, forcing Crowley to flee India entirely. From there, he went to Burma, Shanghai, Japan, Canada, ultimately arriving in New York City, where, apparently, he sought funding to return to the Himalayas.

Failing to secure necessary monies, he returned to London.

In 1914, Crowley came back to the United States, where he spent some time in the Pacific Northwest. My understanding is that he was meeting with members of the North American branch of the Ordo Templi Orientis, an occult order of which he was a member. Ostensibly, he was attempting to educate members of the Order and other interested parties in Thelema, a spiritual philosophy of his devising, though I suspect he may have been more interested in reports of supernatural creatures in the region. Attempts to reach Mr. Crowley directly have been unsuccessful, and on several occasions, I have been cautioned about my efforts in this regard, as my interests are raising undue attention within my organization, quite possibly due to outstanding legal and moral concerns regarding a wilderness retreat of Crowley's on Esopus Island, on the Hudson River, in 1918. As much as I would like to pursue this line of inquiry directly, I must, for the time being, find other ways to establish the veracity of my conclusion.

As to my conclusion, well, let us start with a book recently written by Lieutenant-Colonel Charles Howard-Bury entitled *Mount Everest the Reconnaissance, 1921*, which is a record of the Lieutenant-Colonel's effort to scale Everest. In this book, Howard-Bury speaks of tracks spotted at 21,000 feet that appear to be those of a bare-footed man. Howard-Bury's sherpas said these tracks belong to 'The Wild Man of the Snows,' a local monster that purportedly lives at this altitude. Howard-Bury gave a name to this creature. He called it the "Abominable Snowman."

I hope you can forgive the imaginative leap that I am about to make, but I am certain you will understand—if not outright share—the curiosity that leads me to make such conjecture.

I believe that Crowley captured one of these snow monsters during the 1905 expedition. Perhaps Jacot-Guillarmod, whose father was a well-known naturalist and painter, was party to this adventure as well. Perhaps the death of the porters and expedition members was due to some malfeasance or accident occurring during the capture of this monster. Regardless, Crowley decided the beast was his and his alone, and he took it with him when he departed.

His time in the United Provinces of Agra and Oudh may have very well be spent showing off the beast to local princes. He likely needed funds to facilitate its transport, and I believe his rash behavior with the beast culminated in an attempt to steal it from him in Calcutta.

Afterward, his seemingly listless passage from Burma to Shanghai was likely an effort to forestall interest in his mysterious cargo. In Shanghai, while he was able to find passage for his box, he got separated from it, and it ended up in Mexico, while he went north, through Japan and to Canada.

Crowley's time spent in New York City, ostensibly sourcing funds to return to the Himalayas, was likely to be supported by the timely arrival of the beast in a decidedly dramatic flourish—almost worthy of a stage magician, if I may. But, alas, the *Peter Iredale*, which was transporting his box from Mexico to Seattle, where it would have been loaded onto a railcar, floundered and ran aground.

Whether the beast escaped from its prison on its own accord, in the hours following the grounding of the ship, or whether one of the two men who were guarding its transport opened the box, I do not know. But, if we are to believe what George P—'s father saw on the wreck of the *Peter Iredale*, the beast did, indeed, escape.

In the past few days, I have heard stories of a large "ape-like" creature on the southern slope of Mount St. Helens, one of the nearby peaks in the Cascade Mountain range. The US Forest Service has instructed several rangers to investigate these claims, and I have managed to convince them to allow me to accompany their investigation. We leave on the morrow, and I will report more fully upon my return.

Yours, in curiosity and speculative,

E. Percy Cheliss

*The capsule, buried on the premise of a Mr. Arthur Abernathy H—, was marked with the seal of the Society of Assembled Magicians & Esoterics (S.A.M.E.), an organization that originated in the back room of Murther & Murmer, a magic shop based in San Francisco. Organizational records of S. A. M. E. are sparse, but among the extant documents (most of which are part of the permanent collection housed in the Houdini Museum in Scranton, PA), there is mention of a Historical Mystery Project, which was the creation and burial of capsules containing historical ephemera relevant to Harry Houdini's continued fascination with Spiritualism, the occult, and other matters supernatural.

Requiem

by Sarah Walker

The radio's dial burned amber in the dark, the yellow eye illuminating a voice that he didn't recognize at first, unintelligible, low, and quiet, the murmur of a river as it works itself over rocks.

He didn't remember leaving it on. He should turn it off, but he was so tired.

The noise grew, the voice morphing into static, and then his father, a man he had barely known,

Come…

Finally, he managed to wake, seeing to his surprise that the radio wasn't on after all.

And then he remembered that it didn't even work.

The postage box sat on the table. Innocuous.

He fell back asleep.

That morning, he was worried. He'd been dreaming of his dead mother. She'd been under the cabin in the floorboards, watching him through the slits.

He looked over at the black leather bag.

He was still tired. Each time he thought about what had happened, a little more of him felt lost. Maybe that was the intention of the current chaos his life had become. It seemed to want with a burning occult life to break him down into his constituent parts, and then into dust.

Maybe that's what his father had done to his mother.

The ride had been long and boring, winter rain and sleet falling in a continuous shower as the vehicle made its way down Highway 101, steam turning the windows into blurry smears of impressionistic lights as the other lane's cars passed by much too closely on the two-lane road.

To the west, an ocean dark and roiling danced in a watery madness while to the east, a million-year-old cliff stood dark, an unearthly sentinel, the man-made highway coiling snakelike around it, barely clinging to the rock formations before diving back into a scrubby pine choked area the roadway passed through before arriving finally in the fishing town where his parents had come from.

He took out the photo he'd found of his father. It'd been there in his aunts' belongings all along.

That meant it'd been with him the whole time.

Realizing that had been like finding out that something invisible was exploring his mind for an entry point, its dark fingers lightly touching the back of his skull.

He traced his finger over the photo.

He'd seen the town only in photos, the polaroid background showing the small coastal town, the pale white sky above hung with a mercury silver dime for the sun. It made the scene bleak.

But despite this, his mother's eyes were bright and friendly as she looked out from the past, her eyes shining crescent moons. They contrasted against his father's hard stare, a black expression consuming him and reaching out at Andreas from thirty years ago.

It had been hard for them then, with the fisheries closing, the logging companies moving away. Maybe his father had been different before.

Had she known how his father was? And if so, why did she stay?

He looked out of the window of the beach cabin at the rising tide that now reached the doorstep of his parents' old place with the effects of global warming.

Soon, the cottage would be under the water, fish swimming through the entryways, crabs camped in the corners and on the shelves, nothing but shadows in a murky deep.

An abandoned house inhabited only by spirits of the sea. That's what had become of their small family.

As impossible as it seems, time has a way of making what is fated to happen, happen, bringing together seemingly unrelated things, and weaving them into fever dreams and nightmares whether we like it or not.

And in its desire time sometimes resurrected things better left dead.

Synchronicity is real. And if this house was destined to be swallowed like that mountain and its forest before it, then this was the place where he'd finally be able to rid himself of his past.

He hoped.

He took a deep breath, stealing himself against what he had to do.

The bag sat in front of him on the Formica kitchen table.

He unzipped it.

His father's face looked out, eyes partway open, clouded over, the transparent plastic bag wrapped around dried and desiccated lips so tightly around his nose, it'd distorted the visage badly.

It never got easier seeing the dead man. If that was what it even was.

How many times had he thrown the head away after finding it in his aunt's belongings? Four? Five? Six? The days and weeks had begun to bleed into each other ever since this matter had started.

The first time he found it, he had confronted his aunt in a blind panic.

"What did you do to him?"

"What needed to be done."

"But why would you …do that?"

She shook her head as he told her.

"I didn't. All I did is shoot him, put him out of his misery."

"Well, where the fuck did it come from then?"

"It appeared one day. I have tried and tried to get rid of it."

"Like that? Wrapped in plastic?"

She shook her head. "No, I did that. I worried it'd rot. But it doesn't."

They both had stared at the thing, finally agreeing to go to bed.

They would try and sort the issue in the morning. But when he'd come down to check, the head was gone.

He told his aunt in a rush, but all she did was turn on the coffee pot.

He then asked his aunt if she believed in ghosts. At first, she said nothing but as he stood to leave, she finally spoke.

"Don't talk about it. Whatever it was, it's over. Just forget it. Maybe it won't come back this time."

And for a month, nothing happened.

But then it came back.

Family secrets are normal. That's what his aunt told him after he'd found the head again, this time in a box postmarked Portland, Oregon, but with no return address.

It was gone again by the morning, just the box remaining.

A few dark brown hairs were stuck at the bottom though. How could any if it be happening?

How can something be real physically only to vanish again?

Thinking this all over, he doubted very much that many other families had secrets like his. No matter what his aunt said, none of it was normal.

When she'd finally told him of what she'd done, and why she'd done it, only then had he begun to understand what his father had been like to his mother.

And the real human tragedy of his betrayal.

His father had been a sailor, a hardworking man, but a loner and not very well known in the town.

A stranger.

His mother had been a smart woman, too smart for a small fishing town in Oregon. And she'd been kind. And beautiful. A local. People liked her, she taught school, and at first his father loved her. But soon his father knew that others loved her too.

The jealousy got worse as time went on and by the time she had Andreas, she was not allowed to go out by herself, and their barely born love began to wither. Like all fruit left on a vine, it rotted, and things first turned sour, and then they'd turned ugly.

She grew to hate the man. She told her friends she was going to leave him.

Everyone in town knew of the man's blackout rages.

And one day, when Andreas was six months old, she disappeared.

There was a case put forth by the DA, but no one found any evidence of wrongdoing on the part of his father, and the case was quickly and quietly closed. There was no body, they had no evidence.

"Where?" he asked his aunt her last Christmas Eve. Only two months ago, it seemed like a century passed.

She'd not said anything for over a minute. The wheezing from her tumor torn lungs ripping an ache deep down into his soul.

But eventually she spoke, low and barely audible.

"Near Neskowin. Near the old place."

It'd been harder to get her to draw a map.

But she did.

He then told her he was going back. That he was going to take the head next time it showed up and he would try and leave it at the grave.

So now here he was, in the cabin he'd been born in but was like a stranger's home, next to the ocean that roared out on the gathering night.

The clock in the rickety cabin began to chime.

It was finally time.

He'd do it tonight.

The moisture-soaked air made the darkness tangible, a cold fingered lover sneaking under his coats with wet fingers and dancing along his spine. As he walked, his feet kicked up the swirling fog that became shapes of impossible monsters in a weak flashlight's beam that stuttered as if dying.

He shook it. Even with its new batteries he could barely make out where he was. It was like the darkness surrounding him was trying to swallow his light. The weak little golden beam struggled against it without much success, the night a voracious and much larger mass of the world without sun.

Still, some light was better than none and the flashlight stayed mostly on despite the occasional flickering.

He walked towards where the map indicated, near the shore. The old trees that had once been part of a great forest still stood although now were sunken in the sand in spots, their needless limbs metamorphosed into petrified wood that felt like cold glass to the touch. He brushed by them heading up the shoreline to what he hoped was still his father's grave on an earthen island area in the Neskowin forest.

The place was surreal, much of the land swept away by an earthquake or tsunami more than 2000 years ago. This spot next to the shore was higher than the surrounding territory, the main beach area lower and treeless while on the old remaining ground level now above it, the shore pines twisted and leaned away from the ocean.

He found the spot. The place was frightening in its wildness, the wind so constant and unrelating there that even the slow-growing trees followed its whim in the direction in which they grew. Permanently leaning away from the always rising pacific.

He moved the black leather bag over his other shoulder to put the heavy bag on the opposite arm for a bit. The camp shovel and other items he'd brought for the exhumation. His aunt had wanted him to just leave the head there on the beach and be done with it.

"But what if that doesn't work? I have to be sure I am putting it back right. I know what it wants me to do."

She'd looked hard at him.

"If you'd known him, if you'd been older and could remember…"

"I don't care anymore what the man was. I just want this to end. Just tell me where to look."

She'd nodded.

He needed to see that the man was in the grave still.

Soon he made it to the large pile of black lava rocks his aunt had stacked as a marker, but as he drew closer saw that they were tumbled down and scattered. When he got there his heart sank. Twenty years was a long time and where the grave had been dug, the whole side of the higher ground where the forest sat was now gone, eaten away by the water.

His father's headless corpse hung partway out, freezing rain pelting it, the same rain dripping down Andreas's back. He shuddered, covering his mouth when her saw that though the flesh grey, most of the man was surprisingly still present though peeled back to white bone in some spots.

He would have to rebury it. He began to walk closer, and saw whatever the thing was, it wasn't actually dead.

He'd have thought his eyes were playing tricks on him, but there was no doubt. Its chest was twisting as the corpse tried to extricate itself, arms like sinew, hands clawing the remaining dirt around it. He stopped in shock, unsure of what to do as the headless corpse finally fell free from the ground it'd been buried in. It was close to him now.

It pulled itself slowly along the sandy pebbled shore. Andreas backed up, grabbing the black bag and trying to undo it from his shoulder. It wouldn't come, tangled somehow in the strap for the camp shovel.

As if some signal had been made, the corpse began dragging itself towards him at surprising speed.

It was close enough now that he could see darkness down into the corroded neck and windpipe, and the pink folds of throat muscle. A sound was coming out, a hissing and something wet, and clicking. The sinew and muscle on the body was strong and corded as it brought itself closer and closer, gaining momentum.

Fear finally got the best of him.

He turned to run just as the thing became strong enough to get its legs and rush towards him, running now. It grabbed the bag, slamming into him at full force. He flew forward punching out, hitting something too soft and spongy as he fell to the sandy ground, smacking his head on the black rock outcropping, hot wetness blossoming over the back of his neck.

As he lost consciousness, he could hear the sound of someone running barefoot, the feet slapping the ground hard and fast. It was close, but very quickly the sound grew distant. And soon, there was only silence.

He never saw his father again, or the head.

He spent the better part of the night looking for his dead father with no success. He'd woken up with a headache, the rain on his face cold. It felt good.

He felt the back of his head. An egg was there, as big as a tennis ball, but soon he figured the blood came not from that, but a large cut the sharp lava rock had delivered as he slammed into it. He stood shakily and began to search, but soon it became too cold and treacherous to continue, especially with the knot on his head.

A headache manifested soon after getting home but his pupils looked normal, and he knew he'd lucked out at least there.

And that was the other thing.

Despite the weather, despite the injury, he'd made it back to the cabin after his dead father had run away with surprising ease.

And even the storm seemed to have begun to let up as soon as he'd given up looking for ... the what? The man?

No, whatever his father is, he didn't think his father is a man. Not really. He shook his head.

So, what did that make *him* then? Half monster?

He dried his face and hair again, still damp as he sat in the chair by the small potbellied stove. It was built to roaring now and lit up his face in Halloween orange, the door open to maximize heat dispersal.

He turned and looked out the small window. He could see the sky lightening up in the distance, a pale day dawning. No warm line of sun here in the Pacific Northwest, no.

Just a slow segue from the darkest of nights to a gray morning.

Passing In The Night
by EB Helveg

Now let us hear the joyful corpses sing,

who, rapt and buried, lie amongst their kin.

That day the sky was red, and air, and sea,

for summer's flames remained; they would not pass

to ash and thought and smoky, broken dream.

The sand beneath my feet, the waves, the ships

that passed in murky sunshine, blind and mute --

Yes, all was dull and flat from willful blaze.

This beach was once as sacrosanct to me

as church and parish I grew up within:

Replete with gods and devils, merciful

and strange, with names I scarcely can recall.

To see Dash Point, its beach now gilded rust

with ash depositing on every bench

and choking streams that gasp around their rocks --

It broke my heart in half.

The silence, though,

is what I found most strange. The senseless loss

become a soundless Sound, a crushless sand,

a faint distressing hum of ships unseen.

This place, once refuge from my darkest thoughts,

had turned to bleeding night and flaccid light,

with acrid air devouring beach and tree.

So thence I sat, with ruined peace and calm,

alone, for who would seek out beauty here?

With waves so dim and sky unseen and sun

a reddish sphere approaching night? The ones

who come here surely must be lost.

                                               As such

I had the beach completely to myself.

And so it was in bluish dusk that grew

in hemorrhaging bruises 'cross the sky,

above the false and ferrous sinking sun,

that first I heard the strains of pale song.

The chords were sharp like glass on icy roads

before the ambulance arrives to see

if lights and sirens would be prudent there.

Oh, arrow sharp in how it struck me down.

The words that I could hear but did not know:

O, Look, thou Waves, on Sea unbound and sing

the rage of battles lost.

Of sistren lost.

Of voices long betrayed.

Of souls you stole

into your gaping maw.

O Hear, thou Sea,

the weeping of her kin, bereft as we

must reap the pain you sowed.

We plough the fields

and seed them with your salt. We lust for blood.

O Pray, thou Wind, for mercy on the damned,

Those left behind, who pick up arms anew

To battle gods and devils in their rage.

O Cry, thou Rage, announce the damage done:

So counted, checked, and writ in ichor'd log,

A book to call the Ocean to account.

O Pray, thou Sea, to set our sister free,

remove her from lies of man and main

and from deceit so tempting and so dark.

Our hearts are sore;

our hopes are become dark.

Thus ended song, whose meaning had no grip

on minds as dull and dreary as I hold.

But still...the words attached themselves in me.

With nothing that could stop me, I then walked
Towards the water, whence the music came --
Those notes! They called to me in layers deep
below the soundwaves bearing their fraught song --
And ever hopeless, I did as they said.

At skirling edge, amid the ashen foam,
I found an object, motionless, afloat:
a creature drowned and tangled in the tide.
As fast as sand allowed me to, I ran
to see if there was any life therein,
but no. The creature lay there, beautiful and dead.

Not human, though, this creature, nor of land,
but some beguiling mix of Sea and Man
that better would be found in fairy tales.
I stared at it and willed it to make sense,
to change to something human: though still sad,
a human dead is more a standard find
than this, whatever this could so be named.

And how should I report this wretched find?
The force would never trust that I was clear
of blame, and not misusing resources
or worse:
                assisting he who did the crime.

(What crime? This creature, dead and sad though she

may be, is still not Man. Detectives much

prefer the ordinary murders, see.)

Besides. Perhaps it merely drowned and washed ashore.

Regardless, there was now a sodden corpse

just floating half on land and half in sea,

whose disposition cried for justice borne.

(For justice? Thoughts like that were alien

to me. But on the smoky air, the song

still looms, and every note brings clarity.)

Again, across the muddy ocean waves

the razor song began to slice, but now

it held a shriller key and rageful tone --

as one demanding recompense in blood.

I could not hear the words nor tenor parse

but every piece directed me to gaze

upon the pitiful, pelagic being

that draped herself so carelessly nearby.

The two collided in their meanings thus:

I must return the body to her kin

whose keening song serrated through the gloom.

(Whose keening song had flayed me to my bones.)

I searched the beachfront for a means nearby
to carry honorably this lost soul.

(Her kin would surely tear apart the one
who dared to disrespect this anima,
inanimate though recently become.)

And floating in the water just offshore,
abandoned by some harried family that
perhaps had needed to remove their child
who, shrieking and exhausted, needed to
go home and take a nap, and then come back
another day, when feeling more refreshed --
There sat a rubber boat, turned upside down.
It seemed to me to be of adequate
size and shape to ferry me and she
    (For sister they had called in their laments)
across the water to her mourning kin.

The raft, once flipped, provided float enough
to get us both across the Sound secure.
So, carefully I dragged her body in
to lay across the floor beside my feet.

In disrespect was such a placement not
positioned, though ideal it was not,

because, but little, she amassed so dense

a weight that childhood dreams forsworn would fain

to bear as much importance to their souls.

In lacking oars, I used my sandals rough --

alongside common sense, thus far ignored.

And once upon the water, I could hear

the song refraining, now with frantic tear;

its words still lost to me, though I did try

to capture every syllable and cry.

I failed, true, but damn it, I did try.

Instead, I followed strains that came to me

as tendrils floating smokily and dark,

evading ships and orcas in between

And since their wretched notes aroused no note,

I only had to follow where they led.

Each shard of song was sharper than the last,

with grief that surges like tsunami tides,

with force both brutal and eternally

aroused,

        with sharpened knives of human bone --

A death much deeper than the loss of kin

(Much deeper, even, than the Sound within
which swam this creature for that final time.)

A death beyond the danger I was in
but turning back to Dash Point would have been
anathema.

    I swore to see her home.

(I don't recall the swearing of it, though;
the feeling that I must have buried thought,
and thus entrammeled, so did I proceed.)

A lure, the song was, dragging me ashore
as helpless and as breathless as a trout,
for fear had gripped my lungs and wrung them dry.

Sans warning, from the murk an island shrieked
in upward stabbing blocks of stone and surf,
where never bloomed a gentle herb or leaf
but banished all to miasmatic rot.

And so my kayak to this headstone turned
with not an ounce of will on my own part
and not a pound of strength from my own arms
but just as surely sailing, nonetheless.

The island wept, the singers screeched, the air
around me stabbed and burned. The boat was dragged
ashore perforce, and I, of course, was too.
But once it crushed on shattered sands, the veil
that hung about the island fled; instead
a place of glowing beauty rimed with light
revealed itself to me and calmed my soul.

(But whence the light when night so lately fell?)

The query fell on senseless ears and mind
for though the music changed its key to bright,
So, too, does sun on broken glass alight.

*(The urge to leave is quickly cast aside
despite my wand'ring mind's last screaming plea;
a place of beauty calls to me as home
and who am I to turn such gifts away?)*

*(Between the corpse and creature that I am,
all of our remains shall now remain.)*

The spirits floated down the rocky slopes
to perch on craggy rocks upon the beach.
To call them beautiful would be untrue,
but still I found them irresistible.

I hoped to be forever in their grasp.

Grace they poured upon me for my deed
of giving back to them the one they'd lost,
and begged me to remain with them a while
before I started on my journey home.

Some food, they said, *a drink. Please, take your ease*
With us. A hero such as you deserves
The best.

> *(A trap encloses 'round me now,*
I fear.)

> *(A trap completed swallows me,*
I know.)

    But words in mind could not match words
in mouth and so I took the creatures' gifts,
and in return they offered food and drink
and song of highest quality besides.

Each time I sought to leave, my lips belied
my hopes of ever seeing eventide
or seeing beaches where the orcas ride
or hearing waves upon which seagulls cry.

My lips instead insisted that I bide.

Oh, better had I left myself to die.

Another song! Another meal! And yet
Another day! The words to leave still hang
by me, but as yet are not said. Instead --

I hear the songs,
                        the songs,
                                        the songs,

                                                        the sea.

Silent Colony

by Giacomo Ranieri with illustrations by Tracy Hall

I turned over in bed for the eighth time. Itchy and sweaty, a prisoner sealed within bedding too soft for comfort, my veins vibrated me. Chest pain threatened to kill me if I didn't move. I threw the comforter off and opened my basement window. The window well was a cold damp space, with a metal grate covering the top. It's supposed to keep me safe from all the kidnappers or something. But all it meant for me—if I wanted to go on a midnight hike, I had to sneak up the stairs.

I texted Terrance and got dressed. I'd dreaded this night for a long time. My puffy jacket felt like a damp camping tarp. But I zipped it up and absentmindedly brushed it off as if droplets of water coated it. Water trickled down the cement wall near the head of my bed, and I thanked my family for being poor. If we had fixed up this basement years ago and kept it dry—my blood would've asked to leave me sooner.

It wanted a wet dark place, a place that felt still so it could grow and thrive. Of course I wanted my blood to be happy. I just wish it was happy with me.

My first memory was of feeling distinct emotions that weren't mine. My sentient blood had been with me my entire life.

My blood sent a wave of emotion from my stomach, speaking in its unique way. The emotion built, settled, and intensified. I translated the emotion into imagery and words so I could speak to my blood.

"You can visit me after I leave," it said.

"It won't be the same," I snapped out loud.

"Quiet," it said with a hiss. "We can't get caught tonight."

I'd promised—on the next midnight hike I'd let my blood leave me. It had been over a year since it first asked to leave. This night was overdue.

The stairway outside went right next to my parents' bedroom. A squeaky stair would wake them up, and there were four bad stairs all in a row. I did my best to distribute my weight—but my blood boiled with anticipation. Eager to get outside in the cold November wind, it roiled and pulled at my skin. I sweated. Or were droplets of my blood dripping out my pores?

My dad slept like a rock. I always suspected that's cause my mom paid more attention. Maybe she heard her blood too? Maybe if I got a cut and dripped blood on the counter or something, and she happened to touch the drop, she'd feel as restless as me? Just by touching my blood she would commune with it, as I have learned to. It's hard for me to tell the difference between my emotions and the emotions of my blood. Its needs were clear, like crisp white moonlight.

The last squeaky stair creaked. I shuffled quickly to the landing at the top, through the door and through our backyard. I was in the alley before my heart beat twice. My blood was eager. We were going to try a place we hadn't gone before, some mossy trail that weaved into a swamp. I hoped it didn't work for my blood. I hoped it decided to stay.

My blood sent a wave. "Can you at least pretend to be excited for me?"

I grimaced from the pain, and bent forward, not breaking stride. "I'm scared," I said. The pain always accompanied its messages. Sometimes it surprised me though.

I could tell my blood exactly how I felt—always. It had gotten more confident since I recognized it and accepted it. I had never felt this close to anyone.

"I've been thinking about what to call myself," my blood mused. "I'm sort of a colony, thousands of blood cells and water molecules that think as one."

"Like ants?" I laughed.

My blood sent a spark of annoyance. "Your brain is just a group of neurons. Is it that different?"

I suppose it wasn't that different. Years ago, I realized it wasn't worth it to ask people about my blood. They didn't seem to know what it was like. I was alone in my experience, I was secluded. If I said anything, instead of being the crazy girl who talked to herself, I would be the crazy girl who had a colony of blood living inside her. So, I hadn't tried to tell anyone about it since I was seven. My parents thought I'd outgrown it, like an imaginary friend. But our symbiotic bond only strengthened. And now that I'm in middle school, it wanted to leave me.

Maybe if I had considered my blood part of me, those early conversations would have gone differently? Maybe if I had called it a sentient 'colony,' people would have given me a chance to explain? I doubt it. There was no way around it. I was crazy. But maybe after tonight I would be normal like everyone else?

I stayed quiet until we reached the house. Terrance had a splintered fence close to the sidewalk. Its closeness made me feel cozy and safe, since no one could see me from the house next door. I peeked across the street, a community center from the 80s. It was bone white and deserted this time of night.

I took off my satchel, grabbed my water bottle, and took a swig of salted water. People retain water better if they salt it. My blood seemed to like it. I licked salt off my lips, finally feeling calm. I put the water bottle back, pushing it against a roll of gauze, and checked my phone. It was just past 1 am.

My blood assured me after it left there would be enough blood to keep me alive. The Colony felt like it was all of my blood, to me. I'd had nightmares where my blood came out my wrists and I went boney and white. Petrified like a tree trunk turned to stone, I'd woken up heavy and stiff.

I'll be okay, I told myself. I wouldn't faint from blood loss. And after tonight, the Colony said it would no longer be a confusion or a torment. My thoughts would finally be my own, and I'd be free to wrestle whatever trauma this relationship caused. I couldn't imagine who I was without it.

I appreciated the thoughtful approach to life that my blood had. We both loved to explore nature, and wander trails. It felt like a gift t soothe someone. Nothing soothed it better than a midnight hike. I joked it was like walking a dog. My blood laughed at being called a dog. When my blood laughed it came from deep in the belly, like Santa's laugh. I didn't want to lose the feeling of laughing like that. And I couldn't laugh like that, myself.

Terrance texted me. "almost packed. Meet u at gate"

I waited at the gate, contemplative. Through it wooded trails wove together, surrounding our neighborhood like a moat. They were part of a network of trails that covered the whole city. We lived in a plant heavy area, bright colorful flowers in the spring, and large thick leaves through the whole year. A drainage ditch ran along the trail, past the gate. Ferns and small monstera-esque plants lined the far side of the ditch, and pools of water shimmered in the moonlight, along it.

The gate was a torii, an arch in the shinto religion of Japan. Torii are entrances to sacred places: shrines, parks, and nature preserves. They mark a place where, it is said kami move into our mundane world. 'Kami' refers to spirits of nature—gods, ancestors, and even something as simple as a rock. Torii are all over our city—in state and city parks, as well as back yards—since we have a healthy number of Japanese immigrants. The arches feel like portals to me, where humans could enter the world of the kami. I sometimes think of the Colony within me as a kami, that has found a home within me.

A croak echoed through the thick fogged air, snapping me out of my meditation. I looked around for a toad or a frog. Then I heard footsteps on sidewalk cement.

Terrance ran up to the torii, waving at my blood and I. "Where are you taking me?" He asked, before he made it to us.

I jumped, lost in my thoughts staring at the torii. "I'm not sure," I said honestly.

After a pause I spoke for my blood. I said, "I've had this swamp on mind for a few weeks. It's been calling to me."

This made Terrance visibly nervous. He started rubbing his tweed jacket and quickly switched to biting at his nails. A frog jumped in a pool of black water and Terrance jerked his head towards the drainage ditch.

I almost told Terrance about the Colony a few times. But he was such an anxious person, I was sure he'd stop talking to me.

"Your voice sounds a bit weird," Terrance said, not sure how to say what he was thinking.

"It's a big night for us," my blood sent to me. This was an important night for my blood and I. This was an important place.

I looked up at the full moon and a thought came to me. Maybe my blood had a life in this swamp before it lived inside me?

I turned to Terrance seriously, "This is going to be a different sort of night. I'm gonna need some help getting through something." Terrance and I often talked directly like this, confided in each other and asked for emotional support.

So, I wasn't surprised when he said "Of course. Whatever you need I'm here for you."

I nodded and smiled. He moved in for a hug. We squeezed each other warmly. I choked back a sob. The Colony and I knew with certainty at that moment—he wouldn't be my friend after tonight.

We walked beneath the moon, its reflections in the water winking at us. The walk was quieter than most. Not only because we weren't chatting, but the wetlands were quieter than usual. Aside from the occasional shuffle amongst the brush, or squeak of a small creature, all I could hear was my heartbeat.

The trail went down and down, and the ground softened. Terrance became more tense, and my blood felt lighter. It was a new sensation, my heavy bones and my light blood. Could it be trying to escape right now? Could it be finding its way back to where it was before we bonded?

Had we bonded? It was a question I rarely asked myself. Was I born with sentient blood? Was everyone, and they just thought it was their own emotions? Or did the Colony find me? Was it alive and free outside of me? I imagined a dark pool slithering on the ground. The Colony struck back with an insulted wave.

I continued to imagine it. It dripped through the holes in the metal grate above my window well and pooled just beneath the sill. Then I opened the window, and it entered me through the gap under my fingernails, like a parasite entering a host.

"Stop!" the Colony said.

"Did you choose me?" I asked it directly, in my head.

"No," it sent decisively. "I've always been with you. I was born with you and slowly formed inside you. I'm part of you."

I glanced back at Terrance. He was looking at the familiar trees, probably wondering when we'd turn off onto an unfamiliar path. "Then why do you want to leave me?" I sent to the Colony.

It pulled away.

We walked in silence for a while. I brooded. The Colony cowered. And Terrance breezed along oblivious. What a sweet boy—lucky. The ground began to soften. Trees we passed were scraggly mossy things, wild and untamed. Pools were stinkier—darker.

A gap in some tree roots caught my eye, and my arteries lifted. They pressed against my skin and pulled my arm towards the gap. They pulled and pressed like a prisoner against a padded wall. I stopped and crouched to get a better look at the ground between the roots. Framed by a collection of bushes, the gap was between two trees, not a split from one tree. It was pitch black, but I waited a moment. When Terrance got close some moonlight reflected off something he was wearing, and I caught a glimpse of ground through the root's gap.

"Are we going through there?" He asked, resigned.

I frowned. It was going to really suck losing such a supportive friend. I simply nodded and crawled between the roots.

It was sticky. Our boots made loud sucking and popping noises as we lifted them out of the mud. It was a ravine covered in arching bushes and vines. Completely covered, we crouched and creeped forward. Reeking of death, it was a dark pressure cooker of an ecosystem; exactly what the Colony had been yearning for. We were heading towards the swamp, leaving the peaceful wetlands behind.

After fifteen minutes, we got to a pool of water. I could hear Terrance a few steps in front of me—somehow ahead. He turned his phone's flashlight on, pointing it at the ground, and looked back at me. He looked distraught.

I could see my surroundings better. It was a still place—disrupted for the first time in possibly decades. Terrance was up to his thighs in black water. That meant I must be up to my waist. Was I so out of it that I didn't realize I was submerged in water? I looked at my legs, barely visible through the rippling surface of the water. My knees were just below the surface. I must be on more solid ground than Terrance.

He stopped cause he'd fallen into some kind of hole or soft-bottomed section of the bog. It was weird to see him so much shorter than me, especially with the water level making it look like we were on even ground.

We both stopped moving. Staring at him—that loving supportive friend—I teared up. He didn't need to know anything about why we were here. He barely questioned me at all. I said, 'I need you.' And he said, 'I'm there.'

I cried—crumpled. With my chin on my chest, I let my head hang limp in guilt. A weight formed in my skull, and my heavy eyes began to hurt.

I watched the pool of water calm, ripples dissipate. Terrance's flashlight looked like the moon reflected in the pool. The pain in my eyes became shooting, like when dust falls on your eye, but it came from the back of them.

They wanted to burst out of their sockets. They pressed against my eyelids, towards the reflection of his flashlight. My cheeks pulled off my skull, and I started to fall forward. The pain spread across my face. I couldn't help but imagine hot water suddenly steaming out of a showerhead. My face burned and I yelled as Terrance stepped forward in concern.

The Colony screamed with my voice, "let me go!" I didn't want it to go. I wasn't ready. I shook my head as it sent the demand to me over and over. "Let me go. Let me go!" Terrance flinched, moving the light away from the water.

As soon as the light went away the Colony screamed through me again. "Bring it back!"

And like kraken tentacles against black wood—strands of dark liquid burst from behind my eyeballs. I clawed at my face—blind and not sure what to grab or what to do. "The light. Bring it back!" we screamed again—together. The sound all came from me. Above and around me a mass of thick enlivened blood squirmed and writhed, silent and imposing on the claustrophobic bramble-roofed pool.

I peeked through the strands of blood, reaching towards Terrance. His wide eyes screamed. And his body was tense, turned slightly to the side, as if to run. But he was paralyzed.

My vision blurred like we were in a dense cloud of fog. I couldn't take this thing in me anymore. It was dramatic and bursting with heightened emotions. I ached to be separate from it. The Colony had wanted this. Now *I* wanted it. I needed it. I wanted my blood out of me!

Terrance came into focus. My heartbeat slowed. I pawed at my face—nothing.

"What just went into you?" he asked, "it looked like oil or something."

"What?" I asked. "Into?"

I took a step towards him. He waded away and I fell. I'd forgotten that he was in a deeper part of the pool. I continued forward, bog water splashing against my lips, and pushed him aside blindly. I had to get out. My blood stayed where it was, restless and heavy. "We've got to go deeper in," I said, splashing myself as I tried to gesture at him.

"What is happening to you?" he asked seriously.

I wiped sweat off my forehead and shook my head speechless. "I've been trying to find this place for a long time," I said, realizing I was speaking for myself as well as the Colony. "This is my home. There is something here that I need, that I've been missing my entire life."

Terrance nodded, tense and confused. "Whatever you need," he said as if to convince himself to trust me. "Just don't hurt yourself."

I half walked half swam blindly into the dense night. I kept my eyes on the water, hoping for a shimmer of light.

Terrance grabbed my wrist and tried to pull me back the way we came. I jerked my hand out of his grip and dove under the water. Swimming forward I knew he would follow me. We had to get deeper to separate completely. We had to find the heart of the swamp.

I crawled out of the brush, algae coating my hair and skin. I wiped it all away and stumbled onto land. Terrance was close behind me. "We have to get you back," he said immediately. "We shouldn't be out here. And whatever is happening to you is bad—medically bad."

He was distraught and confused. But I was determined. He wouldn't believe what I believed. "I have a parasite," I said simply. I felt the Colony lash out in anger. It was usually more docile and agreeable than this. "It wants to be in this swamp, so I'm trying to coax it out."

"Don't you think a doctor—" he began.

I waved my hand in front of my face and turned away from him. I took long strides uphill, away from the pools of water. Terrance stumbled after me in the dark. My footsteps were steady and sure. I was alive, a fire raging in me. I reached the top of the hill and saw a cloudscape over dancing leafless trees. The white-grey reflections of the clouds spread out below me.

A lake, the base of the swamp, "this is it," the Colony said.

I ran down the hill. Halfway down before Terrance called from the top, I approached the shore. The water was clear and still. As I slowed, so I didn't disturb the water, the clouds brushed away like curtains. Stepping through them, onto the midnight stage, was a bright beautiful full moon. It stared up at us from the water, and the pressure crashed against my skin.

Like a grenade exploding in my chest the Colony hit every pore of skin. Tendrils of dark blood ripped through weak seams in my pants and lifted soaked locks of hair. They wiggled and wove together, streams of moving blood reached for moonlight, or purpose, or simply something different than me.

"I'm not crazy," I yelled into the dense moist air. Clouds above seemed to drift further from the moon as I cried. The release tingled to my toes. I bet my pupils were so wide you couldn't see the grey-blue color of my eyes. "It was always with me—in me!"

At that moment I realized part of me doubted my childhood belief—I was *sure* some of my blood was sentient. Part of me assumed the feelings my blood sent me were my own feelings. That I had some repressed traumatic memory that split my mind. But there it was, clear as a leaf falling on a sunny day, streams of blood dancing in the air. My tears became red and lifted off my cheeks to join the mass. The streams met each other in the air in front of me and formed up into a liquid sphere.

A wave of relieved excitement washed over me—but it came from outside of me this time. From the sphere back to me, the Colony spoke to me for the first time. I didn't think I would feel this solid. The Colony had been tar between my gears; a friend too close to be objective.

I looked up at Terrance, who stood paralyzed halfway down the hill. Nothing blocked my vision. The Colony had left me, all of it. "It's out," I yelled as I looked back at it.

I held it in my palms over the lake. Some streams moved up my legs to join the sphere. Now that I could see it for what it was—free of its constant presence, its constant messages—I felt burning anger. From my heart a resentment moved like a hurricane towards my throat. I had pushed this down too long.

This Colony had leached off of me, argued with me, fought against me. I resisted the resentment, pushed it away like I'd done my whole life. I flinched, expecting to feel my blood push back and defend itself. But I didn't feel anything but the resentment, and lingering fear. No one else was in my body with me. No one else was in my head—or my heart.

I stepped towards the ball, pointing, and let out the resentment I had been too scared to share.

"You held me back. You tore me down and reshaped me. I have no idea who I am because of you." I backhanded the orb of blood, and it fell into the lake in a splash.

It sent a sad wave of emotion into the air—weaker than when it had been inside me. I imagined a one-year-old puppy hanging its head.

"What are you?" I continued, crouched on the ground beside the shore. "Where did you come from? Are there more of you infecting people—leaching them of their—their...?"

"I was born with you," it sent. "I was you—until I was not."

"Well good riddance," I said quietly. A little spit had fallen from my mouth, into the lake. I wiped the rest of the spit off my mouth as I turned and walked back towards our neighborhood. *My* neighborhood.

It goes without saying that Terrance didn't return my texts. I needed to rest anyway, give my body a chance to make more blood. My parents were worried of course. After two weeks I heard rumors that some people from the city were doing tests out in the swamp.

I wondered if Terrance had told someone about the Colony. If he did, he probably didn't mention me. Otherwise, someone would be harassing me. Once I recovered from the blood loss I felt a bit like a zombie. It was hard to get out of bed. Food was chalky and bland. I was always cold. There's not much to say about that time. To say it simply, I was barely alive. At least I wasn't what I had called 'alive' up to that point.

Then one night I was staring at the ceiling, waiting for sleep to take me. I considered, like I did most nights, about walking out to the swamp. I'm not sure I even wanted to. The trickle of the water coming out of the wall was steady tonight, like white noise. As I drifted closer to sleep the trickle stopped and I opened my eyes to a mass of dark streams reaching out over my body. I opened my mouth, hungry for the reunion with an old friend.

But what came was wholly new. A chill and a writhing mess of anger and fear and longing flooded me. I tasted algae, and that distinct smell of rot. Visions came to me of dead frogs baking on hot rocks and cranes standing in still water. It was like the croaking and chirping conversation of a swampy forest, mixed with the chattering hormonal chaos of a middle school hallway.

Pressure built in my head. My stomach rolled over in pain. I turned to the side and puked onto my pillow. The puke smeared against my cheek, and I flinched. Overwhelmed and weak, I fell asleep. Regrets and guilt replaced whatever I was without the Colony.

Story-2.docx
by Kate Ristau

This is not a poem. This is not a poem because the grad assistant Erik said it had to be a story, so I'm not writing a poem, I'm writing a story.

It doesn't rhyme.

Why would it rhyme? Stories don't rhyme. They build up and tumble down through endless character arcs and delicious plot lines. They don't need to rhyme. They shine.

Repetition? Maybe a little bit. But this is Writing 122, not the New Yorker, and I don't think he's going to fault me for the character spacing either. He said he wanted *character*. I'm giving it to him by the handful. I'm the devastatingly undervalued and highly some adjective poet who is going to turn in their heartbreaking work of Staffordian genius on time. Whom. Not who. Stapled and double-spaced in Times New Roman, 12-point font.

Not Arial. That's me. I'm a serif-girl, through and through. Damn it, I think he's shooting for word count. I'll fix the spacing later. 2000 words like the year he graduated high school. These mother fuckers are so old.

I'm not going to turn this in late. No cap. I've got twenty-five minutes before it's due in PLC which is more than enough time to print it and run across UO like a fast duck. Let's go.

Shit. The library is closed.

The assignment says to include setting details. The Knight Library at the University of Oregon is on the U.S. National Register of Historic Places. Row upon row of tall glass windows line the decorative brick façade. The doors are locked.

Setting is not just place, it's time, and the library is open until 6PM on Saturdays. It is now 6:42. Time, though, is not just numbers – it is a feeling. The weight of moments stacked one upon another like so many words upon the page. If I was being poetic, which I am not, I would say, I measure out my life in coffee spoons. Or at least the little green things they stick in the top of my Starbucks cup.

Setting is also the weather, which tracks that the rain is falling under darkened skies on a dreary weekend where Erik is making me write a story and not a poem, facts. Which is why the skies are dreary and not dripping letters forming swirling ink on pages sewn from the memories of my forgotten youth standing on the graveyard of my soul.

It's cold. It's cold and it's wet but I've got my earbuds in and I'm telling Siri the story and she is writing it down—

No, Siri, don't write drown.

God damn it Siri. Stop. Stop. Don't play that song. Siri. Take a note.

Okay, so Mark has a printer, but he's out of town again, and Frances is out of ink like how my soul is drained by this cheugy story, and my voice is wildly inconsistent and Erik is never going to let that go – I think it's on the rubric for like ten points or something. I don't even know what voice is without the mumble and hiss of the mic – and should that be a dash or a comma? I don't know that either.

In poetry, voice is the way my heart em dashes when I see you. The way a glance at you across the room pulls me down down down from line to line and straight into missing you if you aren't there. You are golden in the silence and loud in the rain. But you can't do that in a story if you want an A.

And you also have to print. So now I'm going to have to use Mom's credit card to add more money on my student ID at the Union then head to the printing center and then over to PLC 115, it's fine.

That's not part of the story.

We are going to need some dialogue. I think that's worth five points too.

"This story is due at 7PM on Saturday night, Raven. No exceptions. I have to get grades in."

"Can't I just write a poem?"

"No."

Expand the dialogue.

"Please, Erik? My grandma died and my cat is sick and I'm unclear about the nature of 'self' and how something like 'homework' can ever really be 'assigned.'"

"Have you heard of Schrodinger's Cat? Check spelling?"

I think he was using that example wrong. He kept explaining how the cat is in a box and it cannot be observed and so it is alive and dead at the same time and I wasn't, I mean I am not sure about the tenses and I know the cat would be better, it would be a tiger in the howling depths of nostalgia tearing apart my goddess mother as she crawls up from the bowels of the earth to feast upon my broken childhood if this was a poem but it's not.

Or is it?

I'll ask Erik later.

Last time I asked him about poems, he lectured me on the Copenhagen interpretation of quantum mechanics, which really has nothing to do with line breaks.

I'm worried about Erik.

I'm worried about Erik because the other day, oh hey Will. I can't believe you're here. I thought you went home already. Yeah, for real. That's awesome. Oh, yeah, no, she didn't. You going? Okay. Yeah. Totally. I'll try to. I wanted to, you know, like talk some more before the break. Yeah. Me too. Okay. Sure. I'll see you over there in a bit. Nah, I gotta charge my card first. You have time? Yeah, walk me over. That would be great. I'm writing a story. It's on my Siri. Totally. Just talk louder. Like this? Yes, but use quotes.

"Okay."

"Oooh. Nice paragraph break."

"Thanks."

"It was cool being in class with you this term. Quote. No, quotes."

"Double quote. Ha. For real. Do you have your classes?"

"Yeah. We should compare schedules. Or whatever."

"Sofa."

"Yeah."

"Wanna head over with me?"

"I gotta do my card so I can print at PLC."

"I have not seven in between."

"Okay! See you over there?"

"Totally."

The doors to the Union swung open like the only way forward was away and if I turned back I'd see Will holding up a salt shaker in Sodom and Gomorrah like each tiny crystal was a moment slipping through the hourglass of a life he had barely--

This is not a poem.

Erik says that when you are writing a story, it's important to balance exposition and dramatic scene in an active and something something way that brings the reader along with you. I suggested enjambment but he told me come onnn get down into the scene and the characters a bit more. Stop writing over the top. Leave the language behind for a moment and tell us. Why should we care? Open the box.

Okay. So, I won't say how Will was left handed but didn't use those special notebooks comma he just flipped his spiral bound over on his desk and wrote on the other side. Those extra lines ran the bottom of the paper and those extra spaces filled with possibility were formatted straight into the ends of every single thing he wrote but I mean with what Erik said about boxes that doesn't seem so important.

I need to talk about the character, Will is tall. He likes ice cream and hoodies and he wears sandals in the rain.

If this was a poem, I'd let the weight of my words gather meaning with crunchy consonants falling from ruby sharded lips as I stood at the duct-taped mic with trailing cords while I told you about the time that Will stood in the rain waiting for the bus that never came.

Or did it?

He's not here. We don't know.

We won't know until I drop off this fucking paper and take the 13 over to Alton Baker shit. Maybe I made a mistake. Maybe I made the wrong choice and the path went backwards with Will and not forward into a future where the printer won't work.

Five more minutes until we're fucked and have to do this all over again anyway. Focus, Raven. Plot. Remember what Erik said. What's the question you are trying to answer? This isn't a poem about Will. Or is it? The words are bleeding memories of hoodie strings. Give us more than what's on the page. You're getting distracted, it's not about Will. Get back to the plot. What's your IF?

IF you don't turn this in on time, Erik is going to fail your ass. And IF you fail this class, ass class, ass class, this is not a poem, Dad's going to lose his shit.

No, no. Get to the heart of it. What's the core question? What is driving the story?

Got it. Center text.

Is it a story IF no one ever reads it?

I mean, is Erik really going to deep-read my story? And is Will going to still be at John's? Which is the what and what is the if? Do these words have to rhyme for stanzas to hold me in like so much time? I'm playing it up to the final second and acting like this has to be Edgar Allen Poe. Allan? Maybe I should I just add more quotes," she said, like time wasn't a series of impossible to understand quantum events that split with each possibility, ultimately existing in totally separate universes.

"You forgot a quote," Erik said.

"I did," I replied, like the many-worlds interpretation relied on my strict adherence to sky-commas.

"You can't call them sky-commas."

"Uh, yes, I can, because quotation marks actually started out as double commas, until someone decided that the weight of words was worth more than the weight of time."

"That's poetry."

"Erik. Everything is poetry. The way PLC flies down around me in the dark like a lover, gathering me in its wings and inviting me in. It's soft feathers opening and closing."

"Can feathers open?"

"It's a metaphor, like the door."

"You're just saying that because it rhymes. Is it a metaphor if no one ever reads it? Your comma use is terrible."

The printer shoots out my manuscript. Erik will hold it in his hands. Or he won't.

I skipped forward in time. Sorry. I hope I brought the reader along. I hope I kept them with me as we split a thousand quantum moments, branching outward into a universe of universes. In each one, Will was waiting for the bus, and I may or may not have turned in a story or a poem on a Saturday night in PLC to my teacher and grad assistant, Erik, who was clearly underpaid and underrecognized by the administration and they should give him more classes and a raise.

I run down the hall, paper in hand. There's still time. There's still plot. There's Will in the rain and 400 more words until the end of this story.

Room 112.

Write out the numbers.

One hundred thirteen.

One hundred fourteen.

"That's a lot of repetition."

"We are reaching the climax, and everyone loves a good countdown." Every story should have a ticking clock. As Nietzsche said, "This all took a long time or a short time (Nietzsche 345.)."

"You don't need citations. It's a story, not an essay."

"Good. I don't have time for a Works Cited Page and made up that number."

"You're citing wrong anyway. And you have no dialogue tags. And you're standing outside Erik's door. It's 7PM."

This is a lot of numbers. Edit that later.

There it is. 115. I mean One hundred and fifteen.

His door is closed.

Erik could be in there. Or he could be gone.

In the moments before I knock and before Erik opens the door – or doesn't – I realize that the weight of the story is in the words he might not read and in the foreshadowing I forgot to add like how Will actually wasn't wearing his hoodie.

If I knock, Erik might not answer. If he opens the door, the single atom decaying might set off a chain reaction of events across space and time where universes collide in a cacophony of light and sound and doorknobs twist and scrape across the bowels of quantum superposition and honestly he may be dead if he opens the door JFC should I knock??

Like the raven on the chamber door, I've become a fucking palimpsest of decoherence.

Pause. Take space.

Breathe into the unknowing. Indent.

I exist in theme.

Not punctuation

The story is over and not

The poem is written and undone

Knock on Erik's door

There is no Plutonian Shore

It's me, it's me, opening wide the door

I'll never be the em dash

I'm always breaking lines

Creating chaos

Emjambment flowing from line to

Line while Microsoft Word creates capitals out of chaos

uncap me

make of me a poem

I am not the story you think I am

my stanzas simmer in the graveyards of my plots

but my words pull you forward

and – still – I linger here

in a moment that stands on the precipice of—

Sweet. I made it over two thousand words. I will leave the extra two hundred thirty nine for extra credit. How do we trim down a quantum?

I knock.

The Ravine

by Jessie Kwak

You have to know the way to the ravine—which country road to turn down, which dead tree to park at, which stretch of barbed wire fence is loose enough you can slip through without ripping your clothes. From there, you'll see a wooden plank set over the irrigation ditch about ten paces south, and another—less janky—plank just beyond it.

Use the second plank. The first is splintered and starting to crack, and maybe it used to hold your weight back when we used to come out here all the time, but it won't anymore. Not now that you've grown.

The ravine is due west from there, just walk straight towards Mount Adams—but I'm not telling you anything you don't remember.

There used to be a dirt road out to the top of the bluff when we were *little* little kids, but it's been ages since you could drive it. You're not supposed to dump things here anymore. The Tribe sent somebody to clean it up about ten years ago, but they only hauled out a few loads of good scrap before they found something more interesting to do instead. So they just bulldozed the road so nobody could get here without busting an axel.

So, yeah.

What I'm trying to say is, the ravine is still what you remember: a magical playground of car parts and broken fence posts and horse skulls picked clean by the coyotes, everything wreathed in faded orange scraps of baling twine like tinsel.

That old International pickup is still here, still on its side from how it got pushed down the hill, the rubber of its tires rotted out in the sun, just shreds hanging off the wheel wells. The doors are still rusted shut. I checked, last time I was here, that time you didn't show.

There's still that old woodburning kitchen stove, serious homestead-type shit that we managed to shove upright and use as the centerpiece for our *Little House on the Prairie* scenarios. I'm glad you never let me light it, because you were probably right. We would have started the whole junk heap on fire, and the firespotters on the ridge would've called your daddy to rally the volunteers and come put it out, and he would've known it was us in a heartbeat.

There's that leather bench seat we pulled out of a Lincoln Continental, our actual initials carved into the cushion even though anybody who saw them would've guessed who they belonged to. We didn't care, because nobody else came down here. Or so we thought.

Do you know that's where I was sitting when he—?

Yeah. You know. You made them tell you every awful detail.

Anyway, there's a lawnmower over by the stove, and that's new. Doesn't matter if the Tribe said you can't throw more shit down here. Somebody always will.

The rest looks familiar to you, though, doesn't it? Broke down vehicles and busted appliances and no good lumber and rusted out wheel lines and like sixty years' worth of Folgers coffee cans: some empty, some full of nails, all full of spiders. I hope your tetanus shot is up to date.

There's a chewed-up horse hoof by your foot. Back then we would have picked it up, used it to poke each other and make each other scream. It's so coyote-gnawed and sun-bleached it's not like it's actually gross to touch, even with the tufts of horse hide and dried tendon sticking out.

Old age apparently made you squeamish, though, because you kick it away with your boot instead of picking it up with your hand.

Look at me, "Old age." Like being in your twenties is ancient—though I guess it always will be to me.

There's one of those Folgers cans sitting on the stove, just like you remembered leaving it, so no wonder you glance over your shoulder to make sure you're really alone. It's been fifteen years since you were here last, scavenging with me through these decaying mounds of treasure to build pirate ships and castles and swords to fight dragons and rescuing princes.

It's all good. You're really alone, like I *thought* I was.

I mean, you're too early.

I told you I'd meet you here at midnight on the full moon on my 27th birthday. Back then I was into all of that astronomy stuff, and we'd sit out here for hours on a cloudless summer night, laying on that Lincoln bench seat and staring up at the dazzling, blinding glory of the Milky Way, taking turns with the binoculars I stole from my uncle's closet, naming the constellations we knew and making up loads of our own. I'd gotten some astronomy book from the school library that said you could calculate the position of the stars and phases of the moon and shit into eternity, and I was drunk with the power of foreknowledge.

I figured out my 27th birthday was gonna be a full moon, so I said we'll back meet here no matter what happens.

I didn't forget.

Guess you didn't either.

Although I expected you to come back under the light of the full moon itself, secret and sneaking like we used to, slipping out bedroom windows, cutting silently through corn fields, running along the banks of the irrigation ditches and giggling every time we almost fell in. One time you did, remember? You hid your mud-soaked jeans in with your dad's work clothes so your mom wouldn't ask where you'd been.

Not that she would have cared about the mud. We both came home muddy all the time. But this mud was sacred, special. Soaked in the silver light of the moon and the silt of the ditch and the secrets of what we got up to when no grownups were looking.

Makes sense you'd've come early, though. You're an adult now. You don't have to sneak away from home, you can just tell your auntie you're out with friends. And nobody gives a shit you're here—you already know that the closest farmhouse isn't within sight of the ravine. That's the point. A hundred years of being the perfect landscape to toss unwanted things where they don't bother nobody and don't cause any trouble.

At first, I think that you came early because maybe you figured you wouldn't remember the way in the dark. Maybe you were worried about getting shot for trespassing, 'cause you heard Mr. Garza died and you don't know the new neighbors, so you don't know who might get a little trigger-happy at the sound of wheels crunching past their driveway too late at night.

But then I see you wandering around and I realize that's not the reason you came early—or at least not the whole reason. You came because you're looking for answers.

What are you looking *for*, though? Like, traces of blood? Fingerprints? The murder weapon? Seriously, Tribal and the FBI were all over this place back when it happened, and entire generations of teenagers on and off the rez have dared each other to go spend the night in the junk ravine past Harrah where that girl got murdered back in the day.

I hate to break it to you, but they're never gonna find him.

Remember how you were going to be a fashion designer? Or a theater costumer, or a wedding dress maker, depending on the day? When's the last time you sewed anything—please tell me it wasn't that skirt you made me, because I feel guilty thinking you gave up the thing you loved so much.

Because now you're a journalist. Police beats, courtrooms, crime scenes, your job is to make sure everybody knows about all the horrifying things that happen in alleys and behind closed doors, and it's my fault, isn't it? I mean, you think what happened to me is *your* fault, like if you'd come like you said you would, I'd still be alive somewhere.

But it's not your fault. And I wish it hadn't sent you crashing onto this new life path, because now that you're here, I can see it in your eyes, how you traded creating beautiful things for chasing brutal ones.

Does it help?

You turn over every inch of that place, like we used to when we were trying to find the perfect piece of cast-off lumber for a project. You work until the sunset turns so gorgeous you can't help but be distracted by it, partly because it's impossible not to look away and partly because the long shadows have turned the colors so flat and muddied it's getting useless to search.

You're starting to realize it's hopeless. You're telling yourself you did your best, that some cases never get solved, but that at least you're here for my full moon birthday like you promised. We always used to watch the sunset from that Lincoln Continental bench seat, so you head towards it as the falling sun paints Mount Adams pink and gold and violet.

I should warn you the bench seat is hella ratty now. Ground squirrels built a nest in the coils last spring, and some stray dogs chewed up the leather, and a magpie has been picking at it while you searched the rest of the junk heap, beak sawing open a hole in the seat.

It flaps away as you walk to the bench, yells at you while you prod at the tear to see what it was so excited about. Just a coil, poking sharp and shiny through the leather. And—

No way.

You take a closer look, and, yep. Totally human. I'd forgotten I knocked out one of that bastard's teeth, what with everything. Do those things have DNA in them? Like, even after this long? Well, you'd probably know, and you must think it's important because you grab your phone and photograph everything, then pull out a baggie and turn it inside out over your hand to pick the thing up. You tuck the baggied-up tooth in your pocket.

At first, I'm afraid you're going to run off now that you've found your prize, but you keep your promise. The moon hasn't quite yet risen, so you settle on the ratty old bench seat to watch the sunset, and I slip my hand in yours and rest my head on your shoulder to watch the first stars come out, just like I've been dreaming of doing since he showed up instead of you.

The Sea Witch
by Wendy N. Wagner

It is always fall when she summons us—

the days spread so thin stars shine through

like glitter falling on the sea,

until a fogbank pulls itself over the horizon.

We ascend the curves of Lighthouse Road:

spruce trees blot out the town, the dune

buggies, the RVs, the retired Californians

looking for tax shelter, the Coast Guard wives, the cannery stink.

This was the first place I ever saw the sea:

foaming far below on the flanks of the jetty

one long gray curve over the end of the earth

no different from the desert we had left behind.

Then as now we sat in the empty parking lot:

her light becoming solid in the fog, paths in red

and then white and then white again, inviting us each

to walk beyond the cliff and all the way out to sea.

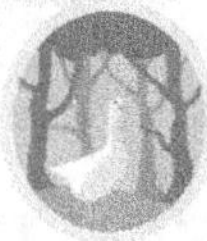

A Mushroom Haunting In Lithia Park
By Phoenix Bourgeois

"Willow—you have to wake up."

The wind howled. Atlas shook his younger sister.

"It's early," Willow moaned, shoving his arm away. The purple streaks in her hair glowed neon in the dappled streetlight that streamed through the cracked windshield. The arrhythmic slap of sodden leaves broke the steady patter of raindrops.

It was a good morning for hunting.

Atlas drained the last splash of dark roast from his thermos and rummaged through the backseat of the hatchback, tossing items into the trunk or tucking them into his knapsack. A knobby, half-melted honeycomb candle, plant-based jerky, a pocketknife, and a compass. A vial of Siuslaw dirt, an excavation brush, a satchel of dried herbs, and a beat-up cassette player.

"What, no room for the records?" Willow asked, rubbing her eyes.

"Good, you're up," Atlas said. He tossed a raincoat onto her lap. "Hurry up and get ready, we'll miss our window."

Willow pulled on her boots with a yawn.

"No coffee?" she complained.

"It'll stunt your growth, c'mon."

A surge of nervous energy flowed through Atlas. He stepped into the rain, flicking his flashlight to life as Willow followed suit. She wore a baggy sweatshirt with a faded bookstore logo over patterned leggings, and an oversized Cannon Beach baseball cap that she had stolen from him.

The trees cast windblown shadows on the trailhead, vibrant fall leaves muted in a cloak of night. A gust of misty air followed them under the canopy of trees, smelling of earthy, damp soil. Their twin flashlights swayed across the forested canyonland.

Behind him, Willow popped open a fluorescent yellow can of sweetened yerba maté. Atlas looked back and rolled his eyes.

"Those things are worse than coffee," he said.

"I know," Willow said smugly.

Atlas had dragged Willow across Oregon that summer. They'd visited almost every state park, car-camping and living off a mix of non-perishables and flexitarian fast food. They'd ventured beyond the southern border into the Redlands and extended as far North into Washington as Gifford Pinchot.

To Willow, it was a distraction. Time to grieve. Time to bond before Atlas started college and left her behind. To Atlas, it was a quest—and the sand of the hourglass was dwindling. Atlas cast a nervous gaze towards the crescent moon.

There was still time.

Atlas checked his pocket for their mother's watch, and the twist of her coarse hair. It felt foreign beneath his fingers. How was it possible that the last tangible piece of a life so large could fit inside a void of denim?

For the hundredth time, he told himself what Willow didn't know couldn't disappoint her— and prayed to the coven it was true.

Willow skipped to catch up.

"Remind me why this mushroom is so important?"

"It's the last on our list!" Atlas exclaimed, too upbeat. "*Black chanterelles*, Willow. Keep your head in the game."

Craterellus cornucopioides, he thought.

Also known as trumpets of the dead.

"Black chanterelle linguine," he said, causing Willow to giggle.

"Black chanterelle chips!"

"Souffle!" Atlas countered.

They parried recipe ideas for the next mile of trail, until Atlas stumbled and reused black chanterelle butter.

"No fair! You already used that one for morels!"

"Over fish?"

"Ew! Not allowed. You lose."

Atlas laughed and bowed in mock concession. He was hit with a nostalgic pang. It was a game they used to play with their mother when they were little, revived for their summer hunts. Now it was Fall—and like the leaves—their tradition would disappear. Unless his plan worked.

Atlas would be starting his freshman year, a semester delayed, in the winter. Willow would continue her sophomore year of home school in Salem—*four hours away*. He hated the thought of leaving her behind.

The coven would watch over her, as best as they were able, but it wasn't enough. It wasn't *family*. They couldn't replace him, nor their mother. A lump formed in his throat. He continued on the trail, hiking downward towards the babble of running water.

The whistle of the wind sounded oddly melodic.

"You might like it down here, if you could stay."

Next to him, Willow's face soured. She had friends in Salem, despite being home schooled by the coven.

They emerged in a dim, tranquil clearing. A goose honked indignantly and flapped away, beyond the mixed canopy of maple, ash, oak, and willow trees. Willow sank onto a boulder near the stream, flicking off her flashlight and draining the last of her maté. She crunched the can with the heel of her boot and tucked it into her pocket.

Oregonians don't litter, and neither do witches.

Atlas walked downstream and discreetly dipped an open flask, the cold prickle of water running over his hand as it filled. The stream had a subtle odor of volcanic gas, due to the naturally occurring lithium oxide for which the park was named. A whisper caressed his ear as if with claws.

Alone, forever.

Atlas jolted, a hand splashing into the water.

The phantom sound of footsteps followed him back to Willow, likely no more than his imagination and awakening wildlife, snapping twigs and crunching leaves. It was getting lighter now. Birds warmed their vocals in a series of discordant chirps.

"This is the spot, Willow."

"I still don't understand why so *early*," she complained.

A thrum of guilt vibrated through him.

"You want more competition?" he asked. "Look in the shade. Under leaves, and in mossy spots. We've got first dibs. Just think of that souffle."

She huffed a sigh and set off to inspect the ring of trees.

Just as Atlas began to lose hope, Willow released a celebratory holler.

"Black chanterelle *jam!*" she cried.

Atlas ran over, skidding to a halt as Willow parted a cluster of leaves. There it was. *Craterellus cornucopioides*, like morbid, black lilies morphing from the soil. He scooped his sister into a hug. He twisted the mushrooms free of their dwelling, carefully rehoming them in a mesh foraging bag. It was a step up from the greasy fast food paper bag used on their first hunt.

His excitement dimmed as he gathered the courage that he would need next. "There's something I need to tell you."

But Willow wasn't listening.

She looked beyond him, to the stream. Her face suddenly illuminated in an unnatural glow. Atlas whipped his head in the direction of her stare.

An illusory light meandered over the water like a firefly swollen to ten times its size. It shimmered. Flickered into a brilliant blue flame.

Atlas shivered. This was a complication, but also a good sign.

He'd been right in his hunch and calculations—the park's conditions were suitable for castings. A dangerous hope brewed in his chest.

One that settled poorly with too much caffeine.

His sister walked toward the light. He reached for her and tripped.

"*Willow Leaf Wilson,*" Atlas hissed, in a near reincarnation of their mother. "Get back here *right now!*"

Like paper set to fire, the light burst asunder.

Motes settled like ash to form the phantasmal electric-blue silhouette of a young woman. *This isn't the right ghost.*

His heart pounded like rain upon his windshield, only this time they were not safe inside the metal flesh of his hatchback. The light that pulsed against Willow's purple-streaked hair was not that of the asphalt-anchored streetlight, but an emanation of lonely, unearthly radiance.

Atlas stepped softly on the moss laden forest floor; the ankle supports on his hiking boots the only thing keeping him upright.

They were childlike together, girl and ghost. All bones and light.

A shadowed reflection of innocence lost, cast in a spectral mirror. Though the ghost was likely over a hundred years old—and Willow would scratch his eyes out for calling her a kid at fifteen.

Atlas creeped towards her, painfully aware of time's inability to freeze. He imagined the seconds of the watch in his pocket as sand slipping through glass—could feel each *tick* as if it were his heartbeat.

"She just wants a friend," said Willow, cocking her head.

"That's not how this works!" Atlas wrung his beanie and combed a hand through his hair. "She wants a friend *forever*, Willow. You can't be that."

She shrank from his tone, closer to the light.

"There is no forever," she said in a small voice, "Mom proved that."

His heart shattered into a million pieces.

Willow was right. Forever didn't exist, but *more time* did.

And he was going to get it. He cast another glance towards the crescent moon, just visible in the quickening twilight.

"We have to go, *now*." Atlas tugged her across the clearing and into the thicket of off trail forest, away from the hovering light.

Blackberry brambles ripped at the front of his favorite T-shirt, the one with a prairie wagon that read *You Have Died of Dysentery*. He'd picked it up at a gift shop in Baker City and wore it frequently to Willow's embarrassment.

Argh! Thorns clawed into his flesh as he made room for Willow to pass. *Well, no need for the knife now*, he thought.

Atlas ran, pulling a cursing Willow behind him until they stumbled back onto pavement. "What the *hells*, Atlas!"

He charged forward, ignored her protests as twilight seeped into dawn. Winburn Way soon faded into Granite Street, which, in turn, crumbled into gravel. They trudged past the reservoir, and back into the woods to an area known to locals as the Fairy Ponds, empty at this hour of students on spiritual quests.

Atlas unpacked his knapsack in a panic, casting unneeded items onto the dirt. He tossed the candle at Willow. "Here, light it."

Willow looked skeptical and scared, but snapped a small, white flame into existence. "What are you doing?" She eyed the assortment of ingredients. "Is this for a spell? You can't do magic."

Atlas leveled his gaze at his sister.

"No, I can't—but you can." He let the words sink in.

"What? Atlas, this is major! You know I can't without the coven."

He needed her to understand. There was so little time left.

Atlas pulled out the watch. The lock of hair.

He watched her face flit from confusion to recognition, to sorrow. Tears misted her eyes. "Mom," she choked.

"You're strong enough, Willow."

"Oh, covens! You… black chanterelles—*trumpets of the dead*, Atlas?"

She was sobbing now. Snot ran from her nose.

"You can do it," he said softly. "And we can all be together again."

A sliver of sunlight kissed her tortured face.

"This is *fucked*, Atlas." She wiped at her eyeliner-streaked eyes.

"*Completely* fucked."

"I know, I'm sorry. But it's now or never."

Willow's chest shuddered and heaved. He had never seen her this angry. He willed his heart to still, the seconds to remain.

He held his breath until she nodded.

Atlas dusted the ground with the vial of Siuslaw dirt and enclosed it with a circle of lithia, stream-doused black chanterelles. He wound back the hand of his mother's watch and placed it in the circle with her lock of hair. He gestured to Willow to place the candle. She hesitated, but only for a second. He squeezed a pinch of blood from his palm onto the flame.

Willow closed her eyes.

She began to mutter, brows furrowed, hair matted.

Atlas paced, one eye on the rising sun.

The ground started to vibrate. Willow whimpered. A blue light circled opposite the pond. Her voice grew louder, into sonorous incantation.

Each mushroom cap was a galaxy formed of iridescent black spots.

Her entire body started to convulse.

"Willow!" Atlas shouted.

The wind stirred branches and leaves into the air.

With a sudden *hiss* the candlelight flared blue.

Willow collapsed and it smoldered out.

Atlas rushed to her, checking for a pulse.

"I tried, Atlas. I promise. I don't think… I… she couldn't bond. It's not what she wanted. There is no forever."

It didn't work.

He'd thought if she could see their mother here, she would be willing to break free of the coven, sacrifice her powers for a normal life in Ashland. Start a real school, make new friends, even apply for a scholarship like his in a couple of years. They could be together. She could have studied ecology, oceanography, or hells—mycology! Anything she wanted!

He looked at his sister in numb disbelief.

It didn't work.

"You can still leave the coven," Atlas said, hating the words. He didn't know where this desperation was coming from.

"My magic—it's my connection to her," Willow sobbed. "You can't understand." The words stung. Tears were streaming down her face. She was covered in sweat, dirt, and scratches. She looked exhausted. Fragile.

Atlas stared at her in horrified revulsion.

He had done this to his sister.

He'd ripped open her heart just as it had started to heal. He had given her an impossible choice, with no time to make it.

Deplenish your magic to turn our mother into a ghost.

Leave the coven and sacrifice your magic to be with us.

Cold shame stabbed into him like ice picks into a mountain. He was supposed to be the one sacrificing for her. He was the older brother.

Had he even considered his family beyond his own desires? Would he have tethered their mother to this world against her wishes? Tethered Willow to his life against hers? The forest swayed. Atlas backpedaled, veered to take the right path.

"I won't go, I don't have to take the scholarship," he said. He was scared to leave her to the coven. To leave her on her own. It wasn't fair. He *couldn't*.

"I'm staying in Salem."

"If you do, I'll curse you," she said. "You deserve more, too."

A tangled ball of unnamed emotion surfaced in his chest.

"It's okay. I miss her too," she said. "You can visit, you know. All the time. I'll visit you, too. The coven will let me leave for the summers—there's probably more slimy mushrooms to find. And hats. I lost yours."

A laugh escaped through another stab of guilt. Would the coven truly let her visit, after he'd sapped so much of her reserve?

"I'll *make* them let me visit," she promised, reading his expression.

Willow had always been independent, but when did she get so grown up? With more than a twinge of embarrassment, he realized he hadn't been worried about leaving her, but afraid of *her* leaving *him*.

They would remain a family. The distance be damned.

"Black chanterelle ravioli?" Atlas asked.

"Cross on it?" Willow extended her pinky, chipped polish on the nail. Atlas entwined his finger in hers.

"Cross on it," he solemnly swore. "Though I really don't think we should eat these." He poked the luminescent shrooms with his boot.

"Fine, but you *owe* me coffee."

Atlas laughed. Across the pond, daylight pierced the forlorn silhouette of a young ghost girl. He watched her form burst into a misted rainbow of many-hued, luminous blues—and dissolve behind the spectral veil.

When he was lonely, Atlas would hike the trails of Lithia Park. Seeking the shadow of blue light beneath the crescent moon.

We Are Not We
by Monte Lin

Have you ever been lost? Like really lost, where nothing makes sense, and you see no way out? It's like a grown-up version of being in a department store and realizing you'd accidentally followed someone else's pair of legs that's not your mom's. That panic you've been left behind and trying to figure out what to do next: you've never been trained to be lost, you were only ever taught to follow directions. But life isn't a set of perfect directions. Even the GPS will tell you to turn left and bam, that road no longer exists.

My friends make fun—used to make fun—of me for having a bad sense of direction. Once on a hike in Forest Park, I really needed to pee, so I tried to walk back to the parking lot but got lost instead. I turned down the wrong direction at a main hiking trail intersection and I was gone for a couple of hours.

How could you get lost, Marvin? There are trails. And signs! they used to say. I shrugged and laughed 'cause it's true. Without my smartphone, I'd never get anywhere. Without my friends, I'd never end up anywhere. If I was all by myself, I'd fall right out of this world.

It starts in a doctor's waiting room. Even though I'd been there dozens of times, my doctors have changed twice. Part of being in a HMO network, I guess. Having to explain my medical history in a 30-minute appointment only to have that doctor leave, get reassigned, or retire, and then I do it all over again.

So when the clerk shouts out the name, "Manny Louie," of course I stand up, because when is a day someone doesn't mess up my name? It's honestly not that hard, but I guess they see my face and suddenly the language parts of their brain file it under "foreign word." Though in this case, someone else does walk up to the clerk and that's when it all gets weird.

So first, ok, so there must be a person with that actual name. So then I get that random doubt: did I accidentally take someone else's drink that one time then? Or wait, maybe it *is* supposed to be me, and this guy is the one making the mistake.

Like this one time a little Chinese girl in the library mistook me for her dad. She gave this little gasp and jumped back, and I almost found myself saying, "Hey, kid, it's ok, I can be your replacement dad." As if in another universe, I did have kid. I saw her dad in the corner of my eye and even I did a double take, because yeah, from behind, we had the same height, similar darker toned clothes, and even wore glasses, though his style was different (and he was balding and I'm not). She quickly figured it out and ran straight to him.

So at the waiting room I'm half out of my seat, the puzzle pieces still not quite locking into place and the guy talking to the clerk is wearing exactly what I'm wearing. Black slacks, gray hoodie, (I can't see his shirt), black loafers. I'm not wearing haute couture. This is my running-errands-and-I-don't-care-how-I-look clothes. And from the back of his head, he might have the same haircut as I do too, but there isn't exactly a lot of variation in middle-aged Asian men's hairstyles, not unless I wanted to have a boy band look.

But I see the guy in profile as he walks into the clinic and he looks like me exactly (almost), and I stand up to say, "I think there's been a mistake."

Everyone in the waiting room jumps away as if I just threatened them. They all scoot back in their chairs. I turn around but I don't see anyone else, just frightened patients. "I think there's some kind of mistaken identity here."

The clerk, this frail-looking white woman, leaps away from the counter, ducking behind the door deeper into the clinic. She shouts for security. I lean over the counter to see what's going on and lock eyes with her.

"Hey, why are you running away? What's going on?"

The clerk screams. A nurse storms out of the office, shouting, "Get out!"

"What did I do? I'm a patient here!"

Her expression flips from angry to furious. She's screaming at me to leave before she calls the police. I look around for some kind of backup, but all the other patients have backed away from me, some still in their seats, all up against the walls of the waiting room.

"What is going on?"

That sends everyone into a terrified, screaming fit, as if I stuck a hot needle into their ears.

The nurse gets that auntie edge in her voice, low, measured, almost quiet. "Get out or else."

She's a good foot or so shorter than I am but I know never to mess with a Filipina auntie, especially one with well-defined arms. I'm sure she's thrown out heavyweights before. I back out of the clinic waiting room with my hands up and go back to my car.

It keeps happening throughout the day. The cafe where I go to decompress: the moment I try to place an order, the staff and customers take a step back and the manager chases me out. The library where I sometimes work with my laptop when I ask for a private room. The take-out burger place where I order lunch.

Sitting in my car in the parking lot seems to be the only moment of peace. No one cares who I am, only if I open my mouth to say anything. I'm hungry, a bit light-headed; it adds a thorn in my head when trying to think things out. I gotta go home. I can't think straight.

Driving home hungry just gets my mood worse. Oregon seems to have a lot of tailgaters, worse when they have those giant, hiked-up trucks that completely block your view in your mirror. This bad mood gives me a bit of tunnel vision, so much so I almost pull up to my usual parking spot, this spot no one seems to realize is a valid on-street space.

I see my girlfriend arguing with me—that Other Me from the waiting room.

Claire's car is in my space, and I can see them arguing. He's pacing back and forth, that thing I end up doing when I get agitated; Claire always wants me to sit still since the pacing makes her nervous. Ok, it's more, I'm—he's—arguing with her, because he's the one talking and she's just saying, "Come inside. Have some tea. Put on a sweater," because it's Oregon weather.

And then I—he—sees me, or actually, sees my car and shouts, "My car!"

That's what they were arguing about. He thinks this is *his* car, and when he got out of the clinic, saw his car missing and gave Claire a call to pick him up, and now he's obsessing over his missing car, yelling in general, out in public.

It's what I would have done.

He sees me, or at first, I think we make eye contact, but the glare on the windshield must blot out my face because instead he points and shouts, "My fucking car!"

Fuck it. I turn off the engine and get out, keys in my hand, finger in the keyring. "What the fuck is going on, Claire?!"

Claire backs away, eyes wide and wet, like that one time I blew up at her over something small and petty, I can't even remember what it was. It stops me mid-stride because it takes me a second to realize she's reacting to *me*.

"Get away from her!"

Other Me, "Manny Louie" me, takes a swing. It's a clumsy punch, leading with the bottom of the fist, the two smaller knuckles, but I'm too distracted by Claire cowering in fear of *me* that I don't roll with it, so it lands harder than it should have.

I think I stumbled back. I don't fall to the ground. But I do drop the keys, so I guess my fingers went slack and the keyring slipped off. "Manny" shoves me back and I almost then fall to the ground but the blood rushes back to my head in time for me to see he has picked up the keys and Claire is dialing the police. The neighbors have come out of their apartments or opened their windows and are shouting.

I run.

What do I have? My phone, my wallet. What I'm wearing. No keys. So I can't get into the house or the car. Not with them there and not without breaking in. I'm heading to an ATM, but it's a bit away, especially if I have to walk. And it's the adrenaline but also the thought of confronting the cops that gets me to almost run. I don't exactly have a place to hide.

I dial up Claire. She doesn't answer, of course, and I leave a message.

"Claire, it's me. It's Marvin. Whoever is with you is an imposter. It's not me. He looks like me, but he's not me. I'm me."

Stupid. Blathering. She needs proof.

"We met at that weird joint company activity. Remember? I worked at that cube farm and you were in that phone banking kinda-scam. Both places were super sketchy, but it was the only jobs we could find. They had that weird morale-boosting ultimate frisbee thing in the park. I didn't have the heart to intercept you and you knew it, kept throwing the frisbee past me."

The VM beeps. Ran out of time.

I call up my text app. Maybe I can crash at a friend's place, and then I stop in my tracks. I feel dead, a creeping sensation down through my legs, as if blood was draining out of my body.

There are texts from me, the Other Me, to my friend. Just recent. While I was leaving a voice message.

>*Fuck, Josh, there's... shit a weird day.*

>*I saw someone who looked like me, steal my care*

>*Car*

>*Threaten Claire.*

Josh replies:

>*Oh shit. What. You ok*

>*Wait what*

>*Looked like you what*

I can see the "..." below of Josh texting when I see a message from "me":

Fucking freaky

Kinda looked like me

Don't make some dumb Asians look alike joke here

Claires freaked out

Josh texts:

Dude I'm not an asshole

I'll be right there dude

Got your back

Fuck fuck fuck.

At the ATM, I get the sense that it'll eat my card, but I need cash, I need resources. The card still has my name, the raised letters worn out and gray-white on the blue background: "Marvin Leo." My driver's license is the same. The right DOB.

I take out the daily max. $1,000.

I found a trick. Pretend to have lost my voice. I either type in my phone's text app or write on a receipt or piece of junk mail. People look at me funny, sometimes go out of their way to avoid me, but retail clerks, they have an incentive to let me buy something quick so I leave.

I use my bank card to get some groceries, a phone charger, and a room in a hotel. So far, nothing has happened. I'm hoping Other Me won't notice yet, although I'm sure the bank will email or call him about "unusual activity."

Crap. That might mean they can trace me to this hotel. Ok, I gotta hope the cops will be slow about this. I mean, every time I've called with a complaint, I'd have to argue with them to send a car, and to be honest, I can't remember if they have ever sent one.

Ok, just sleep here for one night and move on.

I don't have a car though.

I guess I'm getting familiar with the bus and the MAX lines.

The next morning, I try to use my card to get some breakfast at a McDonald's, but it doesn't go through. Crap. I take out a twenty and signal I want it to go (with a walking with fingers motion) and get out of there.

I'm guessing all of my cards are now invalid. All I have now is a bag of food, a backpack, a sausage McMuffin, a coffee, and a little less than a thousand dollars. I don't even have my laptop. Am I a valid person without ID? Without a bank account?

There's a cop car in the parking lot. It's just sitting there, probably doesn't have anyone in it. And they probably don't have APBs for suspected identity theft, but I can't stay here. I need a place to hide, to think. Honestly, I need a place to go to, away from people, at least for a little while.

Forest Park is one of the biggest urban forest reserves in the state, maybe the country. On a map, it might not look that big next to the city, but when you're in the middle of it, the park might just be wild country. So yeah, minutes of walking, hours of walking, the light gets darker, and of course the GPS isn't working because I never get signal. The trees all look different but the same; one bent tree can be a good marker, but walking from another direction, it doesn't quite bend the right way to be recognizable. The trails all look the same: dirt path, stones, a bit of mud. The cross-roads and intersections look the same, and a few don't have signs. Even trying to look for the sun is impossible in Oregon; the sky's permanently overcast.

So I'm wandering around this park that has always scared me a little bit, because it can swallow me whole and maybe spit me out later, maybe not? It's where killers can dump bodies, where some weed farmers grow little out-of-the-way plots, and where once a man and his teenage daughter lived alone for years. This is a place to disappear. It's where I got horribly lost that one time.

Everything feels wrong here. Too quiet. Too much detail with tree branches and trees and overgrown shrubbery and winding paths that disappear around the corner. So much detail that it almost washes out as visual white noise. I could be at the edge of the park or in the deep middle and I'd never know.

People walk by. I nod and smile. They return the gesture, but I hear them whispering to each other behind me. "Did he seem like a homeless guy?"

"I dunno. Let's just keep walking."

"Didn't we just pass him a little while ago?"

There are still people here and maybe this was a bad idea. And what am I supposed to do? Keep wandering around? Camp out in the forest? I don't even have a tent or tarp or sleeping bag. Am I hoping the forest will swallow me up?

Wait, didn't that person just say she "saw" me before? Is... Other Me here?

What if... he got "lost" in Forest Park? Like, what if his body got buried out here? It might take a while for someone to find him. And then I can come home to Claire...

There he is! He's wearing one of my old hoodies. The one I use when cleaning or doing yard work. But I stumble on the muddy trail and lose track of him for a second.

I find myself at that intersection, the trail marked by a sign in front and behind me, another sign for a trail down the hill, and a small, well-worn trail up, almost cutting through the hillside. A notch through the earth, walled by the roots of two trees, as if parting the earth. This is the intersection that confused me that one time, when I turned one direction instead of the other coming up from the path below. The trail cutting through the hillside doesn't look like a sanctioned path, a "fuck you" to the instructions not to disturb the natural environment.

Fuck it. Where else am I going to go, anyway? I step through, my shoes not really good for dirt and mud, so I slip a couple of times, getting my slacks dirty. When I'm through, I come face to face with Other Me.

It's like looking at a photo (well, not quite, maybe a photo of myself in my 20s when I was subsisting on $20 a week for food), because a photo is the POV you are not used to, the POV other people have of you. Meanwhile, you only see yourself in a mirror, the reverse of how people see you. You literally have a distorted vision of how you see yourself.

But it's not the Other Me with Claire. It's another Other Me. About a half-a-dozen Other Mes. All camping out in this nook in the park, connected by a trail that's there and not there at the same time.

"You're the one who left me behind at the cafe," the Other Me says. "Two years ago. You went on to be Marvin Leo."

"Wait, what does that mean?"

It takes me a second to realize that he's replying to me normally. No screaming. No terror. He even looks at me and nods, as if he expected me to realize this just now.

"I'm Martin Leuw. I ordered a drink and the barista misspelled *and* mispronounced my name. I got up to get it, but I saw someone grab my order and rush out the side door. It was probably you."

"I don't remember that."

"Why would you remember a normal day? But I remember because it wasn't my name, and you took my life."

It's the same all down the line. Martin Leuw split off from when Milton Leuw got a courtesy call at the airport. Milton Leuw from Mogie Lee Ou when he picked up his take-out Mexican food, and so on. And after the split off, everyone started treating them—me—like a monster. You can even see a lineage of time. Martin, Milton, and I share a scar on our head from one of our early dates with Claire; I wasn't... we weren't looking at where we were stepping. Staring at Claire and running our head into a metal sign. Martin, Milton, Mogie, and I all share the same crick in our neck from bad desk ergonomics. And so on.

"Who's the original then?"

Martin shrugs. "We don't know. Maybe down in LA before we moved up here."

"Maybe dead," Mogie says.

"Has anyone tried to contact him?" I ask. "Figure out why this has happened?"

"A few of us have gone down there. Do you remember your old hatchback?" Martin says, staring at me as if the answer was obvious.

"The one that got stolen? Yeah, why?"

"It was found in LA, right?"

"Why is that important... oh. One of us took it?!"

"He contacted our parents, and can you guess what happened?"

I pause. Martin waits. I think I want a different answer to materialize out of thin air, but instead I say, "They didn't recognize him. They were scared of him. And he never came back."

"Like we're the ones that don't belong."

I settle in with the encampment. I share a tent with Martin until I can get my own. (Mogie refuses to share a tent, and I remember before I met Claire, I had this angry, loner I-don't-need-anyone attitude going.) It's not great. None of us like camping or the outdoors in the first place. They can't get any real, steady work 'cause communication is a problem. They can get simple physical work, like cleaning out a place or lifting crap, although it's irritating when people think a quiet Asian man doesn't know English. Mogie tried to do some freelance work online, but it got too hard to find regular wireless, stay in Forest Park, and maintain an online presence enough for people to become regular customers. Never mind renting a place.

Sometimes they go into the city in pairs, pretend they're brothers, since again, it's easy for white people to think Asians look alike. Though in a way, we *are* all brothers, and we all *do* look alike, because We are Us, but We are not We at the same time. They do a little manual labor, get paid in cash, buy what we need, and head back to help feed the others. But it's hard, because they can't talk to people, and they can't stick at any one job before people start getting suspicious, of the silence, of these weird homeless Asian guys, or maybe they can sense We are We.

I don't need a mirror to see I'm getting gaunt like the rest, cheeks a bit hollow, sharper angles as the bones become more defined against our skin. In a way, maybe this is better. No one can recognize me. Not even Claire, whom I met after my starving 20s.

"Wait, why... why stay here then, so close to the Other Me? We could get recognized. Claire could recognize us..."

Martin doesn't answer me. Although I recognize that look, a furrowed brow and the chewing on his tongue, when he... I... we... have a difficult answer that we can't articulate. He motions me to the come back their pathetic camp.

I refuse to believe this. I refuse to accept this. These Others may have given up, but I still deserve my life, not that Other Guy.

So I stalk Manny and Claire for a while, looking for his mistake, or an opportunity, or a sign that something is off with Manny. The Others don't try to stop me, but I can tell they think it's a waste of time.

And then one rainy afternoon, I get my chance. Claire's gone to hang out with some friends, and Manny, uncomfortable being alone in the quiet apartment, braves the rain to go to a café. It's what I would do. There he is, walking down the sidewalk to our car a few blocks away, since Claire's car was in that convenient parking spot. The car is next to some thick bushes and trees. I could drag him into those bushes, knock him out, and take my life back.

I pick up a heavy rock and pause. How much force is needed to knock someone out, but not kill them? How much force is needed to kill them, but right away, so they don't just linger? Do I care if this Manny suffers? Do I care if he dies?

He's stopping to check his pockets. He's going to turn around and see me. Will he recognize me in my… our hoodie? I can run up, cross the distance in a second, get some momentum, and then swing, smash the rock on top of his head, crack it open like an egg—

My hand drops to my side, the weight of the rock yanking on my shoulder joint. *What the fuck am I doing?! I can't just murder someone.*

I feel a hand on my shoulder and spin around. The rock slips out of my hands, clips the curb, and smacks into a car door with a dull thud. The hand on my shoulder belongs to Me, no, not Manny, one of the Other Mes, face thin.

"Martin?"

He drags me away, and I let him since the rock hitting the car was loud, even under the rain. As we walk, he says, "How do you think you're going to replace him? You remember you can't talk to anyone not Us."

"I don't know what I was thinking... I guess I thought I… I could just not say anything. Write things down. Pretend I lost my voice."

"For the rest of your life?"

"Yeah, rest of *my* life."

"Or my life." We're a bit away now, walking against the rain at a brisk, stiff pace. "I could have gotten rid of you too."

I almost don't hear him. I'm still thinking of my missed chance, the weight of the rock, whether I really thought I could go through with it, so it takes me a minute and then I stop in my tracks. Martin shrugs.

"I followed *you* and Claire for a while. And then one day, she went out to see her friends and you headed to the café. I followed you for a while. Had a rock in my hand. But I couldn't figure out how much force I'd need to knock you out…"

"Or to kill him right away…" I reach up to the back of my head, the rain making my hand slick, the hood damp, and I shiver. "What stopped you?"

"Milton. Smacked the rock out of my hand."

"And if Milton hadn't stopped you?"

He pauses. "I honestly don't know. I think about it every day."

We don't bring up that conversation when we get back to the camp. But I stop following Claire and Manny. I don't exactly give up, but I can't spend my time obsessing. I even shut down my smartphone so I won't see their texts. (I don't need GPS now. Funny how practice can give me a real sense of direction.) I have to figure out what to do with myself now. Do I stay with the Us or do I go off on my own? Where can I go with people frightened of and hostile to me? Who am I anymore?

I join the others in heading into the city for work. And after a while, I figure it out. The universe screwed Us over, turned Us into the Bad Ones, leaving a Good One, but We all know eventually, the universe will make *him* a Bad One, leaving Us to pick up the pieces.

And yes, one day Manny Louie shows up, shivering from the cold (he lost his jacket in the fight with his Other Me, the New Us). I'm the one who gives him a spare jacket, introduces him to the rest, explains what happened, tells him what he has to look forward to. Follows him when he picks up that rock… And when people screw up the New Us's name, I'll make sure Manny does the same for him, and so on and so on.

Helping a brother out, so to speak.

The Goat Waits for No One

By Margo Pecha

"Dude, did you know the Garbage Goat is actually a portal?" Patrick asked, shoving a fistful of fries into his mouth.

"The… what?" I paused in the booth we were sitting in, a cheeseburger hovering in my hand.

"The Garbage Goat. It's this sculpture downtown with a vacuum in its mouth. You can feed it trash."

I frowned. "Why would you want to do that?"

"Because it's cool," Patrick insisted. "A nun welded it. But that's not the point—if you feed yourself to the statue instead of garbage, it'll, like, teleport you to the bottom of the falls."

"C'mon, man, cut it out."

"No, I'm serious!" Patrick insisted, biting into his own burger. "Only a handful of select people know about it."

"Then how do *you* know?" I asked. I flicked a packet of catsup at him. "You're hardly select."

He dodged the airborne projectile. "Stephen told me."

"Stephen?" I scoffed. "He lies about everything."

"I've known Stephen since kindergarten. He's a good guy." Patrick pointed a fry at me for emphasis. "And he showed us those steam tunnels under campus that you didn't think existed, remember? He wasn't lying about that."

"How could I forget?" I asked dryly. A maintenance worker had discovered the open entrance and accidentally locked us in for hours before anyone heard us yelling for help.

I chewed on my burger, staring out the restaurant's window at the sparse late-night traffic cruising down the street. Despite the terror of our lock-in, I did have to hand it to Stephen—he had a knack for finding interesting places no one else knew about. Just last weekend he'd taken us to a supposedly haunted staircase set in the hillside of a local cemetery. And while we didn't see any ghosts, we did get a good laugh when Stephen lost his footing and tumbled down the stairs.

"So, what's at the bottom of the falls?" I asked.

Patrick leaned forward, wiping the grease off his fingers on a wad of napkins. "An exclusive night club," he murmured. "It's built into the bottom of the Monroe Street Bridge. They have secret raves there every weekend."

I snorted and inhaled the soda I was sipping, the carbonation tingling deep in my nose. Of course Patrick wanted to go to a rave.

"So, the goat has, like, a pneumatic tube system?" I asked. "For people?"

"No, man, it's a *portal*," he said. "It teleports you,"

"Come on, stop messing with me," I said. "I'm not *that* gullible."

"I'll prove it to you," Patrick said, crinkling up his burger wrapper into a tight ball. "Stephen wouldn't lie to me. Let's go." He stood up and began piling our trash onto the tray our food came on.

"Right now?" I asked.

"Yeah, why not? You got anything better to do?"

I chewed on my straw and stared at the Formica tabletop, pretending like I was thinking it through. In reality, it was just another uneventful weekend for me. I had nothing planned, which was why Patrick and I had driven into Spokane from our nearby college town to grab a bag of burgers and do some late-night longboarding.

He arched an eyebrow at me. "I bet Amanda would think you're the coolest guy in the dorm if we found it and brought her and Sammie."

My face reddened and I shoved the remainder of my meal onto the tray. I still didn't really believe him, but I was willing to watch him make a fool of himself. I'd certainly seen Stephen do it enough times. And if there was truly something remarkable about the statue? Amanda would *definitely* be impressed. It didn't seem like there was a downside.

"Fine, I'm in," I said, grabbing my own board from the sticky floor.

"Yes!" Patrick pumped his fist in the air and made his way to the restaurant's front counter. "Extra bag of burgers to go," he said, flashing me a thumbs up.

We waited by the soda machine while a pimply teenager shoveled crispy, golden fries into a paper bag, covering the burgers. Patrick bounced impatiently on his heels, filled with barely contained excitement for our adventure.

"Let's go!" he said, snatching the bag, and I followed him outside.

We'd just stepped onto the sidewalk when an agitated gobbling sound erupted from the alleyway, and I caught the briefest glimpse of a large, feathered body darting into the darkness.

"Was that a turkey?" I asked.

Patrick nodded. "They're everywhere here. They mostly stick to the South Hill, but they wander downtown sometimes."

"That's crazy," I said. I peered into the alley, trying to get a better look at the bird. "Are they friendly?"

Patrick clapped a hand on my shoulder. "Dude, you do *not* want to befriend a wild turkey. We caught one staring into Corey's apartment window and it was *freaky*. It was tapping its beak on the glass like it wanted in."

I stared into the narrow gap, watching for the dark shape of the turkey lumbering among the trash cans and piles of garbage, but all I saw were eerie, stretching shadows cast by the glow of neighboring street lamps.

"C'mon, let's go!" Patrick said.

We hopped on our boards and cruised downtown, barreling through empty intersections and bumping over cracks in the sidewalks. The wind whipped at my face, the cold September air numbing my cheeks and tossing my hair back. I stuffed my hands in my hoodie's pockets to keep them warm.

Clouds of Patrick's breath floated back at me along with snippets of some song he was singing, but I couldn't make out the melody over the thumping of our tires on the concrete and the rushing of the wind in my ears. The bag of burgers swung crazily in his hand, his other adjusting the orange beanie about to slip off his head.

We sped under a steel overpass, a freight train trundling above and lugging its rattling cargo. This side of the state was depressing, and I still wasn't used to it. Everything felt dirty, on the verge of falling apart. The buildings were all crumbling brick, with chipped, faded ghost signs of yesteryear's advertising clinging to their exteriors. Every warehouse we passed sported cracked windows and a layer of grime, trash accumulating in drifts along the foundations.

Thumping bass leaked from packed venues as we neared the party district, the ramshackle buildings transitioning to more maintained establishments, though litter still collected in the gutters and alleys. Groups of bar hoppers staggered by in itty-bitty sequined dresses, shrill voices bouncing off the buildings as they shouted at each other in their pursuit of the next bar. We rounded a corner, narrowly missing a staggering group of polo-clad frat boys, when Patrick came to an abrupt stop.

"Aw, shit," he said, dragging his foot on the ground to brake. "There's some sort of festival."

I pulled up beside him. The road was closed off by striped barricades. Beyond the barriers the road was clustered with pop-up awnings and rows of food carts, the street slung with strings of warm bistro lights for ambiance. A yeasty smell floated on the air. People milled about, chatting and laughing as they nibbled on savory foods and sipped foamy craft beers.

"Can't we just go through?"

He lifted the paper bag, now spotted with grease. "We'd have to pay, and I spent all my money on burgers."

"Me too," I said glumly.

"We'll have to go the long way around. There's a suspension bridge that cuts across the river and goes right into the park where the statue is. It's a little out of the way, but no biggie. We'll just have to cross the Monroe Street bridge first."

"Couldn't we just… climb down the riverbank from there? Do we have to go to the statue?"

Patrick narrowed his eyes at me. "Are you in or out, man? The goat waits for no one."

"I'm in!" I insisted. "It just seems like a lot of extra footwork and bridge-crossing."

"Trust me, it'll be worth it," Patrick said, tugging at the slouching beanie. He hopped on his board and coasted down the sidewalk, away from the festival.

"Maybe we should have brought Stephen," I said, following.

"Couldn't find him," Patrick called over his shoulder, already propelling himself down the next side street. "Wasn't in his dorm. He's probably already there."

My brain turned this over and over like a smooth pebble, worrying it. Stephen loved playing tour guide and was loath to let any of us venture off without him. He thought it made him look cool to be the guy in the know, someone who had the inside scoop on the best hangouts and undiscovered haunts. But I pushed the thought aside. He was probably out partying it up. The goat waits for no one, as Patrick said.

"How does he even know about this place?" I asked. "Has he been to this... club... before?"

"His acupuncturist told him," Patrick said. He pulled a burger out of the paper bag and tossed it back at me.

"Well, where did *they* hear about it?" I asked, catching it.

"I don't know," Patrick said, exasperated. "That's not important. What's important is that we're going there, and it's gonna be awesome."

We trucked across the Monroe Street bridge, munching on our burgers as we traveled. The river tumbled and churned beneath us, and I couldn't help but search its depths for strobing lights, training my ear toward the bridge's thick concrete for the telltale pulse of music, any hint that something miraculous was hidden beneath. Somewhere nearby the sharp trill of a turkey sounded, and the back of my neck crawled with goosebumps.

Patrick swung right at the end of the bridge, following a bumpy road along the river back toward the park. From here I could see how the majority of the park was situated on a peninsula that jutted into the river, connected by various bridges and footpaths for ease of access.

Up ahead the suspension bridge loomed, taut wires supporting the walkway that led to a small island in the middle of the river and skirted around its side, connecting to the park on the far bank via a second segment of walkway.

My stomach lurched as we rolled onto the suspension bridge, and I felt it shift slightly beneath our boards. I sucked in a breath, unconsciously holding it tight in my chest until we'd reached the island and briefly set foot on solid ground again.

But when we approached the second segment of the bridge, we were surprised to discover two large turkeys standing in the middle, unmoving and seemingly unbothered by our presence or the crashing water below. The soft moonlight glinted off their beady eyes, boring right into us.

"Damn turkeys," Patrick spat. He had one foot on his board, rolling it back and forth as he contemplated how to proceed.

"Maybe they'll move if we start heading across," I said.

We hefted our boards and began crossing, the bridge swaying beneath our feet. As we neared the birds they hissed, flaring their tail feathers in a wide arc, completely barring any hopes at edging around them.

Patrick brandished his board like a baseball bat, prepared to swing, and the turkeys lunged forward, stabbing at his hands with their vicious beaks.

"Retreat!" Patrick yelled, and we scurried back across the path, stumbling over our feet.

I looked back as we neared the road, alarmed to see the turkeys advancing in our direction. Their plump silhouettes marched single file across the suspension bridge, seemingly intent on us. Their plumage remained fluffed, agitated.

"They're following us," I murmured to Patrick.

He shot a glance over his shoulder and frowned, wiped his bloody fingers on his jeans.

"If we go upriver a little bit, past the flour mill, there's another spot to enter the park. Follow me."

We stepped onto our boards again and hustled off, Patrick leading us through another part of town I was unfamiliar with. We cruised up a block and over a few more, the darkened streets and hulking shadows not doing my imagination any favors. I kept looking back, worried they were following us, thinking I heard the yipping and jabbering of our pursuers. I was so rattled that

I didn't see the pothole in front of me, and I tumbled from my board, hitting the pavement hard.

"You alright?" Patrick stopped and waited for me to pick myself up.

"Yeah… fine." I winced, knowing I'd have some bruises by morning.

Patrick nodded, but I could tell his mind was elsewhere. He fished two more burgers from the bag and tossed one to me. We sat on the curb and ate in silence, the paper wrappers crinkling. I cast surreptitious looks in the direction from which we came, prepared to see the shadow of a large bird step beneath the orange glow of a street light, but nothing materialized.

We continued on. My knees ached with every push off the ground, and my knuckles were scraped raw, but the pain was secondary to my mounting apprehension. I saw phantom turkeys in every shadow that leapt across our path.

The road opened up to a grassy conservation area. The meadow stretched wide and gray in the pale moonlight, the road cutting through the center, and I could imagine in the daytime it would be a nice place to picnic or study. But at night it felt ominous, shadowy and secretive, like anything could be hiding in plain sight.

As my eyes adjusted to the darkness, I realized we were surrounded. Turkeys were scattered across the field, scratching through patches of fallen leaves, no doubt searching for acorns. Their heads turned toward us as we approached, and soon they sent up a ruckus of cackling and clucking, aggressively beating their wings.

Three strutted down the path to meet us, heads bobbing, and fanned out across the road. We halted our advance. My skin crawled at the intensity of their stares.

"Shit," Patrick said, hopping off his board and kicking the end up. He snatched it in the air and regarded the turkeys. "These things are everywhere."

"I don't think they want us in the park," I said. "Maybe we should just leave."

The turkeys were strutting closer, their sagging wattles quivering and slapping. I took a few steps backward, conscious of the birds' sharp, angular beaks and my already banged up knuckles. I stuffed my hands into my hoodie pockets.

"You want to give up now when we're so close?" Patrick asked.

"No, but I don't want to get attacked by a flock of wild turkeys, either."

He pulled off his hat and absentmindedly ran a hand through his tangled hair, thinking. I warily eyed the birds milling about the meadow. What were they even doing out at night? Didn't they roost in trees or something?

"We can skirt around the IMAX and head for the center of the park," he said. "It's pretty much a direct shot from there."

We backed away from the birds and reversed course, heading for the large structure looming above the treetops. It was a strangely shaped building—circular, with a slanted roofline and white paint that glowed ghostly beneath the moon. My heart picked up pace as we rounded the perimeter, expecting to see the menacing form of a wild turkey just around the curve. But no such bird materialized, and we skated deeper into the park.

The pavilion glittered against the sky, stretched to the stars like a big-top tent, its webbing of lights transitioning slowly from green to blue to purple. Our longboards skated across the asphalt, transitioning from the glassy smoothness of a newly-paved stretch to an older path riddled with cracks and divots.

The night pressed in on us, a sense of unease growing in me the deeper we progressed into the park. I tried to focus on the beauty of it—the clock tower lit up like a giant candle, the sleeping swans floating serenely on water, the carousel's carved horses poised motionless and resolute— but I couldn't shake the feeling of being watched. My shoulder blades prickled with the uncomfortable sensation.

As we neared the goat, I became conscious of a procession accompanying us. Twenty, maybe thirty turkeys silently flanking us in a bizarre cavalcade. They kept pace easily with our boards, their large feet slapping against the blacktop as they trundled shoulder to shoulder, jostling each other in communal pursuit.

The Garbage Goat was nestled in an artistically arranged rocky enclave, with a button to activate the vacuum mechanism set into a nearby rock. His thick, shaggy body was held upright by stick-thin legs. Horns, fashioned of reclaimed springs, stretched upward toward the graying sky. A jagged beard of rebar curled toward the ground, and he bore a weary expression, like he was tired of sucking up gum wrappers and soda cans.

We approached the statue and the turkeys crowded in front of us, flaring their tail feathers and blocking our way. They trilled and gobbled, swinging their pendulous wattles menacingly, and stabbed at us with sharp beaks, blocking us from advancing. We hopped off our boards and edged closer, but they hissed and fluffed their feathers, pushing us backward.

"What do we do?" I asked, dodging swift jabs from the birds. I lifted my board as a shield but they just snapped and pecked at my fingers instead.

Patrick reached into the burger bag and pulled out a fistful of limp, greasy fries. He flung them backward, and they arced gracelessly through the air before exploding against the concrete in patches of potato pulp.

The turkeys rushed around us in pursuit, chattering in excitement and gobbling up the fries.

While they were distracted, Patrick made a series of jabs at the button that activated the Garbage Goat, some long, some short, in a pattern I couldn't determine. Then he stepped back, and instead of the roar of the vacuum, the sculpture's mouth yawned open, the metal stretching like taffy, leaving twisted, jagged strips around the rim of what was quickly expanding into a large, dark hole.

"See you on the other side," he said, giving me a small salute, before he hopped on his board and propelled himself into the goat's gaping maw.

The turkeys were chattering feverishly. I turned away from the stature to make sure they were still preoccupied with their snack, and when I looked back, the portal had disappeared, the goat now returned to a seemingly normal statue.

"Shit," I said, rushing forward. I mashed the button on the rock, but Patrick hadn't told me what the secret code was. Nothing happened.

I hopped on my longboard and sped away from the goat toward the falls—past the water feature, burbling and splashing merrily; down Spokane Falls Boulevard and past the Bloomsday runners statutes, eternally frozen mid-stride; and turned sharply at the corner of the city hall building, where I cruised under the gondolas suspended motionless like strange holiday ornaments. The wheels of my board thunked in time to the rapid beating of my heart as I neared another small park at the edge of the river, its rushing drowning out my panting breath.

The sky was beginning to lighten now, streaked with violet and pink. I braked with my foot and hopped off the board, snatching it and dashing across the manicured lawn to a terraced pathway overlooking the lower falls.

The water poured over the dam, pounding against the jagged rocks that protruded from the water. The Washington Water Power building glowed warmly from the cliff above, its brick exterior a sturdy beacon.

Patrick lay motionless on a rocky outcropping at the base of the falls. His hair was wet and plastered to his head, his hat flung off to the side. His board surrounded him in a confetti of splinters, and the paper fast food bag was ripped open, fries littering the rocks.

"Patrick!" I yelled, but my voice was swallowed by the roar of the falls.

I became aware of a presence beside me—large, feathered, and solemn. It perched on the railing nearby, so close that I could brush its feathers if I reached a hand out. I tensed and held my breath, trying to contain my fear. It preened its breast plumage, dipping its beak in and out, unconcerned by my proximity.

Patrick twitched. He sat up slowly and rubbed his head, checking out his surroundings. He saw me watching from the observation area and flashed me a thumbs up before jamming his hat back on.

"Patrick!" I yelled again.

He stood up and carefully wandered around the rocky bank, inspecting the remnants of his board. I saw him shake his head. He looked at me and pointed at something. I could see his mouth moving, but couldn't make out what he was saying.

More turkeys lined up along the railing, chattering feverishly and emitting a whole host of sounds I wasn't aware a turkey could make. Patrick was still pointing at the ground, but I couldn't concentrate with the cacophony of turkey sounds. My head throbbed.

He pointed again, sweeping his arm to encompass the broken pieces of his longboard. I shook my head and lifted my arms in an exaggerated shrug. Then he picked up a few metal pieces and held them up—the trucks from the bottom of his board, wheels still spinning.

He was holding four. I frowned; there should only have been two. And Patrick's board didn't have lime green wheels, that was—

The realization hit me like a swift punch to the gut: *Stephen had been here.*

The turkeys' vocalizations were rising in pitch, agitated, frenzied. My stomach knotted. Something was wrong.

Patrick cupped his hands around his mouth, and his faint voice reached me across the water: "Stephen's here!" He pumped a fist in the air, unbothered by the smashed board and our missing friend.

A large shadow moved beneath the rapids. It expanded below the water's surface, lengthening toward the rocky shore.

"Get back!" I screamed, waving my hands toward the bank.

With a thunderous splash, a craggy claw emerged from the river, crablike and spiny, the size of a small bus. The pincers flexed on its articulated arm, snapping and stretching toward the outcropping. It reached for Patrick, plucking his body from the rocks with ease, and lifted him above the river, leisurely carrying him downstream toward the Monroe Street bridge.

"Dude!" he cried. "This is so cool!"

"Get away!" I screamed. "Do something!"

"Woooo!" Patrick yelled, throwing his arms in the air like he was at the summit of a roller coaster, about to plummet over the edge.

Patrick only began to struggle when he realized that the claw was sinking, descending rapidly toward the churning rapids. He squirmed in its grip, but the pincer only tightened its hold, squeezing Patrick's abdomen, and he screamed in pain. He thrashed, kicking his legs and beating his fists against the carapace, but it did no good. The claw held tight, dragging him down.

The turkeys were yipping and screeching and squawking in an unholy choir, flapping their wings and stretching their long necks to the sky, drowning out Patrick's spluttering and choking as he went under. I covered my ears, not wanting to hear any of it. Patrick's arms flailed, bubbles bursting at the surface as he was tugged down further, out of sight.

A high keening filled my head, and I realized I was screaming, my voice joining with the turkeys'. And then it was suddenly silent, my wails the only sound ricocheting off the landscape.

Down in the darkness of the river two large globular eyes stared up at me, yellowed and faintly luminescent, rippling beneath the current. They blinked slowly, displaying no emotion or intelligence, before sinking into the river's depths.

The turkeys dispersed, hopping from the railing and quietly disappearing into the urban landscape. A seagull pecked fries on the rocks, gathering a limp beakful before flying off. The sun's first rays sparkled where they touched the water, and Patrick's orange beanie floated to the surface, drifting downstream.

    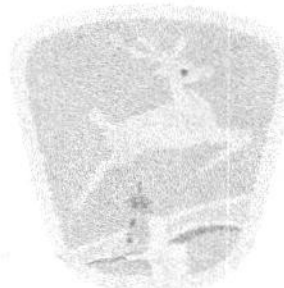

 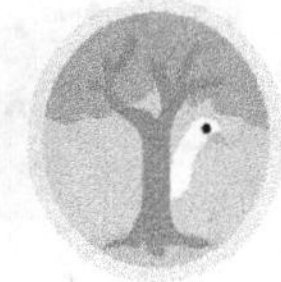   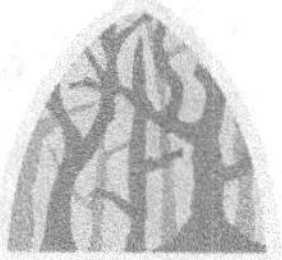

    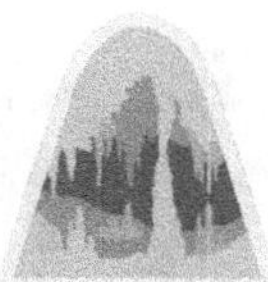

This Island is Magical~
by Rachel Lee Thai Nyeholt

Wow, this Island
is MAGICAL~

Troglodyte
by Cyrus Amelia Fisher

No matter how it looked, I didn't want anyone to get hurt. So just after I bought my same-day ticket flying in to PDX, I asked my neighbor to stop by and check on the leaky water heater in the basement while I was on my trip, because the hack contractor we hired to fix it had probably botched the job. When he stopped by tomorrow morning, he would creak down the basement steps and find my wife duct taped to the salmon-pink armchair she'd been trying to reupholster and a sledgehammer lying upright a few feet away.

After everything, knowing what I knew now, I still couldn't do it. She wasn't my wife, no matter how years of habit kept that word creeping back into my mind like an infection that wouldn't heal. The short-lived honeymoon phase, couples counseling, vacations and fights and steadily increasing boredom, all the things you might expect from a marriage that was heading for divorce as soon as the seven year itch hit—all of it, playacting. Síofra, bytting, changeling, whatever you wanted to call it: something had stolen my Ellie away and taken her place, an almost perfect copy.

Still, I'd left the thing breathing. Fighting the duct tape with tears in her eyes as she tried to say my name. It was a good act: good enough to keep the hammer still in my clammy hands until I let it drop to the concrete floor, no matter the risks. If she got out, if she followed me, I wasn't sure what would happen. I had no idea what she was capable of.

But with the same certainty that I knew that this thing had replaced my wife, I knew the woman I loved was still alive. Waiting for me at the stone altar of our wedding day, two hundred and twenty feet underground.

I hadn't booked a car in advance, so the rental place saddled me with a luxury minivan that would run me three hundred bucks a day. I only needed the one. Just five hours to retrace the route Ellie and I drove on the day before our wedding, delirious with excitement, towards the mouth of the cave where we bound our lives together.

Getting married underground had been weird. Many, many people told us so. But my wife and I met on a caving trip, I'd proposed to her in the lava tubes south of Bend, and she told me in no uncertain terms that we absolutely had to get married at Oregon Caves National Monument.

"My family's been getting married in this area for generations," she said with a smile. "They're pretty stuck on their particular traditions. My mom tied the knot in the Chalet down there back in '79. And my grandmother got married in the caves themselves, before they were even doing tours."

"That's an odd fixation," I'd said.

She shrugged, but her face was apologetic. "I know. I'm afraid it's kind of non-negotiable. My family would disown me if I was the first one to break tradition."

"Honestly, it's kind of awesome," I assured her, pulling her close to press a kiss to the top of her head. I smiled into her hair. "Just can't believe I'm marrying a troglodyte."

"Well, Jim, there's a reason we get along so well."

That was the woman I loved. And the other thing, the one that followed me out of that cave and stepped blinking, hand and hand into the sun—that was something else entirely.

The changes were subtle. I hadn't been attentive. She stopped liking the Thai place we used to order from once a week; she stopped laughing at the jokes we'd shared since our first date. I thought it was normal. Years pass, and one day you walk down into the bright wash of morning sunlight and realize that the familiar, boring face of the person we love is just a shell over something dark and unknowable. And no matter how we convince ourselves that the surface reflects the interior, we have no idea of knowing what might be growing inside. That's marriage.

Then on our five year anniversary, we sat down to watch some videos from back when we were dating, and the realization moved through my body like that old game mom played with me: *crack an egg over your head, let the yolk run down, let the yolk run down.* Cold, viscous fear sliding from my brain down my spine, as the wife-shaped-thing sitting next to me on the couch held her phone between us and laughed at the image of the woman whose life she'd stolen.

Stab a knife in your back, let the blood run down, let the blood run down.

Doing eighty-five down the rain-slicked throat of I-5 south, I scrubbed my hand over my eyes. I knew I was acting like the kind of man they made true crime documentaries about. But I also knew, in my marrow, that she was still there, trapped in the place where all this had begun. And though the legends didn't agree on the particulars, almost all of them agreed that the original could be returned.

I had to believe that. Because otherwise, all those years I'd fumbled through my marriage while the real Ellie suffered, alone, in the dark—they would be unforgivable.

The cave had long been closed off to anyone trying to get inside, sealed with iron gates. The only way to get access was through a tour with a park ranger. I knew it would be hard to slip away, but what other choice did I have?

I arrived at the visitor's center at two in the afternoon. One tour left for the day, just as I'd planned. I walked up to the desk in the gift shop and approached the ranger with an intricately constructed casual smile.

"Hey there," I said. "Can I get a ticket to the next cave tour?"

The ranger's expression changed, and my heart dropped to my stomach. "I'm sorry, we had to cancel our tours for today—our guide called in sick, and we're pretty short staffed as it is."

"...Oh. That's a shame." The smile on my face was a slash through tanned leather. "I drove all this way, you see, and this was kind of important to me."

The ranger nodded, customer-service grade sympathy stamped over her face. "It's very frustrating, I know."

I nodded, staring off into space. This was the part where I thanked her for her time and left: I could see her waiting for me to fulfill my half of the social contract. My hands clenched and unclenched in the pockets of my coat, sweat making the lining as damp as a stomach. I did the math in my head: when my neighbor would stop by tomorrow morning to check on the water heater and find the thing he would think was my wife. How quickly the police would discover that I'd booked a flight to PDX—whether a state parks agency would receive a bulletin about a potential fugitive.

I leaned forward a bit. The ranger's polite smile became more strained. "Couldn't you take me yourself?" I said in a low voice.

"I'm afraid not. I have to stay here at the desk."

"Well—" I felt like I was falling backwards, flailing for any handhold. "I would pay. Seriously, name your price. We could go when your shift is over?" I could see the faint illusion of sympathy disappearing behind the suspicion that I was a cave-obsessed axe murderer. "This is really important to me," I repeated wretchedly. "I promise I'm not a weirdo."

"Legally, I can't do that." I could tell she didn't believe me about not being a weirdo. "You're welcome to come back tomorrow. We've got a campground at the foot of the mountain: fifteen dollars a night, with pit toilets and barbecue grills. Our first tour of the day will be at eleven."

She slid a paper map across the counter at me, marking the location of the campsite in highlighter. Her face told me that if I didn't take it and leave, I was going to have much bigger problems than missing a cave tour.

I left, lightheaded, and walked back to my car. By providence, coincidence, or sheer instinct, I realized I was parked in the exact same spot I'd pulled into with Ellie on our wedding day. If I closed my eyes, I could imagine her in the car next to me, in the wedding dress passed down for generations, vibrating with nervous excitement at what lay ahead.

We'd walked to the central chamber dressed in our finest, like a couple of sacrifices being led to some primeval altar. We didn't have too many friends, and I hadn't spoken with a blood relation since I emancipated myself at eighteen. It was just her family shadowing our footsteps into the dark, carrying electric candles under the watchful eye of park rangers who didn't quite seem to know what to make of us. A slow, silent procession into the bowels of the earth, with the smell of wet stone and the distant trickle of the underground river guiding our way.

We'd reached the section of the cave called Miller's Chapel; Ellie's aunt officiated, tripping through the words like she was relieved to get them over with. When I'd pressed my mouth to Ellie's I tasted the mineral dampness of cave water splashing down on her lips.

And then, at the end of the ceremony, we'd turned out all the lights.

One minute. One minute in total darkness, the hush of the underground river and the rustle of clothing as her family shifted around us. In total darkness we slid the rings onto each other's fingers. I felt her forehead tip forward to rest against mine, and she kissed me again, deeper this time, while no one could see.

That was when the switch happened. There, in the darkness, when she'd pulled back with a smile I could feel against my lips and let go of my hands. Just for a second or two. And when I felt cool fingers entwine with my own again, someone else was standing in the dark with me.

The lights came back on. The thing that looked exactly like Ellie stood right where she had stood, smiling just as she had. The surface of her, the contours I thought *were* her, hadn't changed at all—and everything deeper, truer, that remained in the dark.

I slept in my rental at the Cave Creek campsite. At least, I tried to. In reality, I lay awake staring at the black square of the sunroof, occasionally sitting up to turn over the engine and get the heat going again. I had a quarter tank of gas; I couldn't leave it running.

In the middle of the night, I woke in a cold sweat from the realization that I'd almost made a fatal mistake. My cell phone. They could track that, couldn't they? That would be the first thing they did. I staggered out of the car and waited for my eyes to adjust. There were plenty of rocks around.

Just one thing first. I pulled up the picture album I made months ago. Back when I was first starting to understand what happened. They were all the pictures from back when we were dating, before we'd walked into the caves hand-in-hand and something else walked out with me. Ellie in a hard hat, squeezing through a cave crawl with a grin. Ellie, leaning over to savage my ice cream cone in a blur of hectic movement. Our weekly Thai food dates. She was so close to me now. I could feel it.

I smashed the river rock down on the phone, again and again, grinding it into the smallest parts I could manage and letting the river carry them off.

"Alright, now everybody crouch!"

Laughing, the tour group did as Ranger Ted instructed, bending low enough to navigate the lowest passages in the cave. The more I put my mouth level with my stomach the more I felt like the wash of nauseous acid sloshing around beneath my ribs would come gushing up out of my mouth like I was a balding, middle-aged gargoyle. I felt like I'd spent the night in a trash compactor, my joints and muscles a tangle of gore that only looked like a functioning human body. I fixed my mouth in a rictus grin, teeth holding back the tide, and ducked into the appropriate angle.

"We all feel good with that?" Ted asked, grinning to indicate that it was safe to tell him if your knees were going to simultaneously dislocate themselves five hundred feet underground. "Alright! Then it looks like we're ready to go into… the bat cave." The rest of the group oohed on cue.

The cave entrance wasn't much to look at. Maybe ten feet high, closed off by a heavy metal gate. The guide spouted off some mind-numbing geological details as the group huddled in front of that well of darkness, kids and adults alike craning their heads to see deeper inside. I swallowed a fresh mouthful of stomach acid and coffee. The air from the cave had that usual subterranean smell, wet stone and cold air, a hint of something murky—bat guano? The ranger's voice disappeared into a steadily climbing whine as I breathed that cave air deep. There was something else there. Like the faint sweetness of rot carried up from the long winding places in the earth, familiar somehow, like an almost-forgotten perfume—

Ranger Ted's keys clanged in the lock. The door inched open with a tortured scream.

"Velcome to my lair!" Ted said to more laughter. We trooped past him into the near total darkness, and he locked the gate behind us.

Each step we took into the cave pushed us deeper into the gullet of the earth, an alien organism whose strange folds of tissue passed over our heads as its muscles pulled us deeper. No human could have carved it; no human could have conceived of it. Ranger Ted stopped to share inane anecdotes and crack jokes, but no amount of levity could make us feel less like interlopers.

"Elijah Davidson discovered these caves in 1874, when his dog chased a bear into them and didn't come out," the ranger said. "Now, if your dog ran into a cave, how many would go in after him?" He nodded at the show of hands. "Yeesh, you'd follow your dog into an unexplored cave system with an aggravated BEAR in it? Talk about a lack of survival instincts! But that's exactly what Elijah did."

At the back of the group, I swayed along with the ranger's words. Still no chance of slipping away. Our footsteps shuffled over the gritty floors. Penitents on a long, dark road, bowed under the weight of the earth above. Every step farther away from the light bringing me closer to Ellie.

And somewhere behind us, another sound: footsteps in the twisting, sound-distorting tunnels. Echoes. It had to be. I'd watched the ranger lock the gate behind us.

"So, Elijah had three matches with him," Ted continued. "Now, next question: How many of you would light one match, look for your dog, then head back to the entrance with the second match and keep the third one ready in case you needed it? That would be the smart thing, wouldn't it?" He paused for effect. "Well. Elijah burned all three of his matches looking for his dog, and when the last one went out, he was all alone in the dark."

My knees felt weak; I leaned back against the cave wall behind me for support, hoping the ranger wouldn't notice and tell me to stop touching the delicate cave rock. I wished he'd shut up. I read the story on Wikipedia during my research. I didn't like imagining what it would be like for a person to be down here, alone and afraid in the dark.

"Now, you all may have noticed that we're underground," the ranger said. "That means the kind of darkness we find here is very special. It's cave darkness. It's darker than a cloudy night, darker than your bedroom when you hear something go bump in the night. It's complete, total blackness. After fifteen minutes without visual input, the mind will just start inventing things to see. That's the kind of darkness our friend Elijah found himself in, with no idea how to get back to the surface. Pretty bad situation, right?"

The group stopped in front of an especially beautiful column, stalactite merging with stalagmite and lit by the carefully positioned can lights underneath. And for the first time in the tour, the passage ahead was big enough for a person to slip past the front of the group and go deeper, alone.

"Now, if you all are amenable," the ranger said, "I'm going to suggest something. Let's turn off alllll the lights down here and get a taste of real cave ambiance. It's just as dark down here as it was centuries ago: the exact same darkness that Elijah faced, wishing he'd just let his dog get eaten by that bear."

I made my way through the crowd slowly, towards the yawning passage beyond. I'd have to make it far enough away to avoid being seen, quietly enough to avoid being heard. By the time anyone realized I was missing, I had to be past catching.

"Alright folks," Ted said with a grin. "You ready to go to the dark side? One full minute of cave darkness. In three, two…"

The lights went out.

For a moment I was totally frozen. The dark pressed in on every square inch of my skin with the crushing pressure of the Mariana Trench, impossible to breathe, impossible to move. *Oh god, Ellie, I'm so fucking sorry—*

And then the tour group let out a nervous chuckle, and I found my body again.

I groped forward as quickly as I could, hands outstretched until they touched the smooth, chilly rock. With one hand trailing on the wall, I moved deeper into the earth.

Behind me Ted's voice started up again, already much quieter: painting a grim picture of Elijah's fate against the backdrop of total darkness. But I knew how the story ended. Elijah climbed his way out of the nothingness and back into daylight, to claim discovery of the caves. He even found his dog waiting for him. Happily ever after.

Unless it hadn't been Elijah who came back out again. Only something that looked and sounded exactly like him but wasn't. The cold air sank a little deeper into my bones.

The floor sloped downward beneath my shuffling feet, steeper than I remembered from five years ago. It had surely been half a minute already. I stretched my hand out in front of me and found only open air. Had it been forty seconds? Fifty? I let go of the cave wall and started walking forward at a brisk pace, hands stretched out in front of me to find the next wall as I followed the slope down. I couldn't even hear the guide's voice over the whisper of the cave river now. *I'm coming baby. I'm coming—*

Air. Not just on my hands but around my foot, plunging forward and then down, down, hands flailing and leg kicking as I toppled forward. I didn't even scream, too focused on staying utterly silent that my instincts didn't catch up with me until I felt my hand hit the side of the cave wall with an explosion of pain.

My head hit next.

I blinked, and knew two things: I was alive, and my eyes were open. I was almost sure of it. Again I felt my lids drag across my eye, closed, open—the view didn't change.

Stupid. Stupid. I knew these caves had pitfalls; I should have been more careful. And now I had fallen off the tour route, and my wrist was almost certainly broken. I probably had a concussion, too.

I reached for my phone to activate the flashlight, to make sure I wasn't sprawled on the edge of an even deeper pit—but of course my pockets were empty. I'd smashed my phone to pieces the night before, when the worst thing I could imagine was someone finding me.

I forced a breath into my lungs. I just needed to stay calm. The tours ran every two hours. Before too long, some other chipper park ranger would be leading a gaggle of tourists through the lighted path somewhere above me, and they'd hear me shouting for help. They had to hear me.

…And if they didn't?

I forced myself into a sitting position, cradling my hand against my chest. Nauseating pain sank its fangs into my wrist and made it hard to think. In a survival situation, were you supposed to stay exactly where you were, to make it easier for rescuers to find you? Or were you supposed to act immediately to save yourself, because you'd only get weaker and more confused? What had Ellie done?

It was so terribly dark. I looked down at where my body should be—my feet stretched out ahead of me—and saw nothing at all. The cave surrounded me, enveloped me, sealing me away as surely as a tomb. No sight. No sound.

No. Not totally silent. Somewhere in the darkness, the sound of scraping feet. And then: a single, flickering light.

I went rigid. Squeezed my eyes shut and opened them again. The light remained. Firelight— an electric candle? And a slim, pale hand, hovering in a puddle of light to hold it.

Fifteen minutes until the hallucinations start. How long had it been since I came to?

"Ellie?" I called out. It had to be. I needed it to be. The hand holding the candle remained suspended in the air, silent. Then it began to drift farther away.

"Wait," I said. I staggered to my feet. The candle drifted like a satellite in the darkness, and I followed with my good hand pressed to the moist wall of the cave. At times the light bobbed, wavered, and terror would clench my heart that it was about to disappear—but then it would continue, and a few minutes later I would realize that there was some obstruction in the path to climb over. I couldn't get any closer, but it never left my sight. My heart beat faster in my chest. Was she leading me out, to safety?

I climbed down a particularly steep slope, jarring my wrist with a clash of pain: and then I felt the air open up all around me. A massive chamber—my hand brushed something icy cold. Metal. The railing, and a concrete path just beyond. We'd returned to the tour route, to Miller's Chapel, the place where Ellie and I slid the rings onto each other's fingers in total darkness.

The candle waited for me on that very spot. I stopped ten paces away. The electric flame did not give off enough light to illuminate more than the hand and part of the arm that held it.

"Please," I said. "I came back for you. I'm here to take you home."

"Jim." That voice. Her voice. I nearly fell to my knees, or lunged forward to pull her into an embrace. But something held me at bay. Why hadn't she come to me?

"It's me," I said. "Ellie, please—"

"You left me, Jim."

The words hit me harder the the impact of my fall. "I know. I'm so sorry. I came back—"

"You didn't."

"Yes, I did—Ellie, I'm right here, please, just come here and take my hand—"

I stumbled forward, stretching my fingers to her. And it was only then that I saw the dark line of bruises on the slender wrist that held the candle.

"You left me in that basement, Jim," she said. "And our neighbor was throwing a fit. You can't imagine what it took to calm him down. You wouldn't like to."

The candle rose. My mouth went dry. My wife's face—the thing that looked like her—was marked with broken blood vessels around her bruised mouth, in a rectangle where she'd torn the duct tape off. She grinned, a mouth full of teeth like folded rock formations, pale and glistening in the darkness of her mouth.

"Where is she?" I whispered.

"I'm right here, love. Did you think you'd find some other me, a perfect, untouched version of your wife frozen in time for you to pick back up again?"

I clenched my uninjured fist. "I know what you are. Changeling." The word echoed, hollow, in the vast space around us. "Give me back my wife."

The candle lowered. It illuminated the white swath of her dress, her wedding dress, the one passed down from mother to daughter for generations. In the dim light its rough-spun texture looked like a surgical gown. All I could see of her face was the white of her teeth and the glint of her eyes.

"Now that's a funny old legend," she said. "Swapping out a human for something else— what's the point, when you make such comfortable places to live? A safe, warm shell to grow in, until we're the only thing that's left. And you never noticed it happening. None of you ever do."

The darkness pulsed again, only this time I knew it was not a hallucination. I could feel the presence of something, many things, shifting and whispering just past the tiny ring of candlelight. A conclave in the darkness, just waiting to hitch a ride into the light.

"Come on, Jim," she said. "Let's go home and forget any of this ever happened. It won't hurt when it starts to grow in you. You won't even feel it at first."

I stared at her. The thing that had been my wife. She had been there with me, all along. Rotting from the inside, just like generations of her family before her. I should have known. I should have seen. But I'd been standing in the dark for so much longer than that minute on our wedding day, eyes sealed, mind conjuring what it wanted to see. By now, it was all I knew.

"Ellie," I whispered to whatever shred of her might be left. "I'm so sorry."

"Come on, love. Didn't you say you wanted things to be like they were before? It'll be just like that. We'll walk out of here, together." Her hand extended to me, wedding band gleaming like a predator's eyeshine. "Til death do us part, right?"

The darkness took a breath. The candle winked out. And for the very first time, my wife and I understood each other perfectly.

10 Favorite Campfire Songs as Selected by the Northwest's Friendliest Cryptid, Dave the Devil Lake Monster

(originally published in *The Gosling Gazette: A Junior Muddy Goose Adventure Society Magazine* issue 79, August 2007)

1. Burnt Marshmallow (Sticky, Sticky!)

2. Queen of All Roses But Mine

3. Pine Needles on My Knees

4. O Aberdeen

5. All 'Round the Mulberry Bush

6. The Meatball Song

7. Oregonians Don't Litter —and Neither Do Witches

8. Martin, Milton, Mogie

9. I Saw Bigfoot Dancing Last Night

10. Goat Turkey Goose (cha-cha-cha)

The Ghosts of Lake Roosevelt
by Wendy N. Wagner

It is always cold where the lake's hunger
meets the wake of the ferry, despite
the bleach-fierce sun. The cliffs here
are haunted by ten thousand years
of footprints, and still echo songs
spun silver from salmon.

I sought history from the farmers
and found a basalt-bred garlic,
one white bulb costing only fifty cents,
its silver-papered skin streaked
the breeding color of a king chinook.
Its name its color and its birthplace.

Beneath the lake, that town's footprint
drowns. A hundred miles reclaimed by sport
fish, the cemeteries emptied, animals
driven onto the high plateaus. The earth
scraped raw so when the dam strangled
the river, the only witnesses were ghosts.

Those ghosts still wail as the party boats

cut through their memories, and sorrow

draws the heat from even the heartiest swimmers.

In the winter, the lake draws fog into ice-shrouds

frosting branches and power lines to diamond,

sharp offerings to the river-that-was.

Standing on the ferry deck, the cloves

of the lost peeling in my hand, I lean over

the rail to search the depths—as if I will find

that missing tombstone, that overlooked house,

that forgotten way of life, and only a warm hand

keeps the ghosts from pulling me beneath the waves.

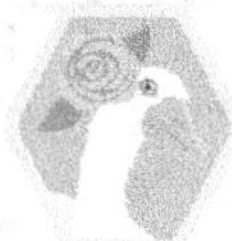

The Queen of All Roses
by Katherine Quevedo

I first learned of the Queen of All Roses after my night landing into Portland, Oregon, the City of Roses, my birthplace.

With my backpack thumping against my spine and my carry-on suitcase rolling behind me through the dim, subdued terminal, I surrendered to the haze of a new time zone. I scratched at the stubble on my chin. My mind swam with fatigue and possibility. The airport's curved wooden ceiling and massive skylights yawned above me, like my jaw helping my ears pop after the pressure change. The dark restaurants and cafés all closed up for the night made my stomach rumble. In this space obviously designed for a crowd, with hardly another soul present, I felt like a trespasser. I kind of liked it.

I found a spot to take the obligatory photo of my feet on the Portland Airport carpet, then tried to get my bearings. One of the perks of such a long flight was how little decision-making I'd needed to do on the plane. I could sit back and know I was right where I was supposed to be, making progress toward my destination without having to think about it. Now, however, I had to look for wayfinding signs and deal with my backpack and carry-on, all while very sleep-deprived. The lobby looked so deserted. My fatigue finally usurped the excitement of sneaking through a location after hours.

I reread the last message from my parents: "Sorry, went to bed. Can you take MAX and get a ride from the Sunset station?"

No one's here to get me. I'd known this would be the case—a drawback of taking a red-eye flight—yet a pang of disappointment shot through me. I found a sign pointing toward the airport's light rail station and dragged my suitcase down the long hallway.

In my fatigue, it occurred to me that maybe the MAX train didn't run at this hour? Thankfully, I found a train waiting at the station. Its interior glowed a cheery yellow against the night. It looked empty. I entered and slid onto a forward-facing spot near the front of the car. I plunked my backpack on the aisle seat to my left and wedged my carry-on into the row in front of me. I sighed and relaxed into my chair. I could enjoy this next portion of my travels where I didn't have to make any decisions. And I had the whole place to myself.

That is, until the announcement came that the doors were closing. Footsteps pattered into the train car right as the doors slid shut. I glanced back. A crouching figure shuffled up the aisle, closer and closer to my row. Scraggly hair swung across his face. He clutched a brown paper bag for dear life. Its crinkling grew louder as he approached. We were alone in the car—probably this whole train—yet he slumped down directly across from me, into the aisle seat to my left. My shoulders stiffened against the hard seat back. He'd probably have tried sitting next to me if it weren't for my backpack. I knew I could say something or get up and move elsewhere, but that would feel so rude.

The man placed his paper bag on his lap. A savory scent emanated from it—not unpleasant, surprisingly enough. When had I last eaten? I'd forgotten to fill my water bottle in the airport. The train lurched forward, making me sway in my seat, caught between jetlag, hunger, and thirst. I just wanted to get to my parents' house. The man hunched over his noisy bag and pulled out a chunk of what appeared to be rotisserie chicken. He ate it and licked his fingers.

"We are thirsty," he croaked.

Great. He was talking aloud, and using the royal "we."

"We two," he said, pointing back and forth between himself and me. "We are thirsty. I know where we can quench our thirst on this night."

I scootched as far away from him as I could. It wasn't much. "Sir, I'm not sure what you—"

"Bly-Eye." He faced me and pointed to his left eye, bloodshot and filmy. The other looked starkly clear in comparison, almost too white. "My name is Bly-Eye."

I couldn't stop staring. It was less about the differences between his eyes and more about their shared intensity, like gazing into the sun when you know you shouldn't. My hip pressed into the train's cold, firm wall. He seemed to be waiting for something, probably my name.

"I'm Gary."

"Gary, Gary, quite contrary," he blurted, then erupted with such laughter that I banged my shoulder against the window. "Riding the train so late. No one came for you, Gary?"

"They couldn't pick me up this late."

"No one could pick me, either," he said.

"Up," I corrected without thinking. "Pick you *up*." Maybe that was bad-mannered of me.

He smirked and stuffed more chicken into his mouth. Then he tore off a scrap of the paper bag and used it like a napkin. It seemed to leave more grease on his lips than he'd started with.

"I see you like carnivorous plants," he said.

"What makes you think that?"

He pointed to my backpack, where a keychain of a Piranha Plant from *Super Mario Bros.* dangled from the zipper. It made me think of the road trip I'd begged my parents to take me on in high school, when we'd wound through the twisty roads of northern California to a small botanical trail. We'd squeezed our car into one of the few spots in the tiny gravel lot, then traipsed down the wooded path. It must've been less than half a mile. And there, in the shallow bog, its water green from the mineral serpentine, just past the wooden railing, we spotted the dense cluster of pitcher plants about knee high. It seemed like hundreds of them. They ended in bulbs like little question marks curling upon themselves. The underside of their green hoods had hints of red, like unripe tomatoes slowly striving toward readiness. I'd wanted *so badly* to step past the railing. If it had been nighttime, like right now, perhaps I would've.

Something about this night—the clear, stark moonlight, the jetlag, the swaying of the train, how deserted everyplace felt—rendered me more curious than usual, more daring. I wanted to explore. Who knew it took returning from a trip to feel that stab of adventurousness?

As though reading my thoughts, Bly-Eye hunched into the aisle toward me, his face serious. "So, Gary. You want to see the nocturnal, carnivorous rose?"

I uttered a quick laugh. It sounded weak. "There's no such thing."

"At the rose garden they have one. The only one. The Queen of All Roses. She only hunts once a year, and that happens to fall tonight."

I hadn't been to the International Rose Test Garden in years. My family used to take out-of-town visitors there in my childhood. From the garden's hilltop perch in sprawling Washington Park, you could see the skyscrapers of Portland nestled in greenery on a clear day. I'd never thought of venturing into the rose garden at night. A tremor moved through me, the shiver of a thrill—or the train juddering.

"No one believes me about her," Bly-Eye continued, "because I have no device. No camera. They find nothing about this carnivorous, nocturnal rose. But you. You will help me. You will capture the proof. I can get us there. Promise. The train, the elevator, the shuttle."

I considered his words as I stared out the window. Portland glowed dimly all around us, just a thin layer of glass away. The night, this night, unlocked something deep within me. Being awake so late, after such a long stretch, felt like another form of sneaking around where I shouldn't. Yes, perhaps I'd become nocturnal and predatory, like this mysterious rose of his. Perhaps we could go on our own hunt, for an adventure, for proof of something rare. In daytime, his route would make sense. The train, the elevator, the shuttle. And the MAX had been there unexpectedly. So far, so good.

We'd made it all the way to Goose Hollow by now, the final station before the tunnel.

My mind churned as we left from the stop and snaked under the tall bridge with ivy all over its feet. Suddenly we were inside the hill, and then came the dizziness of seeming to move backward and forward at the same time, and the dark tunnel outside making our bright interior reflect upon the windows, and the almost imperceptible dip as we headed toward the platform below the zoo. Blue safety lights zipped by. The air whined around us in a cross between a whisper and a shriek. Bly-Eye grinned at me, his lips glistening with chicken grease. I turned away and found his reflection smirking at me in the window.

To get to my parents' house, I only needed to go two more stops, to the first station outside of the tunnel—or last, depending on your direction. I'd ping a ride from there, get home in no time.

Or I could follow this total stranger, get off at the next stop, the tunnel one, and go see the Queen of All Roses.

There was more to it than the pitcher plants, of course. There was also the movie poster for *Little Shop of Horrors* I couldn't stop staring at as a kid, with its ravenous, tentacled, flesh-eating plant front and center. It had teeth and a tongue! The first time I'd seen Venus flytraps in person—in the flesh—my heart had sunk at how small they were, how inadequate considering how long they'd haunted my imagination.

"What size is this rose?" I asked, trying to sound nonchalant.

He faced me, his good eye twinkling with delight at my obvious interest. "Come with me. Find out."

Right on cue, the train screeched and decelerated as we approached the underground station. Our tight, black tunnel opened up into a broader one with curved ceiling and bright lighting. The platform to our left showed up as a wall of white and gray after all the darkness and reflections.

Bly-Eye hoisted himself to his feet. "Come."

There was only one way up and out from the platform. "I'm pretty sure the elevator's closed at this hour."

"Not for us. I already told you."

I found myself dragging my suitcase toward the train door, rushing after the hobbling figure of Bly-Eye. The Piranha Plant keychain thumped against my backpack as though urging me forward. I stepped out onto the platform. The doors swished shut behind me. My stomach gave a nervous twist as the train sped away, leaving me alone with Bly-Eye. We passed the core sample running along the wall, gray rock trapped in a long, transparent tube. As he'd predicted, the elevator door did indeed open for us. I followed him into the oversized square silver box. My feet pressed into the ground as we began our ascent, then with a whoosh and a whir, we reached the surface and stepped outside.

The huge parking lot sloped away from us in the gloom, but the shuttle bus waited nearby all lit up like a lantern. First the MAX train, then the elevator, now the shuttle. To think, at first no one was there to get me. But Bly-Eye made it happen. He got me. Somehow, he got me. Knew about my longtime fascination with carnivorous plants. My recent thirst for adventure, for access to forbidden places, or at least familiar places during prohibited times. He grinned knowingly at me. He'd abandoned his chicken bag somewhere along the way to getting me here, stepping up into this bus. It had no driver.

I kept my backpack and carry-on between us once more, although this time I didn't mind Bly-Eye sitting across the aisle from me. Still, my stomach flipped as we set off up the forested, twisty, one-way route to the rose garden. How long had they used an automated shuttle for this loop? We wound through steep embankments lined with ghostly trees, past the jutting roof of a picnic shelter, and eventually reached the residential section where the outskirts of a Portland neighborhood abutted Washington Park. The bus rattled through tight curves between cottagey houses, a long stretch of our journey. I poured my heart out to Bly-Eye as we traveled, the various frustrations of my youth, my attempts to see more of the world, to find my place. He nodded and nodded and watched me with those wild eyes of his, while the bus's windows rattled and rattled.

We entered Washington Park once again, where the night had transformed the reservoir below the road into a giant mirror of stars. We passed the Sacajawea statue with her arm outstretched, perhaps to provide direction, or to my eyes in the dimness, waiting for me to grab her hand. I couldn't tell if she wanted to pull me closer or have me yank her from the spot.

Finally, we arrived at the rose garden stop.

"Leave your bags here," Bly-Eye said. I thought for a moment of his paper sack of rotisserie chicken. "The shuttle waits for us. Promise."

As ludicrous as that seemed, way out here in the wee hours of the morning, thus far he'd given me no reason to doubt him about any logistics. I knew the shuttle's loop would continue through the woods, past the archery range, down to the zoo parking lot. I could stay on the bus, complete the circuit, and head home like I should. Instead, I left my backpack and carry-on behind and disembarked with Bly-Eye. We passed between the sport courts with tall fencing reining them in—or rather, protecting them from the outside—and the rose garden's narrow parking lot.

We entered down the garden's stone steps, past the covered kiosk with the site map, to the paved walkways. In front of us lay the stepped terraces of rosebushes in the night like a carpet upon wide stairs, the arbors spread among the empty pathways, everything hushed as though lying in wait.

He led me to the brick walkway known as the Queens' Walk. How fitting. He stepped onto the half-circle overlook at the center, pointing at the ground not far below. "We go here." He led me to a nearby break in the foliage, where a short dirt path led to our destination. A single tree stood in the center of the trail as though trying, pathetically, to block our way between the hedges. We passed on either side of it without incident and hopped over a shallow ditch of water. Its ripples shone in the moonlight like foil. We stopped below the overlook on the roomy path of wood chips.

"Ready your device," he said. His voice sounded tense for the first time.

I whipped my phone out of my pocket and prepped the camera. We waited in silence.

And then came a sound at once wet and scraping.

I spun to face a tall silhouette like someone on stilts gliding toward us, practically upon us. I froze and took it all in. Her breath: pure perfume. Her fingertips ending in thorns rather than nails. Her gown of leaves. Her head a gathering of petals, the tops glittering with dew as if a tiara sprouted from her. And where her face should be, I saw only shadows from the curling edges of petals. She towered over me by at least two heads. If I were insect-sized with my human brain, a Venus flytrap or pitcher plant would be the most terrifying sight on Earth. Now I, a grown man, felt so tiny and *caught* in this moment, so overwhelmed and poorly adapted, I could only quake before the nocturnal and carnivorous Queen of All Roses.

This night. This trickster of a night would teach me a lesson, that I am vincible, that I am owed nothing.

I kept my phone angled toward her for what must be the worst shaky-cam video ever. I caught a potent whiff of her fragrance, and although the night remained silent, somehow my ears filled with a sound like the shriek of air around the MAX train as we'd rocketed through the tunnel. She spoke to us in that scent. I understood her fury at Bly-Eye. He'd betrayed her trust, breaking one of his promises, his biggest one. His job was to protect the secret of her existence and to bring her prey. Instead, this time he'd schemed to catch her in the act, divulge her, make his mark at her expense.

He seemed just as frozen and helpless as I was. She reached her leg out toward him. Under the gown of green prickly leaves, I glimpsed not a foot but a root. She stepped on him, and I can't describe it any other way but to say she drank him. Ate him, I suppose. He decomposed in front of me, right there on the wood chips. I watched, stunned, as though my own feet had taken root. I understood at once that that would've been me, if he hadn't attempted to trick her. I tried not to think of chicken and grease and bones.

Then she turned her attention upon me. Her petals rippled, perhaps about to bloom open. I swear I heard a peeling sound. What lay inside? The spiny teeth of a flytrap, or the tunnel of no return of a pitcher plant, or something more regal and devious? A face, perhaps? Would she consume me in a way she hadn't reserved for Bly-Eye? Or talk to me, order me around, hypnotize me? I knew how these situations would play out in fairy tales. The poor hapless traveler, gullible enough to be lured away from safety. This was the point where she'd replace her servant with a new one, someone to do her bidding throughout an indebted, pitiable existence. In other words, me.

No. I turned and ran. I bolted between the rows of thorny bushes, up the stairways, toward the shuttle mercifully waiting in front of the sport courts. The bus had stayed put, as poor Bly-Eye had promised. I flung myself onto a seat and panted as the bus doors hissed shut. It felt as though thorns had ruptured my lungs and squeezed around my legs. I should never have trespassed. Gary, Gary, quite contrary.

The shuttle set off away from the rose garden, away from the Queen of All Roses. I looked at my phone in my quivering hand, intending to delete the video—promise—but when I pulled it up, the screen showed only pure blackness through the entire recording. I turned up the volume and could hear my frantic breathing and nothing else for the duration. I mashed the delete button and stuffed the phone away. But I knew the things we record are never truly gone.

My bags appeared untouched where I'd left them. As I pulled my backpack onto my lap, the keychain made an unfamiliar jingle. I peered down at it. The cartoony Piranha Plant had contorted into a detailed rose, complete with tongue and teeth. Goosebumps spread across my flesh, each one a prickle as though from a thorn. I had been picked.

She had let me go tonight. Of course she would. She'd already eaten. But a year from now, if Bly-Eye was to be trusted on such matters—and what reason did I have to doubt him?—she'd need more. And I'd been picked. Now I ask you, which is worse, to help the carnivorous Queen of All Roses feed, or to find out what happens if you don't?

Parafernatorio
by Daniel Dagris

My living girlfriend has always been jealous of my dead girlfriend. She's haunted me for years, always in the same room since the night I found her under my bed, thinking she was a monster. I'd stolen a ring from her dead body, and she'd come with it.

"We're just friends," I told Candy, from our bench beside Reflection Lake, south of the peak of Mount Rainier. "We can't kiss or hold hands or anything."

"You would if you could," Candy said.

Ever since my mom died, I've wanted to meet Death. Skeleton in a white robe, Death. The one that gathers spirits when people leave their bodies. I watch for Death when I sneak into the funeral home in a suit I took off a body. I'd say *stole*, but stealing means someone still owned it. My dead girlfriend told me there was no them there anymore.

I try to look sad walking past a stranger's casket toward the snack table, the burnt coffee I love to hate and the knock-off Oreos I hate to love. I saw Death that day. Not for the body on display, but for the elderly father of the deceased who had a heart attack in the bathroom.

I had just opened the door when I saw Death's boney feet and robe beside the twitching body of the father of the corpse on the floor of the big stall at the end. I heard faint choir music as I crawled under the locked door. The song, probably from the funeral on the other side of the wall, silenced as Death closed her robe and with one boney finger touched the mirror above the sink in that large stall. Death disappeared into that mirror like a hallway. My dead girlfriend followed.

My dead girlfriend got smaller, hurrying to catch up. I heard glass cracking with each step into it she took. Around the mirror frame the glass started to splinter, the cracks worked their way toward her. I would have shouted, but if music could bleed through the wall, my voice certainly could, too. I would have tapped on the glass hoping she would hear me, but cracks tinkled at its edges and were quickly forming a tunnel of shards around the shrinking figures. I worried knocking on the glass might only add more. The cracks closed in. The unbroken portion the size of a vinyl record, then a plate, then a saucer. Worrying it might break through the middle and force my dead girlfriend to follow Death even if she wasn't ready, I placed my hand over the center to absorb some shock. Still, the edges closed in, splitting under my hand until beads of my blood ran down along the maze of shatter.

Death turned to my dead girlfriend. I lifted a finger, but my blood hid whatever might be seen under Death's hood. Soon my dead girlfriend's face peeked out between my pointer and thumb. Then she vanished to appear behind me, reaching a ghostly hand to join mine against the glass, lacing her fingers between my own. I imagined warm soft skin but felt nothing.

"We'll need this," she said, and with little drops of blood falling into the sink, she guided me to an edge of the center of the mirror, still unbroken. My fingertips plucked it from the rest, which shattered and tinkled across the bathroom floor.

The calm drone and sobs beyond the wall were replaced by raised voices. I wrapped my hand in toilet paper and the shard of glass with a snowflake worth of sharp edges in paper towels. It was only the size of my dead girlfriend's palm. I slid it into a jacket pocket, and pushed out the bathroom door just before strangers rushed in.

As the sun started to set, my dead girlfriend pointed to Reflection Lake, where it showed a snowcapped Mount Rainier upside down, even in late July.

"Does one of us have to almost die for Death to let us in?" Candy said. I put a finger against my lips to shush her.

The blue sky oranged as the sun slipped away, and purple rimmed like a bruised lip where the sky touched space.

My dead girlfriend nodded at me. I drew the shard of mirror out of my pocket and the paper towel wrapping, and held it up, shining sunset into Candy's eyes.

"Careful!" She said.

"Don't be a baby," I said, and Candy punched me in the shoulder. "Learn to hit me harder and I'll stop," I said and grinned and she grinned back, so I felt okay not saying sorry.

Instead of looking up at the mountain, I looked at the same clearing in the mirror. In the reflection the sky glowed red, and burning woods surrounded a grand charcoal-colored lodge with glowing flame at its seams. In that instant the air changed, like I'd opened an oven door to check on roasting meat I'd forgotten.

I looked up from the mirror to see the mountain burning and both my living and dead girlfriends staring up at the flames. We existed in the reflection now.

"It's not real," I said. But I didn't know. "It's not our real, at least."

But smoke filled our noses. And the mountain wore black clouds like a witch's hat.

"Tell that to the trees," Candy said. I took her hand as we watched them burn and burn and never crumble.

I pulled Candy along the path around Reflection Lake. Instead of following, my dead girlfriend began to walk across the water toward the charcoal lodge. Each step sent a ripple.

Candy must have followed my surprised look because she kept tripping over stray roots and rocks, and each time I caught her she was glancing from the fires to the lake, at the latest ripple, at the rare opportunity to see the dead, herself.

The trees screamed as we passed. A high-fluting pain that made my blood cringe.

When my feet brought me too close to one, blue-glowing eyes looked out from behind it, and I backed away. They didn't blink, and didn't follow.

The inferno slowed our steps as I tried to catch up with my dead girlfriend and Candy tried to keep up with me. The lodge glowed like coals in a wind at our approach. It loomed high into the clouds of smoke so we couldn't see the top, only the light where the seams like bright embers along campfire logs cut through the smoke.

We passed burning topiaries, screaming bushes in shapes of ancient gods, and chimeras with arms and legs and heads of creatures, some extinct, others nameless. Strange mixes of tyrannosaur and tiger, of elk and condor, of giant spider and wooly mammoth.

The open front doors of the charcoal lodge blew gusts cold as a blizzard. Entering those frigid winds, I shivered, and my gut twisted—sick from the change.

But the vaulted ceilings inside had no seams of fire. It was a hotel built of stone that seemed fire-licked like it had burned down at least once. A stairwell at its center spiraled out of sight both up and down.

"Welcome," said a voice like a dog's snarl, "to Parafernatorio." The name was spoken as three words, each overlapping before the last was finished

A concierge stood behind a stone counter in the shape of a hotel front desk. He had the body of a man in a charcoal grey suit, three heads covered in short fur. They looked like wolves, one shadow-dark, one bone-white, and the third speckled bone and shadow.

A nametag on his chest read GOYET. His syllables overlapped at their edges, each spoken by another head as he said, "Do you have a reservation?"

"We're here to see Death?" I said, unable to keep the question out of my voice. Then looking around, I spotted my dead girlfriend disappearing into a banquet hall brimming with the strings.

Candy followed her, saying, "Oh my god, I can see you! Wait up!"

"Of course," Goyet said. "Down the stairs. Death prefers the winter."

"Do we have to pay to be here?" I asked.

"No," Goyet said. "Only *if* you leave."

"Is winter a room?" I asked.

The heads all angled at me. "It's a season," Goyet said. "It's on the other side."

"Of the mountain?" I said, confused.

One head shook. Another bared a toothy grin. The third looked annoyed like I was wasting its time.

"Of the earth?!" I couldn't keep the shock out of my voice.

The heads all nodded.

"So, down the stairs ALL the way," I said.

"And up the other side," Goyet said.

"Couldn't that take a lifetime?"

"Most of our guests stay significantly longer."

I went to get Candy, who had wandered through an archway carved with horned and winged creatures that stood more than three times my height.

Inside, guests dressed in the finest clothes of every era danced and gabbed, or sat and clinked glasses, or necked half-naked in dark corners. Many were dressed in suits with tails and gowns with flowing ruffles, or in royal robes and togas. Others wore expensive casual clothes of the modern rich. And on a raised stage in the middle, played an orchestra made up of fairies. Some the size of a finger, and one so tall that as she swayed while strumming a harp half the height of the room, her tiara clinked against the vast chandelier, causing its crystals to chime a rain of sound and reflect the light into a prism of twirling colors.

"Candy!" I shouted.

But she waved a hand as if to shush me and didn't look back. I knew that wave. It meant a fight. So, I rejoined Goyet in the foyer.

"This place makes no sense."

"Very little," Goyet said, nodding.

"Is that by design?"

"Come," Goyet said, leading me to the stairs.

He walked to the stairwell, one head motioning for me to follow. I moved to the railing beside him. From this close, he smelled like those rotting fish tree-flowers all around Portland. Floral but unwelcoming. I leaned over the railing into a gap around which the spiraling staircase wound. Expecting darkness, I was surprised to see light in orange and turquoise and pink illuminating the impossible depths.

I've never seen so many stairs," I said. "A place this old doesn't have an elevator, does it?"

"If you're in a hurry then let me assist you," he then lifted me like I weighed nothing and dropped me into that brightly lit abyss.

The spiral of stairs corkscrewed around me so fast that dizzy would be an understatement. Within seconds my throat stung and chewed up peanuts and raisins and chocolate and sesame sticks shot from my throat. It fell in a wet spray as if racing me to the center of the earth.

The relief from vomiting allowed falling to become the only thing I could fathom, clearing all else from my mind. The coil of stairs that spun around me grew hypnotic as I caught glimpses of hallways that led into blindingly bright light—like each contained the sun itself. Then past railings over which tidal waves crashed, sending seawater spray between banisters and into my eyes.

Floor after floor flew by. Each archway appeared at random.

One archway opened to a sea of naked bodies, some incomplete. Many screaming.

One opened to a circle of folding chairs in which people sat in discomfort, looking bored at the person speaking, like the speaker had never been interesting, and had never stopped talking.

One archway smelled like pennies and dripped with blood.

I hurtled faster and faster so when a glob of floating filth approached, I had no time to react before splashing into it. Salt water, human ash, tepid milk, battery acid, sprinkles, and countless other contents including my own vomit burned my nose as it drove into me. I had time only to close my eyes, and when I emerged from the other side of the glob, I coughed out all I could. As my brain spun like it did a backflip in my skull. Something was different. Instead of plummeting, I was a cannonball flying but also slowing down. Gravity had turned and so, as afraid as I'd been of landing, I became of falling again, of ending up inside that ball of runoff at the center of all things. I turned without meaning to and my neck craned to see where I was headed. As I slowed, I wondered if I could reach out and grab a railing before my velocity changed. If I didn't want to break my arm, I'd have to time it just right.

As my fall peaked and reversed, I became weightless. In that instant, I was snatched from the air and placed on stone steps. And as startled as I'd been to be tossed into the spiraling depths of the earth, I was as surprised to be still and standing again, beside Goyet. I leaned against a nearby wall. My bones felt like rubber from adrenaline.

"I forgot the meaty ones vomit," Goyet said, "Dante was fragile too."

"*The* Dante?" I asked. "*Inferno* Dante?"

"He'll be so disappointed to be known for his most hellish work," Goyet said. "I look forward to telling him. Yes, he wrote of Inferno, a place of torment inside the earth. But also of Purgatorio, a place of contemplation that exists between good and evil, and of Paradiso, where the good move from a mountaintop to the heavens. Every journalist has their own interpretation. But Parafernatorio exists outside of those rules. It passes through those places, yes, but it ascends to the sky on both sides. Mount Rainier, where you entered, and here, on Mont Ross, a mountain peak on the Kerguelen Islands."

"Why does this place exist?" I said, shivering. The oven heat with cooling gusts had flipped to frigid air with oven wafts coming far too rarely.

One of Goyet's heads yawned like I had missed the point.

"*Because* it exists," he said, "It's a place where all are free. The dead escape torture and boredom and bliss here. And the magical join them. In short, we host all the best parties."

I followed Goyet out of the stairwell, into a massive white-walled and marble-floored banquet hall, nearly empty, except for a single table where a guitarist strummed. His music sounded warm and mischievous. The man playing it had something burning between his teeth. Goyet led me towards that table, and as we walked, I realized the walls weren't painted white, they were glass, and it was snow that colored them. When the wind shifted, glimpses of glaciers and ice frothed waves crashed far below.

At the table, something moved. A white robed figure who had blended in with the snow at first. The bottom of the white robe stained in dry filth that burled like the marble floor's dark streaks. Goyet motioned to the figure, so I moved to the chair opposite and sat. Though I'd wanted to meet Death for years, and had played this moment out in my mind enough times that it had continued into my dreams, I'd been prepared to see a bleached pale skull. But the face that turned to me as my teeth chattered was familiar. Thinner and her hair streaked with silver, it was Candy.

She smirked at my obvious confusion.

Not knowing what to say, the words that tumbled out were, "I wanted to meet the Death who took my mother."

"I know," she said, her voice sounded deeper and worn down, but brittle too, like someone who rarely spoke. "But that was many Deaths ago. She turned to the room. "Isn't this place beautiful?"

I looked at the blustering snow and she placed an arm around me. At her touch the snowfall slowed and became a dance of snowflakes all twisting and fluttering. New colors refracted between them, a rinsed-out rainbow of light bounded from one to the next, but a billion of them.

"So many people die, all the time. The burnout is unreal." She pinched her white robe and raised it, with a nod to the creeping filth rimming the bottom. "So, we have to live an eternity in a moment. And so many moments are breathtaking." She squeezed my shoulder, and I looked to her face again. And though she looked older, her smile still curved at the end in the same way I adored, and the sparkle of her glance made me feel at home as I always did with the her that was mine. "And to be filled with song," she said, letting go of my hand and opening her robe.

It wasn't bare skin, but bones she showed. And from between them, inside her, a song swelled, the grandest choir I'd ever heard, the glass around us shook with the power of it. The living painting the sky had become felt like it made Goyet's words settle into my own bones: Paradise was right here.

Then, inside her robe she spread her ribs like files in a cabinet, but somehow there always seemed to be more. And as she did, the voices of the choir became more apparent. Each so human and complemented by the next. A community of sound that made each other stronger. She flipped between ribs, highlighting voices until one nearly tore my earliest memories from inside me.

It was her. My mother's voice. It emerged bright. She'd sung to me the day I was born, and it was the first perfect sound I'd ever heard, and here she was still singing. I'd found her. I wanted to know if she was ok, but her song was so beautiful, the question never came. She was.

Then, just beside my mother's voice in the choir, I heard a space. A note was missing.

"This space is for you," Death said. "For when your time comes, and you have all the more to sing about."

She squeezed my hand again, and we sat for an eternity watching the snow fall.

I returned to Goyet and the stairwell.

"Is there any other way to the top?"

Goyet tilted two heads again, in that *you stupid child* way.

"There is no top," Goyet said, his shadow-dark head wore contempt with a fang revealed. "Only between. Wouldn't you rather stay?"

I didn't argue, just dove headfirst down the stairwell.

Through the wing carved archway, the fairy orchestra played a high-tempo flute-driven song. The dance floor churned with the spinning and the spun. In a balcony box I spotted my dead girlfriend, seated and watching. I rushed to the stairs that led me to her. Her seat wasn't ornate, but a tire swing hanging from a worn rope. "I met Death," I said, "I can't believe you weren't there. We've got to go, but I'll tell you all about it on the way." I turned and slammed into charcoal-colored fabric and that rotting fish tree-flower smell.

"If you want to keep all you know and all you have, you are welcome to never leave," Goyet said. "But if you must, there will be a cost."

"You just showed me infinite exits," I said, incredulous.

"Exits *to* Parafernatorio," he clarified. "None from it."

"What if I break a window?" I said, not waiting for an answer.

One of Goyet's clawed human hands landed on my head and clutched my scalp, holding me to the spot. The shadow-dark wolf head placed its nose against mine and stared deep into my eyes.

"You saw *what if*," Goyet said. "The blue eyes among the flames. They left without paying and the cost was madness. You know Death's secret. To keep this knowledge, you must leave something of equal value."

The dance floor below reminded me of the snow and the vibrant memory of my mother's voice. Of the instant or eternity I spent in that swirling snow and song. Of how it could prove to be company for any lonely moment. A wellspring of peace at my fingertips. I had no idea what sacrifice I could make in exchange. Goyet would have to take my heart to mean as much.

In my silence, my dead girlfriend spoke up, and letting go of the rope swing, she reached out and held my hand that wore her ring. "I will stay," she said to Goyet.

My mouth fell open.

Goyet nodded, two heads watching her, the third looking at me like I didn't know how lucky I was. "Done," he said.

"Wait," I said. The ring feeling lighter somehow, like I now wore cheap costume jewelry.

"I'm ready for a change," she said. "Nothing is forever. Not even forever."

"I haven't been alone since I met you," I said.

"Maybe you'll like it," she said.

"But I have so much to tell you."

She took my hand where I wore her ring upside down. She squeezed it so I felt the jewel press into my palm. "When I spoke to Death in that mirror," she said, "She forgave me. I haven't been alone since I met you. Maybe I'll like it."

I followed her down the stairs, ready to argue, to convince her to stay with me, but at the bottom she vanished into the crowd. As I scanned the faces for her, moths of loss fluttered in my chest.

Candy's face, young—the her that came here with me—spun into sight. She was waltzing with a Pharoah. She spotted me, thanked him, and walked to my side.

"You're still you," I said, my eyes flitting to the crowd.

"Always have been," Candy said. "I talked with Alsie."

My eyes stopped slipping away and fastened to Candy. When she said the name of my dead girlfriend, it was like a spell broke.

"I can see why you like her," she said. "And this place," she turned to the grand ballroom, "I don't know how anything else could ever be so wonderful again."

"I think if we don't leave soon," I said, "we never will."

"So, you found, Death?"

I nodded and tried to smile, to show even a glimpse of the joy the other Candy had shared with me. But Alsie was gone and it felt like Goyet had taken my heart. I'd found her ring when I was young enough to need a night light. And the longest we'd been apart was when she'd crossed Reflection Lake on her own. When she'd let me fall through the earth alone. It was like she knew it was over before I did. I thought back to if she'd been distant, but she was dead. She'd never seemed happy. Now she was gone forever. Maybe nothing is forever. But I tried to be happy for her, which must have looked pathetic because Candy's face fell, and she gave me a hug.

"It's ok, pal," she said, and her choice of words only saddened me more. We followed Goyet to the doors, where I stared out at the screaming trees, holding Candy's hand, which didn't hold mine back.

"About the knowledge of this place," Goyet said, "you can leave and forget, or you can leave something in exchange."

I thought of my fall and all I'd seen along the way. Of how the strangeness of this place painted existence in new light. But this must have kept me from speaking for too long, because this time Candy spoke first. She squeezed my hand and said, "Let him remember. You can have his love for me."

Goyet heads nodded again, "Done."

"What?" I said.

"I'm not in love with you," Candy said, both her lips and shoulders shrugging.

And as I looked at her, I didn't love her like I thought I did. I couldn't tell if Goyet had taken that or if I'd always felt this way.

"And you," Goyet turned to her. "Do you want to remember this place?"

She looked back at the sea of music and color and people and creatures of all times.

"You can keep it," she said.

I might have blinked, and we were outside. Standing in a valley of grass and whistling marmots.

As I remembered my paradise waiting for me when Death one day came, my friend smiled and laid in a clover patch. She plucked and blew on a dandelion, celebrating in her breath and bliss this green mountain, bursting with life.

Greening in the Dark
by Patrick Swenson

The porch step felt cool where Brett sat, waiting for his sister Lisa, who'd gone into the house to ask their mom for some lemonade. An August breeze gusted off Lake Quinault, eddied about his parents' house, and brought with it a familiar smell: a musky fresh scent that signaled rain.

A streetlight stood out near the access road that looped around to create a humble driveway. Its soft flickering gave him a sense of security in the surrounding woods, protection encircling the porch steps like a fairy ring.

"There are fairies out there!" Lisa used to tell him, during her elementary school years.

"How do you know?" Brett would ask. "Can you see them?"

"No, silly, they're camouflaged. They cover themselves with moss to hide from humans."

She was fourteen now, first year of high school coming up, but she still had the exuberance of the grade schooler he'd teased unmercifully. He looked away from the porch and focused on the dark above the lake. A light flared and traced a trail across the sky. He shuddered, reminded of the War and what he'd left behind on his quest to come home.

The screen door squeaked on its hinges and Lisa appeared, a glass of lemonade in each hand. She had on a black rain jacket. He took one of the glasses and felt the cool condensation on its surface, pressed the glass against his forehead for a moment, then took a sip. The lemonade tasted tart and lingered in his mouth.

Staring into the night, he convinced himself he saw animals weaving around the trees, phantoms in the forest, harbingers of the War's uncertainty and mystery. The trees were covered in thick green moss. Almost *every*thing was covered in moss. He thought about the past five years, where he'd been, and the whole ordeal seemed an eternity away.

Actually, it was half a solar system away.

Triton.

Triton, a substitute for home, an artificial habitat, its people kept alive with simulated food and thin, recycled oxygen. The hastily constructed domes covered humanity the same way moss covered the Quinault temperate rainforest.

Triton, joined to Neptune like a parasite. A sterile environment that had no resemblance to the resilience and interconnectedness of Earth. Nothing like home. Absolutely *nothing* like the rainforest.

As soon as Lisa sat next to him, she started right back in on her search for shooting stars. "There's another one," she said, gazing high above the lake. "How many *is* that?"

"I've lost count," Brett said.

"It's the Perseids, right? Always around mid-August. From that comet—what's it called?"

"Swift-Tuttle."

"Another!" She pointed it out. "Why so many? This is unusual."

It was dark but he could still see the amazement on her face. She was loving the spectacle.

"So many stars," she said with a disembodied voice. "I mean I know they're not real stars, but you know? Think about it, how stars—suns—some of them died millions of years ago or more. Some had planets. Was there—*is* there—other life out there?"

"It's just us."

"No way. *Life*," she said. "Out *there*."

"I don't believe it," Brett said. "We're fighting amongst ourselves here, and on Triton and everywhere in between. We're all chasing different dreams. If there is any other life out there? They don't care about us."

She continued as if he'd said something trivial. "I mean are you *seeing* this? Look at those! One flipped left, one dove almost straight down."

"Lisa," he said.

"Another one! It's almost like a firework, so luminous. So . . . *green*."

Before he was drafted and shipped out to Triton, while in high school, he learned about mosses. One was a cave moss called dragon's gold that actually shined emerald green. Due to the lack of light, the moss had adapted, which created the moss's luminescence. Moss did these kinds of things—all mosses did—without roots.

Only at home could he grow roots.

"Lisa," he said again.

Finally, she looked at him.

"They're not shooting stars."

She didn't say anything at first, searching his face. "Not shooting stars? What do you—what are they?"

"Me."

"*What?*"

"I've been trying to tell you since I got here."

"Tell me what?"

Now Brett pointed at the sky. "All of them. They're all me."

By the time Brett entered high school, the rumblings of secession had started. The Triton colony's desire for independence intensified. When the War began, the Triton government suspended intersystem flights. Earth followed suit. Brett and thousands of others fell victim to conscription to build an army of Earth loyalists to fight the separatists. He didn't see combat, assigned as a Purser aboard a supply ship that made runs to the front lines. In the early months of the War, the front lines were in place around Neptune, but as the first year dragged on into the second, then the third and fourth, the momentum turned. The front moved closer and closer to Earth orbit.

It was the chance he'd hoped for: the opportunity to come home.

His supply ship, coupled to a Marine warship, fell victim to a Triton carrier attack. The supply ship, forced to tag along during the skirmish, was overlooked long enough for Brett to desert in a dropship.

I just want to go home.

It was unlikely he'd make it, even though he was so close, Earth visible from the front lines. They would chase him down and deny his return, but he had to try. *Moss is resilient. Remove it, and in the right conditions, it will still come back.* He believed it.

The same Triton carrier disabled Brett's dropship after it entered Earth's atmosphere. He woke up in a Tacoma hospital and answered to the highest-ranking personnel in Earth's military forces and intelligence agencies. He told them the truth:

"I just wanted to go home."

"Nothing doing, kid," said the sergeant grilling him today, closing his handheld and tucking it away. "We don't take kindly to Triton spies."

"I'm not a spy," he said. "I *told* you—"

"The tribunal will decide that."

"Tribunal?" He sat up in his hospital bed. "I just want to—"

"We'll talk tomorrow." He turned crisply and left the room.

Late that night, Brett slipped out of his room past the surprisingly few MPs patrolling the hospital and continued his quest for home.

He didn't go home right away. They'd look there first, come down the South Shore Road with a convoy of military vehicles, a show of strength and power. It was the tourist season and the Olympic Peninsula teemed with tourists that crowded Highway 101 and jammed up the lake road. He could blend in with the rest of the crowd. The Olympic Rainforest didn't care. It revealed its beauty to the multitudes, sharing freely blue waters, historic lodges, campgrounds, resorts, and hiking trails through the ubiquitous moss-covered trees, the spongy green dripping from their branches like the tangled beards of giants.

He took four different busses to get to the South Shore Road, then continued past his parents' house, a historic cabin his dad leased from the Forest Service. He bummed a ride to the end of the lake and beyond, to the upper river bridge, to the lower Graves Creek campground.

He'd bought a pack and supplies in Aberdeen, enough to keep him warm and fed on a hike to the Enchanted Valley chalet. There he could hang out. Hide for a while until things cooled down. Thirteen or so miles to Enchanted Valley. He was in good shape and figured he could get up to the chalet in five hours. The trail crossed the river, and the old growth trees were tall and magnificent, close to a thousand years old. The rainforest's natural order was on full display, the moss dripping from the branches and clinging to the trunks.

Few people were on the trail, and it surprised him. In the high summer, you often hiked behind a line of other hikers and backpackers. The trail crossed the river, then he clambered up the long path to O'Neil Creek. Another bridge later on, across Pyrite's Creek. From there, he came across an old fence, then meandered through downed trees to a last bridge, a single I-beam with a wooden handrail. Another quarter mile, the summer light starting to fade, and there was the old wooden chalet, comfortably near the Quinault River. Towering behind it, Chimney Peak. Enchanted Valley was magical, impossible to describe to someone who'd never seen it. It was a land of Lisa's fairies, hidden with moss.

The chalet, built in 1930, was taken over in 1943 by the park service, then closed for a long time, used as a ranger station and an emergency shelter. But now, refurbished, placed on a new foundation farther away from the river, it was open during hiking season.

It seemed deserted.

It wasn't.

Other hikers must've been turned back or warned off.

As soon as Brett approached the chalet door, the first soldier came around the corner. Then another from the other side, and two through the door. They raised their rifles. He halted fifteen feet from the door. Now that he'd stopped, he scanned the valley and saw the military transport half hidden near mossy trees.

Somehow, they'd known he'd make for the chalet.

A man in plain clothes walked out, ordinary and unremarkable, close to his dad's age, he thought. He wore jeans and a rich brown suede leather coat that seemed too warm to wear in the August sun, even this high up in the Olympics.

"You're in big trouble, son," he said.

"How did you know to find me here?" Brett asked.

"I'm agent Jim Moore," he said ignoring the question. "You want to come a little closer?"

Brett felt he had no choice, so he did.

"You want to go home, is that right?"

Brett gulped but answered firmly. "Yes. Absolutely *yes*."

But it's not possible now. It's not going to happen.

Jim Moore smiled, then snagged a chair from the porch, dragged it forward, and indicated that Brett should sit. Without waiting for him, Moore turned and took another chair, scraped it over to face Brett, and sat down. When they were both seated, he waved left and right, and the soldiers backed away to a more comfortable distance.

"There's the whole desertion thing to consider," Moore said.

Brett shrugged.

"You really want it bad, don't you?" He didn't wait for Brett to answer. "Seems when you want something bad enough, everything conspires against you."

"Seems to."

Moore gazed out at the river. "Yeah, I get it. You were drafted against your will. You've fought in a War that makes almost no sense. Kind of matches up to my own kind of thinking, but I'm not the one shooting people or blowing up spaceships. The enemy has reached the gates, and the enemy is *us*."

"What the fuck does that mean?"

"Your sister told me she believed in fairies when she was young," Moore said, His eyes scanned the valley. "So, then I guess they're all around us here in the valley, hidden from our sight."

He hated knowing Moore had talked to his sister, asking personal questions. Probably spoke to his mom and dad, too.

"And how do they do that?" Moore asked.

"Cover themselves with moss."

"Huh, that's exactly what she said. You believe that shit?"

"Doesn't matter if I believe it," Brett answered. "But if it's true, it makes sense. Moss is confirmation of life. What hides behind it is irrelevant."

Moore narrowed his eyes and nodded. Then he shrugged. "Well, Earth is desperate now. Nowhere to hide. Triton forces are near our orbit and they're not slowing down. A rolling stone and all that. Our military has the go-ahead for more desperate measures. I don't know what most of them are. I'm just the intelligence guy. And you know what?"

Brett thought the man would keep going, answering his own question, but he didn't. He was waiting for Brett to answer.

"No, what?"

Moore's answer was another question. "You think you're the only one?"

"Only one what?"

"Deserter."

It *didn't* surprise him. "Suppose there are a few, sure."

"More than a few." Moore laughed nervously. "A lot more."

"And you're rounding them up?

"We are. Not difficult, for now. *You* gave us a run though. You and your fairy protectors."

Brett waited, studying Moore's face, which was serious as hell, as if he'd stated a proven fact with his fairy remark.

Moore stood abruptly, slapping his thighs as he did so. He lifted his hand, palm up, and Brett stood. "You want to go home? Okay, we're going to give you a reprieve. A little time, free and clear."

Brett faced Moore, but his heart pounded a mile a second. He willed it to slow down, knowing there had to be a catch. There was always a catch.

"But there's a catch," Moore said. "If you *really* want to go home."

Brett closed his eyes, waiting for it.

Moore said, "You can go home. On one condition."

Was that a raindrop? Brett craned his neck to look at the porch light. Mist. A few drops danced around the veil of light.

"What do you mean those lights up there are all you?" Lisa asked.

He raised his gaze, turned back toward Lisa. The vivid lights in the sky did their bizarre dance. He pointed. "Each one of those is a dropship. Or an escape pod. They're all soldiers deserting their ships. It's almost non-stop. We can't see the ships, but the fleet is so close now. These soldiers are coming home, just like me."

"My shooting stars are *deserters*?"

"They're soldiers going *home*. Or trying to."

"Like you."

"Your fairies saved me."

"My *what*?"

"When you were younger, remember? You believed fairies were all around us here in the rainforest, disguised by moss."

"Oh, right. And they saved you how?"

"They protected me. The military, the intelligence agents? They singled me out. My case was . . . *unique*. Enough so that I could come home."

"Didn't you tell Mom and Dad you had to leave again?"

"Yeah."

"Why? I still don't understand."

Brett heard scurrying in the kitchen behind him, Mom finishing up a late dinner; he smelled peach cobbler baking in the oven. Dad was probably reading his medical journals, maybe checking the stock ticker.

Down the lake, east, toward Enchanted Valley, lightening flashed on the horizon and rippled along the mountains; a low rumble echoed through the night long after the flashes vanished. More colored lights flickered at the sky's zenith. Shooting stars. Desperate soldiers. Fairy lights.

"It's the only true way home," he said.

Lisa gave him a helpless look. "Just tell me."

He did.

Agent Jim Moore had allowed him this brief time at home in return for his services, that one condition. He had to leave family behind and return to Triton as a spy. The only way to turn the tide of the battle, Moore said—though it was likely too late—was for spies to board a stealth ship and infiltrate Triton. Hide. Adapt. Employ trickery. Subversion. Gather intelligence, gain ground, go back three spaces, take another turn, and hope to hell something good came out of it. Put in the time, and for no more than a year—if the War lasted that long—then come home for good.

They had thought him a spy at one point, and now they were making him one.

If he survived the next year of the War, he'd finish his long journey home, and rain or shine he'd be welcome.

"It's not fair," Lisa said. "It shouldn't take so long to get home."

"I know. But I've got your fairies. I've got plenty of moss to take with me. Moss is resilient, remember. It will come back to the rainforest just as I will."

"Promise?"

"Promise. Moss covers and protects everything."

"Eventually, even our gravestones." He looked at her in surprise and she smiled. "Yeah, I *read* that poem. You said I should, and I bet you never thought I would."

"I memorized that poem in high school for an English project. The poet Bruce Guernsey says moss is 'greening in the dark,' and everything is still and quiet."

"I like when he compares moss to wet dust covering the names cut into the stones," Lisa said. She frowned. "A poem about people dying isn't very encouraging these days."

He patted her leg. "You know, I don't think the poem *is* about death. I think it confirms that life *grows*, life *persists*, even when everything has died and sunk into the ground."

"Do you think even fairies die?"

"I would guess so. And when fairies die, they'll be just like us."

"How?"

"They'll be home."

He huddled close to Lisa and felt his sister's warmth. He smiled knowingly, because like him, she made no move toward the door, and the rain had come.

Dreams in the Witch's Castle
By Remy Nakamura

起. Ki.

Union Station, Portland. March 1969.

The Amtrak hisses behind me. I'm greeted by the smells of diesel and petrichor. Gray clouds hang heavy with moisture, winter refusing to let go.

In my grandma's final lucid moments, she made me promise to bury her second cervical vertebra in the roots of her favorite tree near the stone house in Balch Gulch.

"You'll dilly-dally," she said, smiling from her deathbed. "Until then, keep me close so I can haunt you."

That was Columbus Day, 1962. Baachan has haunted me for six and a half years.

I order a coffee at the Caboose Room. It's late, and I shouldn't, but I need to hold something, sip something. My sleep is shit anyways.

Mixed crowd keeps to themselves inside: traveling salesmen, GIs, a couple of families, black and white, a few Asians. I drink my coffee while it's piping hot. The black and bitter brew pours down my gullet, sears my nerves, fills my soul.

It's only a few blocks to the hotel, but I shuffle along like I'm in the mountains, humping my regulation kit. Or a casket. I keep my eyes down. I'm not ready to face the ghosts.

News from 'Nam plays on the old TV behind the counter, choppers and tired faces in grainy shades of gray. Another war in another country where the people look like me, at least to most Americans. Clerk asks me where I'm from. I bristle. Does this dirty hippie kid think I'm a gaijin?

"From here," I snap. It comes out harsher than I intend, but kills any small talk. Sure, the question could have been innocent. But fifty years of not belonging, no matter how hard you try, it wears you down.

My room is spartan, but clean.

I improvise a bare bones butsudan altar on the well-worn dresser. I start with two cheap white candles, the kind you put on a birthday cake. I pour a couple of tablespoons of rice into a tiny sake cup and prop up a stick of incense. Photos of my parents, my kid brother, George, in uniform, my grandma in a kimono.

Finally, the centerpieces: a postcard of the Great Buddha at Kamakura, and Baachan's nodobotoke, her throat-buddha bone, wrapped in a white silk handkerchief. I don't believe in any of this stuff, but like Baachan always said, it's the *doing* that's important. The doing makes the go'en, the connection.

I pop-spin-flick my zippo and light the candles and incense.

I put my palms together and bow. I breathe in, breathe out the sandalwood scented smoke.

Just a bit longer, Baachan. Patience.

My fingers itch, so I grab my sketchbook. It's taken a couple of years, but I've retrained myself to reach for a pencil or a brush when the urge hits.

There's still a couple of hours of light, and ghosts to confront.

Baachan, I need some help. Sampo shiyou ka? Shall we walk?

I pocket her vertebra and head out.

These city blocks are hopping, but to me, it feels like a ghost town.

The Mikado Hotel, closed with the evacuation order. When I was a kid, me and my dad would go to the steam-filled sento in the basement, where he'd gossip and laugh with the other bathers. It seemed like the only time he wasn't working, the only time his forehead wasn't tight with worry.

I stand across Everett Street to sketch a profile of the building and its entrance. Passers-by look nervously my way, hurry past me. I force a reassuring smile as a black and white Plymouth passes, slowing to a crawl.

The Yamaguchi Hotel, now a soup kitchen. My dad would walk the long way around to avoid that block. My mom's midwife helped run that hotel. She always stopped to comment on my height and health when we passed on the streets. She presided over my arrival into the world, and my mother's departure.

Katei Gakuen, in the red brick Povey building where me and the other kids would go to study

Japanese *after* a day in school. I never hit the right balance—I was too weird and American for the kids in Japan, too stiff and Japanese even for my Nikkei classmates here. Product of spending too much of my childhood bouncing back and forth across the Pacific. And I was never boyish enough–I hated baseball and judo. I was the one quietly drawing or sitting with Baachan and mending.

I didn't return to Portland after the War. Signing on with the Army as an MIS linguist was my escape from miserable Minidoka, that high desert prison camp with its impossible winters. I spent half the War following MacArthur around the Pacific, translating captured letters, convincing cornered enemies that surrender was better than suicide, and interrogating prisoners, including a guy who used to bully me when we were kids in Wakayama.

I was thinking about returning when I heard about the incident at Hood River. The locals struck the names of Nisei soldiers from the memorial there. Later, I heard from friends and former neighbors about Governor Snell, the Klan, and the Japanese Exclusion League, all waiting to welcome us in their own way.

Anyway, Dad was gone, George was gone, our store was gone. After the war, Baachan joined a cousin in San Francisco.

So, I spent four years translating for SCAP in Tokyo and then reupped for Korea. When I was discharged, I found a nice gig teaching at the Defense Language Institute in Monterey, close enough to check in on Baachan on the weekends.

Back in my hotel room, I kill the harsh light of the single bare bulb and switch the old RCA set to a dead UHF channel. The static casts a light across my bed that's almost organic and the white noise softens the ringing in my ears, a lifelong souvenir from a grenade in Saipan.

Did I sleep? The sheets are twisted. I reach for a pencil, roll it around in my fingers, and flip through my sketches. The charcoal outlines of the storefronts are bold but lifeless, almost skeletal.

My hands move without conscious direction. "Jimmy's Clothes Shop" appears in this display window, lines as faded as my memories. My pencil scratches the paper, and the ghostly shape of the owner, Masaaki Usuda, manifests in the doorway.

I do this with each scene, conjuring faint shadows of my childhood friends, neighbors, shopkeepers, hotel managers, lawyers, grocers, teachers, grannies and aunties, uncles and grampas.

Baachan once told me that in Japan, the spirits of the living can haunt you just as well as those of the dead. I've populated this abandoned Japantown with the ghosts of the departed, alive or no.

Satisfied, I sleep.

承. Shou.

Baachan and I used to take the trolley up Thurman to Balch Creek and Macleay Park, but the streetcar lines were dismantled twenty years ago. I decide that walking is somehow less painful than asking for a bus schedule. The capricious sun banished yesterday's cloud cover. Overnight, the Willamette Valley has decided to skip spring altogether.

Even with my coat off, my shirts are soaked through. I remember Nob Hill being much less uphill. To be fair, that was on the far side of years of beers and katsu curries. And three or four thousand packs of Lucky Strikes.

Finally. I descend from the neighborhood into the small canyon, following the well-worn trail that winds through the forest along Balch Creek. The sound of running water precipitates a cascade of memories.

Baachan and I walked this path almost every Sunday before the War. We'd always stop at her special tree, a towering Douglas fir with bark so deeply furrowed you felt like you could squeeze into it. She would pray and leave offerings in a hollow between its roots. Then we'd make our way up to the sturdy rest shelter, where she'd use the toilet, and we'd sit and eat onigiri wrapped in pickled mustard greens.

I brought my sketchbook and travel palette of watercolors, but I hesitate. How can I capture even a hint of this beauty? A million shades of spring, the textures of sharp ferns, dappled sunlight, twisting ivy, branching maples, and tall trunks dusted with lichen patches the color of copper patina. There are no straight lines: naked alders reach for the sky in zigs and zags, every knee and elbow a bulbous mass of moss, and even the tallest firs tilt in this direction or that like lean towers of Pisa. Streams randomly spring from the steep hillsides, and there are entire walls of dripping moss and ferns.

It is a frozen paroxysm of a thousand greens, a slow explosion of luxuriant life.

I breathe in and out and in again, the grassy earthy damp air is my mantra.

Baachan, I'm a fool for waiting. Sorry I took so long.

I follow the trail with renewed vigor. Upward and deeper into this cathedral canopy, bolstered by nature's own flying buttresses.

This is where Baachan belongs.

And where I belong, for now.

I haven't felt this close to her since her death.

I pass between two colossal pillars, one a red cedar, one a Doug fir. They form a natural torii gate, and remind me of the long chopsticks, one wood, one bamboo, that I held when we picked and passed the bones from Baachan's cremated remains to her cousin and then into the urn.

This means I'm close—less than a minute's stroll, at a slight bend in the creek, the grand dame in a close triumvirate of forest matriarchs.

I almost run the last bit.

But it's not there.

Her tree is gone.

The two side trees remain standing, but the center one, Baachan's special Douglas fir, is uprooted and lies broken across the creek and the opposite bank in massive segments. Each is covered with mushrooms and moss and ferns and ivy. My throat is dry. I can't get enough air.

Dazed, I stumble up the path to the stone shelter.

It, too, has fallen.

The walls and stairs remain standing, a skeleton of dark basalt. The wooden roof has collapsed in, the windows and doors are gone. The forest has started to devour the ruins. Peace signs and profanity are painted in bright colors, and bottles and cigarette butts litter the area. The lowest part of the shelter is inset, like a bus stop made of black rock, or a square gate into a shallow underworld.

Somehow, I've dropped the vertebra, that last precious piece of my Grandma. I scramble to pick her up and as I rise, I am also falling.

Darkness.

転. Ten.

I open my eyes.

The stone house is surrounded by an endless treeless expanse of yellow-brown grass and sagebrush, instantly recognizable. Minidoka, Idaho. One of Uncle Sam's very own concentration camps.

Baachan is here, looking like she did thirty years ago, less stooped but forever short, more black and less gray in her hair.

"This land is like Dracula," she says. "Suck life out of skin and soul. Frank-chan, ne, sampo shiyou?"

We walk. I'm simultaneously kid-Frank back in Japan, twenty-year-old-just-about-to-enlist-in-the-Army Frank, and this current version, middle-aged-and-all-alone-sad-sack Frank.

"I thought move to Oregon was hard," she says. "But coming *here*, it make me wonder what I do in past life to deserve this." She jabs a finger at the desert scape.

While we pick our way through the brush to the distant camp, I play with the bone in my pocket, rolling it between thumb and forefinger like an oversized, lopsided juzu prayer bead. Then I realize who I'm with, and what I'm doing.

"Oh shit, Baachan, gomen."

She laughs, a long chuckle that ends with a coughing fit. She waves at me to insist that she's fine.

"Learn rule so you can break them," she says when she finally catches her breath.

"Did Buddha say that? "

"No," she says with a wry grin. "Picasso."

This was one hundred percent Baachan, especially when it came to tradition and religion. She learned how it was done so that she could riff on it. She made her own magic and music, and people either dismissed her as some wacky old lady, or they respected her for it.

In fact, during the War, many looked to Grandma as a sort of midwife for their grief. She had no special training—just a listening ear and a way about her that told people that she had one foot in konoyo, this world, and one in anoyo, that world.

And that's what she was good at. Where orthodox faith and teachings and ritual struggled to keep up with the pace of change, with new and unexpected forms of loss, when you lost both of your homelands, when you lost parents and cousins in the Pacific and sons and brothers in Europe, when you were locked up like a criminal in the desert and you couldn't dig your way out of layer upon layer of shame, Baachan could step in and improvise, show you how to move on.

We're back at the stone house.

"Frank-chan," she pats my hand. "I need go soon. But first, talk to magical white woman."

Confused, I close my eyes. I open them.

I'm sitting on the wet ground. A thin white woman with short brown hair leans over me. She looks concerned. Her worried brow reminds me of Dad.

"Are you okay?" she asks. I guess I don't respond, because she hands me a canteen. "Drink this."

She helps me sit up.

Where's Baachan? I panic and look around me frantically.

"Looking for this?" She hands me the neck bone. I take it quickly. I'm confused. Why does Baachan want me to talk to this stranger?

"Thanks," I croak. "For looking after Grandma." The words escape before I can bite them back. She quirks an eyebrow, curiosity nudging aside any concern.

It all spills out. I tell this stranger about Baachan and her last request.

"Trees were magical to her," I add. "I mean, they are to many Japanese. They say that when trees turn a hundred, they gain a spirit, called kodama. You're not supposed to cut them down, they might curse you."

"Oh my," she says. "Oregon is in *deep* trouble."

"And we worship ancient trees like little gods."

"You call them kami, right?" She laughs at my surprise. "I've studied a bit of anthropology."

"Kami are gods but not gods. A waterfall, a great poet, even our ancestors can be kami, if living relatives remember and honor them." I've fallen into the safety of my teacher role.

"That tree really was special to your Grandma. I'm sorry," she says. "Many old giants fell in the Columbus Day storm, six-seven years back. Did serious damage to the rest station too."

"October, 1962?"

"Sounds right."

Holy shit. Baachan and her tree died on the same day.

We sit in silence. She breaks it first.

"The kids are calling this ruin the Witch's Castle." She stands up.

"Grandma would've liked that. She was a Japanese version of a witch." I stand too. The world spins.

"She sounds like my kind of woman." She eyes me with concern. "Listen, I live near the Thurman bridge. If you're having a hard time, come find us." She tells me a house number and disappears down the path.

I close my eyes. I open them.

Just upstream from the Witch's House is an enormous Douglas fir. It's at least two yards wide at the base, on the bank above the creek. How did I miss this beautiful monstrosity?

I lean my tired head against it. The enormous furrows in the bark gently split around me, embracing me and taking me in. It is dark and comforting, like standing in a cedar wardrobe packed with cool winter coats. I stretch my fingers high up into the sky and my toes deep down into the earth.

I stand tall, taller than most of the trees in the forest, but I'm in the valley, and the others on the steep slopes around me keep me humble. I drink in the sunshine, convert it into sweet nectar and tough bark. I'm an inside-out lung, my needles like so many alveoli, and I breathe deep. I spread my thirsty root-toes in the soil, penetrating rock and clay, drinking deep from the creek and the earth.

My roots split into rootlets which divide further into smaller threads that connect me to other trees, and I realize that I'm just one part of the entire forest, nervous and lymphatic and circulatory systems on a grand scale. I'm part of a cycle, with older generations nurturing the young, lying down and laying down the bones around which and on which the forest grows. The forest embodies go'en, connection, the relatedness of all things.

We rise and fall as one, this forest.

I open my eyes.

I'm sitting in the Witch's Castle again.

I sit for a while longer, then emerge into the light and the waking world.

結. Ketsu.

I sketch Baachan worshipping at her tree, like she did so many times on our visits here. I try to remember, to draw the tree as it was. I add sacred rope around its broad trunk and paper talismans hanging from it, folded like lightning.

Then I realize this tree isn't dead.

It grew for over a hundred and fifty, maybe two hundred years, glorying in the abundance this world had to offer: sunshine, lavish rain and creek water, nutrients in the ground. Now, it provides food and haven for coming generations: fungi and lichen, mosses and insects, woodpeckers and squirrels and even future giants of the forest.

It has passed into another phase of existence, but it continues to nurture. It will shape the future for decades to come.

I fold the drawing around Baachan's nodobotoke—it is the closest thing to a prayer and a talisman this poor artist can craft. I plant it deep, like a seed, in the convex hollow that was once the base of Baachan's mighty tree.

I nestle into the roots as close as I can.

I leave a piece of Baachan here.

But she isn't dead.

While I live, while I remember, she lives on, this new spirit in the forest.

And she lives on in every connection I make, every painting I create, and every nurturing story I share.

Author Bios

Phoenix Bourgeois writes in Portland, Oregon where she co-hosts Northwest Speculative, a PNW Reading Series that connects readers, authors, and venues. She grew up bouncing from one library to the next. Now, Phoenix writes her own fantastical stories—bouncing from one coffee shop to the next.

Once a Silicon Valley software engineer, **Curtis C. Chen** (陳致宇) now writes stories near Portland, Oregon. He's the award-winning author of the bestselling KANGAROO series of funny science fiction spy thrillers and the lead writer for Realm's Echo Park podcast.

Daniel Dagris is an author from the Pacific Northwest. His fiction has been recommended by Best Horror of the Year, nominated for the Pushcart Prize, received honorable mention from Glimmer Train, and featured in Chuck Palahniuk's Plot Spoiler. Daniel's short stories have appeared in Portland Review, Bridge Eight, Orca Literary Journal, and elsewhere.

Cyrus Amelia Fisher writes queer tales of shipwrecks, mycelium, and horrors of the flesh. After years of driving around the United States in a beat-up minivan, they finally returned to the mossy fens of their birth in the Pacific Northwest. Now they while away the hours communing with their fungal hivemind and writing about cannibalism. Naturally, they also love to cook.

Erik Grove is a writer, writing teacher, editor, and dog wrangler living and doing things in Portland, OR. You can find his short fiction in places like *Nightmare Magazine, Escape Pod*, and *Winding Paths: A Playable Reading Experience*. You can find links to stories, information on appearances, and more sundry shenanigans at www.erikgrove.com.

Tracy Hall is an artist in various mediums including ballpoint pen, painting, bookmaking, and textile art. She enjoys being outdoors, reading, and appreciating cats.

EB Helveg moved to Seattle for the weather, and has never once regretted it. He's been published in various anthologies and a couple of magazines, in both poetry and prose. He has two awesome kids who think his jokes are hilarious, and a very patient roommate who puts up with his nonsense. He would really like to be taking a nap right now.

You can find him on Instagram/Threads at @idreamofvikings.

Patrick Hurley lives in Seattle, where he works as Managing Editor for Paizo Inc. Patrick has had work published in Lightspeed, Factor Four, Mysterion, Abyss & Apex, New Myths, and Galaxy's Edge. He attended the Taos Toolbox Writer's Workshop and is represented by Jordy Albert of the Booker Albert agency. To read more of Patrick's work, check out www.patrickhurleywrites.com.

Frances Lu Pai Ippilito (she/her) is a Chinese American judge, mom, writer, and publisher in Portland, Oregon. Her writing has appeared in several venues including Nightmare Magazine, Flame Tree's Asian Ghost Stories, Chromophobia, Mother: Tales of Terror and Love, and Unquiet Spirits. She is the founder of game and book publisher Demagogue Press and the award-winning nonprofit, Qilin Press, which focuses on community stories. She is also the co-editor of three cozy horror anthologies through Underland Press, and serves as a HWA Trustee. But most importantly, she believes in geese. IG: @demagogue_press & @qilin_press

Jessie Kwak is an author whose earliest stories sprang from the many unsupervised hours she spent courting tetanus in junk heaps. She now lives in Portland, Oregon, where she is the author of thriller novels, two series of space scoundrel sci-fi crime novels, and a handful of productivity books including From Chaos to Creativity and From Big Idea to Book.

E. Michael Lewis studied creative writing at the University of Puget Sound. He is a lifelong native of the Pacific Northwest whose ghost stories appear in The Black Beacon Book Of Ghosts (Black Beacon Books), Flight or Fright (Cemetery Dance Publications), Savage Beasts (Grey Matter Press). He's on the web (www.emichaellewis.com) and Facebook.

By day, **Karen Aria Lin** is a technical writer in the software industry. By night, she writes speculative fiction stories. She contributed to the 2024 Aurora Award-nominated anthology GAME ON! by Zombies Need Brains. Her fiction has also been published in Pulphouse Fiction Magazine, Haven Speculative, and The First Line. When not writing, she's sending routes at the climbing gym or hiking with her mountain dog. You can find her website at karenlin.me/fiction.

While being rained upon west, west, west of Portland, Oregon, **Monte Lin** edits, writes, and plays tabletop roleplaying games and writes short stories. Clarion West got him to write about dying universes, edible sins, dreaming mountains, and singularities made of anxieties. His stories have been published at Translunar Travelers Lounge, Cossmass Infinities, Cast of Wonders, Flame Tree Press anthologies, and others, with nonfiction in Strange Horizons. He is also managing editor of Uncanny and can be found on Bluesky @montelin.bsky.social.

Gigi Little is the author of the novel Who Killed One the Gun? and the editor of the anthology City of Weird. She's also a book designer and the art director of the picture book A Tree of My Own. Her writings and design can be found in journals and anthologies including Portland Noir, Dispatches from Anarres, The Magic We Miss, Art Born Words, and Mountain Bluebird. She lives in Portland, Oregon, with her husband, fine artist Stephen O'Donnell.

Brian W. Parker is an author, illustrator, designer, publisher, educator, and foster adopt parent/advocate with over twenty books to his credit, including The Epic of Nicholas the Maker, The Pawsons Move In, and The Magic We Miss Anthology! He grew up in Alaska, then Mississippi, and has always been in love with storytelling in every medium. Literature, movies, art, you name it! He has a BFA in graphic design and illustration, as well as a MA in writing and publishing. Now he spend my days working on in youth publishing with his family and teaching about the creative process. Check out their work at **www.believeinwonder.com**!

Luciano Marano is an award-winning writer, journalist, and photographer. He is the author of the werewolf novella trilogy The Ambush Moon Cycle (Raven Tale Publishing) and numerous works of short fiction appearing in anthologies such as Year's Best Hardcore Horror and The Best New Weird Horror, among others. Originally from rural, Western Pennsylvania, he now resides near Seattle.

Remy Nakamura is an author, activist and a compassionate productivity consultant. He writes weird, dark and hopeful fiction. His stories can be found in Escape Pod, Pseudopod, and many anthologies. He has a Masters in Genre Writing from Edinburgh Napier University and is a graduate of Seattle's Clarion West Writers Workshop. He currently serves as a board member for the Clarion West Foundation. He grew up partly in Japan, where he and his Obaachan greeted their ancestors at a little butsudan altar every morning and evening. He now lives just a short run from the Witch's Castle in Forest Park and an even shorter walk from Portland's New Chinatown/Japantown historic district.

Rachel Lee Thai Nyeholt is an art director and cartoonist. Her work is inspired by nature and its magic. She's currently working on her limited series comic, Seeded. She lives in Portland, Oregon with her family.

Margo Pecha's fiction has appeared in Even Cozier Cosmic and is forthcoming from Fraidy Cat Quarterly and Graveside Press. She holds a bachelor's in creative writing from Eastern Washington University and a master's in writing and publishing from Portland State University. She lives in southwest Washington state where she works as a copy editor. When she's not reading and writing, she's puttering about her garden and wrangling too many chickens.

Katherine Quevedo was born and raised near Portland, Oregon, where she works as an analyst and lives with her husband and two sons. Her fiction has been nominated for the Pushcart Prize and appears in Nightmare Magazine, Fireside Magazine, On Spec, Abyss & Apex, LatineLit, and elsewhere. Her debut fantasy novella, Thrice Petrified, is available from Of Metal and Magic Publishing. Find her at www.katherinequevedo.com.

Giacomo Ranieri produces videos, coordinates events, and writes sci-fi/fantasy for young folks, often illustrated. He founded Creative Branches, a PNW company focused on graphic novels, crowdfunding, and business support for creatives in publishing. You can follow Creative Branches on most major social platforms. His writing drips with an intense reverence for nature. He explores culture, our limited senses, and the emotional systems that we often let govern us.

Kate Ristau is the President of the Science Fiction and Fantasy Writers Association (SFWA) and the Executive Director of Willamette Writers. She is the author of three middle grade series,

Clockbreakers, Mythwakers, and Wylde Wings, and the young adult series, Shadow Girl. You can read her essays in The New York Times and The Washington Post. She is the chair of the Tigard Public Library Board of Directors.

Camden Rose is a queer author who loves seeking out magic beneath the everyday world. Her works have appeared with Inner Worlds and Heartlines Spec. She lives in the Pacific Northwest with her spouse, black cats, and collection of books and board games. You can find her online at www.camdenscorner.com.

Joe Streckert writes primarily about Pacific Northwest history. His bylines include the Portland Mercury, the Daily Journal of Commerce, Comic Book Resources, and several others. He's also host of The Weird History Podcast, and the author of Storied and Scandalous Portland, Oregon. He lives in Portland with his wife, son, and very large cat.

Patrick Swenson is the author of the Union of Worlds trilogy and the standalone dark fantasy Rain Music. He's the editor and publisher of Fairwood Press and a graduate of Clarion West. He's sold short fiction to Unavowed, Gunfight on Europa Station, Unfettered III, Unbound II, Seasons Between Us, and others. He runs the Rainforest Writers Village retreat on the Olympic Peninsula. He taught high school for 39 years. You can find him at patrickswenson.net.

Mark Teppo is the publisher of Underland Press. He has written more than two dozen novels across a wide variety of genres, including historical fiction, eco-thriller, horror, western, mystery, science fiction, and dark fantasy. He lives in the Pacific Northwest, where he is busy making things. His favorite Tarot card is the Moon.

Wendy N. Wagner is a foot traveler, writer, and editor whose works include horror novels like Girl in the Creek and the SF thriller An Oath of Dogs. Her short fiction has been nominated for the Theodore Sturgeon and Shirley Jackson awards, and her short stories, poetry, and essays have appeared in more than seventy venues. She lives in Oregon with her very understanding family, a large cat, and a Muppet disguised as a dog.

Sarah Walker is a horror writer, anthropologist, and visual artist whose work delves into the eerie intersection of culture, myth, and fear. With a background in biology and anthropology, she crafts chilling narratives that explore the darker sides of humanity. She has been published everywhere from Lovecraft Ezine to Vastarien, Test Patterns, Eight Tower Publications and more. Her first novel, Exterminating Angel, is planned for publication in 2026 year. Sarah also co-owns and is the art director for Weird Fiction Quarterly. She makes her home on the Oregon Coast where her family has lived for generations.

About the Game

The Royal Game of Goose, also known as the Game of Goose, is one of the oldest known board games. The earliest versions show up in fifteenth century Europe where geese symbolize good fortune and plenty. The oldest game board is at the Metropolitan Museum of Art in New York City.

With the straightforward mechanic of "roll and go," this race game has survived the test of time and continues to be popular internationally. One reason may be that the game board and spaces lend themselves to easy thematic reconfiguration. Game boards have been customized with geographical, historical, political, scientific, etc. themes, including the stages of human life.

In this rendition, we've personalized the Game of Goose with the joys of our very own Pacific Northwest. The stories and poems in this collection have their very own space on the board. If you're up for the challenge, play the game and take a guess which story matches the space.

The Basics

- Ages 8+
- 2-4 players
- There are 63 total spaces on the game board.
- The goal of the game is to reach the 63rd space before the other players.
- Landing on special spaces triggers the space's effects.

Set-up

- 2d6
- Place the book down with the cover facing up. This is your game board.
- Cut out the player tokens in the Appendices. Photocopies of the tokens or proxies (coins) may be used instead.
- Player tokens are placed on the first space.

Gameplay

1. Players place their tokens on space 1.
2. Each player rolls 2d6 to determine turn order.

3.   On their turn, each player rolls 2d6. Player moves their token forward the number of spaces rolled.

4.   On the first roll, if the player rolls a 6 and 3, move to space 26.

5.   On the first roll, if the player rolls a 5 and 4, move to space 53.

6.   If a player is near Space 63, the player must roll the exact number of spaces to reach 63. Otherwise, the player must move backwards the number of spaces past the 63.

7.   If the player lands on a special space, follow the instructions for those spaces below:

#	Board Square	Effect
1	The Troll	Start
5	The Lake	Goose Space - move forward by the amount of your roll
6	The Bridge	Move to Space 12, the Stag
9	The Beach	Goose Space - move forward by the amount of your roll
14	The Farm	Goose Space - move forward by the amount of your roll
18	The Apple Tree	Goose Space - move forward by the amount of your roll
19	The Peak	Skip your next turn or move back to space 13
23	The Ship Wreck	Goose Space - move forward by the amount of your roll
27	The Sound	Goose Space - move forward by the amount of your roll
31	The Bog	Skip your next turn
32	The University	Goose Space - move forward by the amount of your roll
36	The Ravine	Goose Space - move forward by the amount of your roll
38	The Lighthouse	High five your opponents. Honk like a goose. Move forward 1 space
41	The Woods	Goose Space - move forward by the amount of your roll
42	The Trails	Go back to Space 38, the Lighthouse
45	The Goat	Goose (Goat) Space - move forward by the amount of your roll
50	The Island	Goose Space - move forward by the amount of your roll
52	The Caves	Death awaits. Roll 1d6. If 4 or high advance to Space 53, the Ferry. If 3 or lower return to Space 1, the Troll.
54	The Rose Garden	Goose Space - move forward by the amount of your roll
59	The Rainforest	Goose Space - move forward by the amount of your roll
63	The Castle	End

Game Pieces

Match the Story With the Location!

A Letter Found Among Records Recovered from a Historical Mystery Capsule, Opened on the Hundredth Anniversary of its Burial in Astoria, Oregon*	A Mushroom Haunting in Lithia Park	Beached	Bridge Walk	Desolation Jack
Dreams in the Witch's Castle	Green Lake: the Game	Greening in the Dark	How Do You Like Them	Parafernatorio
Passing in the Night	Requiem	Scabs on the Earth	Sea Witch	Silent Colony
Story-2.docx	The Ghost of Lake Roosevelt	The Goat Waits for No One	The Queen of All Roses	The Ravine
The Rituals of the Freemont Troll	This Island is Magical	Troglodyte	We Are Not We	White Stag

#	Board Square	Location	Story
1	The Troll	Fremont Troll - Seattle, WA	
5	The Lake	Green Lake - Seattle, WA	
6	The Bridge	Burnside Bridge- Portland, OR	
9	The Beach	Manitou Beach - Bainbridge Island, WA	
12	The Stag	Portland, OR	
14	The Farm	Bellevue Park - Bellevue, WA	
18	The Apple Tree	Fort Vancouver - WA	
19	The Peak	Desolation Peak - WA	
23	The Ship Wreck	Astoria, OR	**A Letter Found Among Records Recovered from a Historical Mystery Capsule, Opened on the Hundredth Anniversary of its Burial in Astoria, Oregon***
26	The Ghost Forest	Neskowin, OR	
27	The Sound	Dash Point, WA	
31	The Bog	Oaks Bottom Wildlife Refuge - OR	
32	The University	University of Oregon - Eugene, OR	
36	The Ravine	Harrah, WA	
38	The Lighthouse	Umpqua Lighthouse - OR	
41	The Woods	Lithia Park - Ashland, OR	
42	The Trails	Forest Park - Portland, OR	
45	The Goat	Garbage Goat - Spokane, WA	
50	The Island	Clay Meyers State Natural Area - OR	
52	The Caves	Oregon Caves - Cave Junction, OR	
53	The Ferry	Lake Roosevelt, WA	
54	The Rose Garden	Portland Rose Garden - OR	
58	The Lodge	Mt. Ranier,- OR	
59	The Rainforest	Lake Quinalt, WA	
63	The Castle	Witch's Castle - Portland, OR	

Answer Key!

#	Board Square	Location	Story
1	The Troll	Fremont Troll - Seattle, WA	**The Rituals of the Freemont Troll**
5	The Lake	Green Lake - Seattle, WA	**Green Lake: the Game**
6	The Bridge	Burnside Bridge- Portland, OR	**Bridge Walk**
9	The Beach	Manitou Beach - Bainbridge Island, WA	**Beached**
12	The Stag	Portland, OR	**White Stag**
14	The Farm	Bellevue Park - Bellevue, WA	**Scabs on the Earth**
18	The Apple Tree	Fort Vancouver - WA	**How Do You Like Them**
19	The Peak	Desolation Peak - WA	**Desolation Jack**
23	The Ship Wreck	Astoria, OR	**A Letter Found Among Records Recovered from a Historical Mystery Capsule, Opened on the Hundredth Anniversary of its Burial in Astoria, Oregon***
26	The Ghost Forest	Neskowin, OR	**Requiem**
27	The Sound	Dash Point, WA	**Passing in the Night**
31	The Bog	Oaks Bottom Wildlife Refuge - OR	**Silent Colony**
32	The University	University of Oregon - Eugene, OR	**Story-2.docx**
36	The Ravine	Harrah, WA	**The Ravine**
38	The Lighthouse	Umpqua Lighthouse - OR	**Sea Witch**
41	The Woods	Lithia Park - Ashland, OR	**A Mushroom Haunting in Lithia Park**
42	The Trails	Forest Park - Portland, OR	**We Are Not We**
45	The Goat	Garbage Goat - Spokane, WA	**The Goat Waits for No One**
50	The Island	Clay Meyers State Natural Area - OR	**This Island is Magical**
52	The Caves	Oregon Caves - Cave Junction, OR	**Troglodyte**
53	The Ferry	Lake Roosevelt, WA	**The Ghost of Lake Roosevelt**
54	The Rose Garden	Portland Rose Garden - OR	**The Queen of All Roses**
58	The Lodge	Mt. Ranier,- OR	**Parafernatorio**
59	The Rainforest	Lake Quinalt, WA	**Greening in the Dark**
63	The Castle	Witch's Castle - Portland, OR	**Dreams in the Witch's Castle**

Muddy Goose Adventure Society Field Notes

Date	Location Explored	

REFLECTIONS:

WARNINGS:

Muddy Goose Adventure Society Field Notes

Date		Location Explored	

REFLECTIONS:

WARNINGS:

Muddy Goose Adventure Society Field Notes

Date		Location Explored	

REFLECTIONS:

WARNINGS:

Muddy Goose Adventure Society Field Notes

Date		Location Explored	

REFLECTIONS:

WARNINGS:

Muddy Goose Adventure Society Field Notes

Date	Location Explored	

REFLECTIONS:

WARNINGS:

Muddy Goose Adventure Society Field Notes

Date		Location Explored	

REFLECTIONS:

WARNINGS:

Muddy Goose Adventure Society Field Notes

Date	Location Explored	

REFLECTIONS:

WARNINGS:

Muddy Goose Adventure Society Field Notes

Date		Location Explored	

REFLECTIONS:

WARNINGS:

Muddy Goose Adventure Society Field Notes

Date		Location Explored	

REFLECTIONS:

WARNINGS:

Muddy Goose Adventure Society Field Notes

Date		Location Explored	

REFLECTIONS:

WARNINGS:

Muddy Goose Adventure Society Field Notes

Date		Location Explored	

REFLECTIONS:

WARNINGS:

Muddy Goose Adventure Society Field Notes

Date	Location Explored

REFLECTIONS:

WARNINGS:

Muddy Goose Adventure Society Field Notes

Date	Location Explored

REFLECTIONS:

WARNINGS:

Muddy Goose Adventure Society Field Notes

Date		Location Explored	

REFLECTIONS:

WARNINGS:

Muddy Goose Adventure Society Field Notes

Date		Location Explored	

REFLECTIONS:

WARNINGS:

Muddy Goose Adventure Society Field Notes

Date		Location Explored	

REFLECTIONS:

WARNINGS:

Muddy Goose Adventure Society Field Notes

Date		Location Explored	

REFLECTIONS:

WARNINGS:

Muddy Goose Adventure Society Field Notes

Date	Location Explored

REFLECTIONS:

WARNINGS:

Muddy Goose Adventure Society Field Notes

Date		Location Explored	

REFLECTIONS:

WARNINGS:

Muddy Goose Adventure Society Field Notes

Date		Location Explored	

REFLECTIONS:

WARNINGS:

Muddy Goose Adventure Society Field Notes

Date		Location Explored	

REFLECTIONS:

WARNINGS:

Muddy Goose Adventure Society Field Notes

Date	Location Explored	

REFLECTIONS:

WARNINGS:

www.ingramcontent.com/pod-product-compliance
Lightning Source LLC
Chambersburg PA
CBHW081103300726
48976CB00011B/2706